Praise for the novels of Cathie Linz

Luck Be a Lady

"You can always count on Cathie Linz to create a feisty, non-stereotypical librarian in her stories . . . Linz has written another fast-paced romantic comedy with just the right amount of heartfelt emotion." —*Booklist* (starred review)

"Filled with an assortment of odd yet engaging characters, this funny, madcap adventure is lively, sweetly sexy entertainment that fans won't want to miss." —*Library Journal*

"If you're looking for a book that will make you laugh out loud and allow you to walk away feeling completely satisfied, then this is the perfect story for you to pick up!"
—*Night Owl Reviews* (4 stars)

"Once again Cathie Linz gives us a character that just can't be stereotyped. Wisecracking, well-endowed and smart to boot, with Megan West she broke the librarian mold. *Luck Be a Lady* is a fun romp filled with some bizarre, lovable, quirky and endearing folks." —*Fresh Fiction*

Mad, Bad and Blonde

"For lighthearted contemporary romance, it's hard to beat Linz. Filled with believable characters and witty dialogue, her books never fail to entertain."
—*Booklist* (starred review)

"Lively pacing, a pair of magnetic, thoroughly appealing protagonists and well-defined secondary characters . . . make this sexy story sparkle with humor and pizzazz, while great geographic and cultural Chicago detail, an intriguing mystery and a dash of *Romeo-and-Juliet* add complexity."
—*Library Journal*

continued . . .

Smart Girls Think Twice

"The brainy girl and hunky guy have never been so much fun. No need to think twice about grabbing this book when you're looking for pure entertainment."   —Susan Wiggs

"Readers will be captivated as they watch the introverted academic get in touch with her inner warrior and realize her true potential. Funny and poignant by turns, Linz's latest is sure to charm."   —*Booklist* (starred review)

"A prim heroine with a fiery core and a haunted, searching hero who thrives on the rush of adrenaline join with an abundance of quirky characters to drive the classic plot of this funny, spicy romance to a satisfying conclusion.
     —*Library Journal*

Big Girls Don't Cry

"The characters spring to life, and readers will be thrilled to find that individuals from Linz's earlier novels pop in and out like old friends. And kudos to Linz for creating a heroine who looks and acts like a real woman."
     —*Booklist* (starred review)

"[A] sweetly charming, splendidly funny and supremely satisfying contemporary romance."   —*Chicago Tribune*

"Another keeper."   —*Contemporary Romance Writers*

"A must-read. Top pick!"   —*Romance Reader at Heart*

Bad Girls Don't

"Cathie Linz gives her beautifully matched protagonists lots of sexy chemistry and some delightfully snappy dialogue, and the quirky cast of secondary characters gives *Bad Girls Don't* its irresistible charm."   —*Chicago Tribune*

"Linz, known for her fast-paced, snappy romantic come-
dies, once again sparkles in this heartwarming, funny tale.
And her secondary characters . . . make an already excellent story exceptional."   —*Booklist* (starred review)

"Linz's characterizations are absolutely wonderful. I fell in
love with the protagonists from the first page . . . It has
always been a pleasure to read her books, but I must say
that this one is a fantastic novel!"   —*Rendezvous*

"Totally delightful."   —*Fresh Fiction*

Good Girls Do

"Humor and warmth . . . Readers are going to love this!"
—Susan Elizabeth Phillips

"Cathie Linz is the author that readers of romantic comedy
have been waiting for. She knows how to do it—characters
with depth, sharp dialogue and a compelling story. The
result is a charming, offbeat world, one you'll hate to
leave."   —Jayne Ann Krentz

"Sometimes even good girls need to take a walk on the
wild side. Linz deftly seasons her writing with her usual
delectable wit, and the book's quirky cast of endearing secondary characters adds another measure of humor to this
sweetly sexy, fabulously fun contemporary romance."
—*Booklist* (starred review)

"Sexy, sassy and graced with exceptional dialogue, this
fast-paced story is both hilarious and heartwarming, fea-
turing wonderfully wacky secondary characters and well-
developed protagonists you will come to love."
—*Library Journal*

"Lively and fun, and you won't be able to put it down."
—*Fresh Fiction*

Berkley Sensation Titles by Cathie Linz

GOOD GIRLS DO
BAD GIRLS DON'T
BIG GIRLS DON'T CRY
SMART GIRLS THINK TWICE
MAD, BAD AND BLONDE
LUCK BE A LADY
TEMPTED AGAIN

Tempted Again

. . . .

Cathie Linz

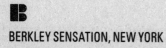

BERKLEY SENSATION, NEW YORK

THE BERKLEY PUBLISHING GROUP
Published by the Penguin Group
Penguin Group (USA) Inc.
375 Hudson Street, New York, New York 10014, USA
Penguin Group (Canada), 90 Eglinton Avenue East, Suite 700, Toronto, Ontario M4P 2Y3, Canada
(a division of Pearson Penguin Canada Inc.)
Penguin Books Ltd., 80 Strand, London WC2R 0RL, England
Penguin Group Ireland, 25 St. Stephen's Green, Dublin 2, Ireland (a division of Penguin Books Ltd.)
Penguin Group (Australia), 250 Camberwell Road, Camberwell, Victoria 3124, Australia
(a division of Pearson Australia Group Pty. Ltd.)
Penguin Books India Pvt. Ltd., 11 Community Centre, Panchsheel Park, New Delhi—110 017, India
Penguin Group (NZ), 67 Apollo Drive, Rosedale, Auckland 0632, New Zealand
(a division of Pearson New Zealand Ltd.)
Penguin Books (South Africa) (Pty.) Ltd., 24 Sturdee Avenue, Rosebank, Johannesburg 2196,
South Africa

Penguin Books Ltd., Registered Offices: 80 Strand, London WC2R 0RL, England

This is a work of fiction. Names, characters, places, and incidents either are the product of the author's imagination or are used fictitiously, and any resemblance to actual persons, living or dead, business establishments, events, or locales is entirely coincidental. The publisher does not have any control over and does not assume any responsibility for author or third-party websites or their content.

TEMPTED AGAIN

A Berkley Sensation Book / published by arrangement with the author

PRINTING HISTORY
Berkley Sensation mass-market edition / January 2012

ISBN: 978-0-425-24454-8

BERKLEY SENSATION®
Berkley Sensation Books are published by The Berkley Publishing Group,
a division of Penguin Group (USA) Inc.,
375 Hudson Street, New York, New York 10014.
BERKLEY SENSATION® is a registered trademark of Penguin Group (USA) Inc.
The "B" design is a trademark of Penguin Group (USA) Inc.

PRINTED IN THE UNITED STATES OF AMERICA

10   9   8   7   6   5   4   3   2   1

This book is dedicated to the incredibly brave Andrea Markell, her husband, Vic, and her kids, Katie and Victor, as well as all those affected by the terrible tornadoes in the South and in Joplin, Missouri, in the spring of 2011. My thoughts are with you all.

Special thanks go to Amy Alessio for her help regarding Young Adult librarians. My heartfelt gratitude goes out to all you readers who have been there for me over the years, as well as the hundreds of librarians and booksellers who have given me your support. Please know how much I value each and every one of you. You are simply the best!

Chapter One

. . . .

When in trouble seek shelter. Marissa Bennett had learned that lesson at an early age. She'd had to. Seek shelter from the storm. And there was no safer haven than her hometown of Hopeful, Ohio.

Or so Marissa hoped. Not that hoping, wishing or even praying had helped her out much lately. The bottom line was that her life had completely fallen apart over the past year. And now here she was, heading back home in a used and dented lime-green VW Bug. The eyesore of a car was a necessity not a choice.

Hopeful hadn't changed much since Marissa had left to go to college more than a decade ago. As she traveled along Washington Street, the main highway into town, she drove past the oak tree–filled campus of Midwest College. The ivy-covered brick buildings glowed in the May sunshine. It was Saturday afternoon so the campus wasn't as bustling as a weekday when classes were in session, but groups of students sat out under the trees enjoying the fine weather.

Her father was a history professor at the college and had been for years. One of her earliest memories was of him carrying her on his shoulders to touch the abundance of crabapple blossoms lining the entrance to Birch Hall, where he had his office.

Marissa's parents had wanted her to stay and attend Midwest College, but Marissa had her heart set on attending Ohio State. She'd been eager to spread her wings and fly, excited about the world of possibilities open to her.

No, Hopeful hadn't changed much . . . but Marissa had. Divorce and disillusionment did that to a woman. Knocked the stars from her eyes and turned her dreams to dust.

How different would her life be right now if she'd stayed in her hometown instead of leaving?

She wouldn't have met and fallen for Brad Johnson. Wouldn't have married him. Wouldn't have caught him in their bed with another woman.

The humiliating memory cut clear through her and Marissa shoved it out of her mind for the time being. She'd been doing that a lot lately: shoving thoughts away and locking them up somewhere deep inside her as if they were radioactive waste. It was the only way for her to cope with the fact that she'd lost the life she'd built. Living a mere hour outside of New York City had given her the best of both worlds—the culture and excitement of the big city and the suburban lifestyle. But that was all over now. Gone.

Infidelity had ended her marriage. Budget cuts had

ended the job she loved at the local library. The divorce had ended her ability to stay in the compact English-style cottage home of her dreams she'd shared with her husband. Her situation had started to seem hopeless before she'd been given this second chance in her hometown.

"What makes you want to return home?" library director Roz Jorgen had asked during Marissa's interview at the Hopeful Memorial Library several weeks ago.

"The fact that my life is a mess" was not a suitably professional response, so Marissa had come up with an alternative statement about not realizing the value of something until you were away from it for a while.

Marissa must have said something right during the lengthy interview with Roz and the library board, because they'd eventually offered her a job and in doing so offered her a lifeline when she desperately needed one.

So now she had a position at her old hometown library, where she'd gone to Story Hour as a kid and worked as a page shelving books while in high school. She slowed as she drove past the library building on the corner of Washington and Book Streets.

There were so many memories here. Her father had taken pride in telling her that the white Doric columns guarding the library's front entrance were the same style found on the Parthenon in Greece. She wondered if her dad was proud of her now that she'd returned home after messing up so badly. Beyond the words "Good luck," he hadn't said much when she'd come for the library interview several weeks ago.

Marissa had felt so stupid and useless after the divorce. Signing the divorce papers on her one-year anniversary hadn't helped. She couldn't even stay married for twelve months. How lame was that?

"You are *not* falling to pieces," she fiercely ordered herself. "Not in front of the library's book drop. It's been six months. Your falling-to-pieces days are done. You're starting over. Focus on that. Your new life. New job."

Yes, the pay was low, but it was a job and Marissa was grateful to have it. And yes, she'd have to stay at her parents' house for a week or two until she got her act together and her first paycheck. But there were worse things, right?

The threat of tears came suddenly and intensely as it often did since walking in on Brad in their bedroom doing the nasty with a female intern from his office. Blinking frantically, Marissa turned on to Book Street and found an empty parking place along the curb. Needing a moment to collect herself, she put the demon VW into park. She missed her Ford Five Hundred, but she hadn't been able to afford the car payments so she'd had to trade it in. This rust bucket was the only thing in her price range. She'd told the car dealer, "Any color but green." Yeah, right.

"Beggars can't be choosers," Marissa muttered, glaring at the rusty lime-green car hood.

"Are you lost?" The question came from a woman leaning on the open passenger-side window. "Do you need help?"

Yes, Marissa wanted to reply to both those questions.

"Marissa, is that really you?" the woman asked.

That was the question. Was Marissa really sitting there staring at her high school guidance counselor, Karen Griffith, who always described her as "smart and perky"? Or had Marissa fallen into some kind of parallel universe? Was this all just a bad dream and she'd wake up to find herself in her sleigh bed with her husband . . . her totally committed, non-adulterous husband?

Not gonna happen, her inner voice told her.

"Are you okay?" Karen was staring at her with concern. In high school, she'd always invited the students to call her by her first name and cared about their well-being.

"Yes, I'm okay." Marissa wished she sounded a little more confident.

"Are you sure? You look a little pale."

"I'm sure." Not really, but Marissa had become a fairly good liar. Sometimes she could even lie to herself. "Are you still working at the high school?" She'd learned that diverting attention away from herself was a useful tactic.

"Yes. I saw your mom at the grocery store the other day and she was bragging about how you're coming home to work at the library. I remember you were an avid reader in school. You always had a book in your hand. You knew early on what you wanted to do with your life. You had a plan. Not many students do."

Yes, Marissa had had a plan but it certainly hadn't included a failed marriage or ending up broke.

"Well, I'd better get going. It was nice to see you again. Welcome home." Karen waved and walked away.

Before Marissa could put the car in drive, her cell phone rang. The ringtone of Bon Jovi's "Livin' on a Prayer" let her know her mom was calling. At fifty-two, Linda Bennett was a huge Bon Jovi fan and a self-confessed worrywart. She'd called Marissa every hour since she'd set out very early this morning from just west of New York City, her former home.

"Where are you?" her mom demanded.

"On Book Street by the library."

A souped-up Camaro pulled alongside her VW with rap music blaring at rock-concert decibels, making it hard for Marissa to hear what her mom was saying. "What?"

". . . go around the barricade."

"What barricade?" Marissa asked.

No answer. Marissa's phone was dead. She'd forgotten to charge it before heading out. No big deal. She was only a few blocks from home . . . her safe haven.

• • •

Connor Doyle surveyed the crowd gathered for Hopeful's Founders' Day Parade. As the town's sheriff it was his job to make sure that things remained peaceful. Not that Hopeful was a hotbed of trouble or crime. Coming from Chicago, where he'd been an undercover cop in the narcotics division, he knew all about trouble and the worst that humanity had to offer. The brutal murders, the gang violence.

Connor had been a third-generation Chicago cop. His grandfather, his dad, his brothers—all Chicago cops. Well, his younger brother Aidan had recently moved to Seattle, but he was still a big-city cop. Connor's family didn't understand why Connor had left Chicago two years ago for "a hick town." Their words, not his.

Connor had his reasons and they were nobody's business but his. No one expected him to spill his guts. That wasn't the way his family worked. It certainly wasn't the way a cop worked.

The bottom line was that his years working undercover had left a mark on him. A permanent mark. Connor absently rubbed his left shoulder where a jagged scar remained to remind him of a knife fight that had almost ended his life.

Connor's older brother Logan had once told him that undercover cops were great liars. They had to be.

Connor had certainly been damn good at his job. So good that the lies had nearly consumed him.

His gaze traveled over the crowd. He knew most of the people he saw. The six Flannigan kids, all age eight and under, were present with their parents front and center. The kids had dripping ice cream cones in their hands. The only exception was the baby still in the stroller, who was reaching for her sister's cone, her face screwed up on the verge of a hissy fit.

Farther down, the older generation was well represented by a group from the Hopeful Meadows Senior Center. The women outnumbered the men by ten to one today.

Beside them was Flo Foxworth in her folding chair. Flo always reserved a curbside front row seat for every city event—from parades to concerts to fireworks. She worked in the post office and knew who subscribed to what magazines although she didn't share that knowledge with many. Not far behind her was Digger Diehl, the best plumber in town, who proudly wore his DRAIN SURGEON T-shirt with his denim overalls.

The mayor, Lyle Bedford, wore his customary red vest with his suit as he walked at the head of the parade with the Girl Scout Troop holding the large blue-and-gold FOUNDERS' DAY PARADE banner. Looking at him now, you'd never know that the guy had had open-heart surgery six months ago. A lifetime resident of Hopeful, Lyle had been mayor for nearly two decades and his popularity showed no signs of decreasing. Lyle loved Hopeful and the town loved him back.

Behind him was a Brownie Troop then a group of Boy Scouts. Trailing them was one of the town's shiny red fire trucks with Connor's buddy Kyle "Sully" Sullivan at the wheel followed by the fully decorated Chamber of Commerce float.

Next came the Hopeful High School Marching Band playing the theme song from *Star Wars*—playing it badly but with a lot of enthusiasm. The teenagers' faces were hot and sweaty from the above-normal May temperature, which was already in the low eighties. At least the predicted storms had held off for the parade.

The arrival of the perky cheerleaders waving their pom-poms was greeted with cheers from the men at the senior center—both of them. The football team was met with cheers from everyone for their impressive winning record last season.

Connor looked away to check the crowd. A second later, he heard a murmuring among the parade-watchers. Turning back to the parade he was surprised to see a rusty lime-green VW Bug crawling along the parade route at about three miles an hour, blaring some rock song he didn't know.

He expected to see some rebel teenager at the wheel, someone who'd pulled this stunt on a dare. Instead he saw a woman. Not a senior citizen who might have gotten confused, but a fairly young woman. Her smile was a little strained as she held up her hand and waved at the crowd as if she were royalty. Her face was flushed and she wore no ring on her left hand.

There were no markings on the car to indicate that it was part of any city organization or group.

Who is she?

Connor didn't realize he'd said the words aloud, until the woman beside him turned to answer him. "That's our new librarian," library director Roz Jorgen told him.

"Is she part of some library entry in the parade?" he asked.

"The teenage pages and members of Friends of the Library are participants in the book cart drill team . . ."

"That VW may be small but it's no book cart."

Roz shrugged sheepishly. "I don't know what to say."

"No problem. I know what to say."

Connor walked around the barrier and headed for the rowdy VW with the out-of-state license plates. "Stop your vehicle, ma'am," he said.

"What?" she yelled.

"Turn down the music."

"I can't. It's broken. It turns off and on by itself."

"Green Day," a teenager yelled from the sidewalk. " 'Boulevard of Broken Dreams.' Awesome song."

"Pull off at the next intersection," Connor ordered the librarian, shouting so he could be heard over the music.

She flashed her brown eyes at him, startled perhaps by his bossiness. She shouldn't be. He was a cop, after all. Giving orders went with the badge. And he was in uniform, complete with sunglasses so there was no mistaking who he was.

Several things about her startled him. Her eyes, for one thing. They weren't just brown, they were a light brown that reminded him of fine whiskey. Her shoulder-length brown hair was loose around her face.

He moved a barricade so she could turn off the parade route onto a side street.

Putting the car in park, she hopped out of the car before turning to face him. "If you can figure out how to stop the music, I'd appreciate it."

He reached in and twisted the keys in the ignition, turning the car off.

"I should have thought of that. But then I'd be stuck in the middle of the parade and I didn't want to do that." Her smile was a little wobbly. "I wasn't expecting a police escort."

"I wasn't expecting an unauthorized rusty VW to appear in the parade," he said.

"Are you going to give me a ticket?"

The dread in her voice made him curious. Not that most folks were eager to get a ticket. But there was something more in her case.

"Since you're new in town, no," he said.

"What makes you think I'm new?"

"Aside from the out-of-state plates, you mean?" he said.

She nodded and nervously twisted a strand of her hair before tucking it behind her ear.

"Most local folks would know better than to crash a parade," he said. "And Roz told me that you were the new librarian."

"She saw me in the parade?"

He nodded, watching as a blush covered her face. She looked good all hot and bothered. "License and registration, please," he said.

"Or course. Um, do I take them out of my wallet or just hand you the wallet?"

"Have you ever received a ticket before?"

"No, of course not!"

She seemed upset that he'd even ask such a question.

As she reached for her wallet he noticed the paleness around her left ring finger.

According to the New York driver's license she handed him, her name was Marissa Johnson. She was born in 1983 and was five foot six.

"Well, Ms. Johnson, welcome to Hopeful. I'm Sheriff Connor Doyle." He removed his sunglasses to give her one of his trademark reprimanding don't-mess-with me stares. Did he imagine her startled recoil just then? Hell, on the don't-mess-with-me scale, the look he'd just given her barely rated a two. He could be much more intimidating without even breaking a sweat. "You really do need to pay attention to the barricades and other traffic signals in town."

The signals he was getting from her abruptly changed from nervous uncertainty to downright irritation. He wondered what had caused the transition. He'd let her off with a warning and even welcomed her to town. What more did she want? Why was she eyeing him as if he was rodent shit all of a sudden?

Connor's expression remained impassive as he slid his sunglasses back on. "You could have caused an accident. Could have hit someone in the parade," he said.

She remained silent. She was biting her lip, which strangely enough made him want to reach out and save her lush lower lip from such abuse.

He definitely had not imagined the change in her attitude. Maybe she had a thing against cops? Then why had she acted all sweet and polite in the beginning? No, he was willing to bet it wasn't all cops, it was something about him in particular that got her all riled up.

Connor was used to riling up women. His brothers often kidded him that he was the womanizer in the family, which was bullshit because the truth was none of the Doyle men had trouble with the ladies. No trouble finding them, that is. Definitely some trouble keeping them. Connor's older brother Logan and his dad were both divorced.

Connor had lost track of how many times his dad had hopped on the marriage-go-round. Logan had recently remarried and hooked up with a librarian. Connor had been the best man at their Las Vegas wedding in December. That hadn't changed his personal aversion to getting hitched, however.

Connor eyed Ms. Johnson carefully before contacting dispatch to run a check on her plates and license. The response came back negative. Clean record. Not even a parking ticket.

He returned her license to her. She made a point of avoiding touching him as if they were in first grade and he had cooties. What was her problem?

"What are you doing to my daughter?" a woman demanded as she marched toward them. "You don't think she has enough trouble, losing her job and her house and her husband? She could be having a nervous breakdown."

"Mom, what are you doing here?" Marissa said.

"Flo called to tell me you'd been arrested."

"I was just giving her a warning," Connor said. "If she's unstable, however, she shouldn't be driving."

He knew it was the wrong thing to say the instant the words left his mouth.

The librarian turned into an infuriated woman warrior ready to do battle. "I am not unstable," she growled at him. "And you have no right saying that I am."

She stood there, in her white shirt, jeans and sandals

a good six inches shorter than his six-foot frame and dared him to say something else.

Of course it was a dare he accepted. "And you have no right crashing a parade," he said.

"I didn't crash it. I was very careful not to hit anything. It was a mistake, that's all."

Connor was starting to think it was a mistake not to ticket her for giving him a hard time.

He had the feeling that things in Hopeful were about to get much more interesting with her arrival. He wasn't sure if that was a good thing or not.

Marissa couldn't believe it. Of all the cops in all of Ohio, she had to be pulled over by this one. Connor Doyle. The guy who'd taken her virginity back in high school.

Okay, so he hadn't "taken" it. She'd willingly given it to him. Practically thrown herself at him. She'd been a high school senior and he'd been a freshman at Midwest College. An out-of-towner from Chicago. A sexy bad boy with a romantic streak. He'd followed his high school sweetheart to college but they'd broken up halfway through the school year.

Marissa had been working beside Connor at the popular Angelo's Pizzeria for five months by then. She'd gone by the nickname of "Rissa" in those days and had dyed her short hair ink black. She'd had a humongous crush on him from day one.

When she'd heard Connor was available, she'd been thrilled. Not that she was the only girl to try and catch his eye. But she had the advantage of knowing him for months—knowing what made him laugh, knowing his favorite songs, the way he thought.

So she'd screwed up her courage and "Rebel Rissa"

had kissed him one night as they'd left the pizzeria. He'd pulled her closer and kissed her back.

"You taste like tomato sauce," he'd murmured against her mouth.

"So do you," she'd murmured back.

They'd done a lot of murmuring in those days. A lot of kissing. He'd introduced her to the art of French kissing and she'd become hooked. They were a couple. Not that she went around bragging about it and not that she told her parents. What she and Connor had shared was too fiery and intimate to talk about. Their actions spoke louder than mere words.

And their actions had escalated with every heated embrace or tongue-seducing kiss. She'd wanted him to make love to her and he had. She hadn't told him she was a virgin because she didn't want him to have second thoughts.

Her first time had been awkward and a bit painful but he'd been so tender and loving afterward that she'd fallen even deeper in love with him. Her second time was much better and her third time was awesome. So were the multiple times after that. She was on the pill and he used a condom so they were being careful. But she hadn't been careful with her heart.

So she'd been totally blindsided when their three-month relationship ended at the end of the school year. He'd dumped her and gone back to Chicago. No explanation. Nothing.

She was starting to see a pattern here. She'd been blindsided by her first love and blindsided by her last love, her husband, Brad. Men sucked.

How dare Connor show up here in her hometown. This was supposed to be her safe haven. And despite the badge he now wore, there was nothing safe about Connor Doyle. Not one solitary thing. He still had those hard-to-define blue-green-gray bedroom eyes, broad shoulders, and lean build. Age hadn't seemed to do anything but improve his looks.

No, there was nothing safe about Connor. He was trouble she didn't need.

When in trouble, seek shelter. But how the heck was she supposed to do that when the trouble was right here in her own backyard?

Chapter Two

. . . .

"George, we're home," Marissa's mom happily announced as she tugged Marissa into the living room.

Marissa's dad, Professor George Bennett the Third, did not reply. Given his lack of response or appearance, her mom said, "He's probably working on his laptop in his study and listening to his medieval madrigals on his iPod with the volume cranked up."

"We shouldn't bother him then," Marissa said.

"He's your father. You'd think the least he could do would be to greet you when you come home."

"That's okay. Really."

Her mother sniffed her disapproval. "You could use a little paternal moral support after almost getting arrested."

The truth was that her dad had never been real big in the moral support department. In fact, the last time

Marissa remembered really bonding with him was . . . well, she couldn't actually recall. Sure, he'd shown her the trees lining the entrance to the college but she'd only been five or six then. He must have said he was proud of her once or twice since that time, right?

She certainly didn't want him knowing about the parade-crashing incident. That would definitely not make him proud. "Let's not tell Dad about that unfortunate incident regarding the parade, okay?"

"I suppose you're right." Her mom reached for her cell phone. "I should call your sister and tell her you're finally here."

"Can we hold off on that until I get settled in a bit?" Marissa's relationship with her younger sister, Jess, was complicated at best. Marissa couldn't label it as either good or bad. It just . . . was. Sometimes they argued and sometimes they got along.

Her mom set the phone down. "I guess we could wait a bit. I've got your old room all ready."

Marissa knew from her brief visit for the library job interview that her mom hadn't changed anything in Marissa's room since she'd left for college. But it still shook her a bit to walk in and see the purple walls and all the mementos from that time in her life. A time when there were so many adventures yet to come. A time when she'd had a mega-crush on Connor.

She'd burned any photos of him after he'd dumped her and gone back to Chicago. The pics on the cork bulletin board on the wall were of other events during her high school years, not that one. And there were photos of her dog Bosco, a rescue from the local animal shelter who'd died in his sleep at the ripe old age of fifteen. They'd gotten Bosco when Marissa was two. She and

Bosco had grown up together. They hadn't gotten another dog after his death because there was no replacing Bosco.

Marissa set her backpack on the bed with its paisley Indian cotton cover and pulled her wheeled suitcase farther into the room. The west-facing windows allowed the afternoon sun to pool on the hardwood floor and also afforded Marissa a view of any oncoming storms.

The storm thing was important to her after surviving a major tornado that had swept through Hopeful when Marissa was eleven. She'd been home alone with Bosco at the time. Thankfully, the storm hadn't damaged the house other than broken and cracked windows. But it had completely destroyed houses at the end of their block. So much for living on Tranquility Lane.

When in trouble, seek shelter.

Marissa had sought shelter that day, racing down to the basement with Bosco when the storm hit as tornado sirens blared in the distance. Then the roar of the twister overwhelmed all else, shattering glass and shaking the entire house.

She'd hugged Bosco close and buried her face in his fur as the two of them had crouched low and shook together. She could still remember those moments with photographic clarity. The storm had snuck up on her. The sun had been shining half an hour earlier.

To this day, she still had tornado nightmares. And she had a thing about being able to have a window with a western exposure because that's where most of the storms came from. After the disaster, which had killed half a dozen people, Marissa had insisted her bedroom be moved across the hall to the former guest room so she'd have a western exposure to see bad weather approaching.

This room was meant to be her sanctuary. All of the high school items around the room had personal meaning, from a quirky *Peanuts* cartoon with Snoopy and Woodstock to her Oasis poster. Their song "Wonderwall" had been one of her favorites

Noticing her interest, her mom said, "Last time you weren't here long enough to really enjoy looking at all your things. I hope it makes you feel at home."

Marissa turned to hug her. "Thanks, Mom."

"You know you can stay as long as you want. The room just sits here empty. Frankly, I'd enjoy the company. Your father certainly doesn't provide much companionship these days. I've told him I'm going through menopause and huge hormonal changes. But does he care? No." Her mom waved her hand in front of her increasingly red face. "Hot flash. Hot flash! It's too damn hot up here. I'll bet your father messed with the thermostat again."

"Maybe he's trying to conserve energy. You know, because of global warming and everything."

"I know all about global warming. It starts right here." Her mom vehemently pointed to her own chest. "There's a damn blazing furnace inside me." She impatiently wiped away trickles of sweat from her face.

"Have you talked to your doctor?"

"The man is useless."

"Maybe you should try another physician then."

"I'd hurt Dr. Matthews feelings if I did that."

"You just said he was useless."

"That doesn't mean I'd want to hurt his feelings." She

stepped out into the hallway to yell downstairs. "George, turn up the air-conditioning. I'm boiling here!"

"Maybe you should go down and check it yourself," Marissa said.

"You're right. If you want something done, do it yourself. Can I get you something to drink while I'm downstairs? Or to eat? I made some lemonade with real lemons, just like you used to love."

"No, thanks." As her mother departed, Marissa wished she could have a shot of tequila about now. The day had not gone the way she'd hoped. Crashing the Founders' Day Parade had been bad enough, but seeing Connor again sucked.

She hadn't noticed any sign of him during her brief visit a few weeks ago to interview at the library. And no one had mentioned that he was the town's sheriff. Of course, no one knew about her earlier relationship with him so there was no reason they'd make any connection.

She didn't want a connection with Connor. At this point in her life, she didn't want a connection with any man.

And even if she had known about Connor's presence in Hopeful, what difference would it have made? It's not like she had any other job offers or other options.

Then there was the fact that she refused to allow Connor to rule her life. Just as she refused to allow her ex to rule her life.

She waved her finger in a circle at her slightly bedraggled reflection in her dresser mirror. "They aren't the boss of me!"

She leaned closer. Oh God, was that a gray hair? She plucked it out and studied it. "No, not gray. Must have been the light or something. You're okay. You're going to be fine. Just breathe. Don't hyperventilate. Everything is going to be okay. Say it often enough and you'll eventually believe it. Sooner or later. Sooner would be better," she told herself. "So work on that."

• • •

"Who was the stranger who crashed the parade?" Mayor Bedford asked Connor as they both stood around the fairground area at the end of the parade route. This was the starting point for the historic district garden tour among other festivities. Booths had been set up in aisles offering food, from funnel cakes sprinkled with powdered sugar to grilled corn on the cob. The mayor always made a point to stop at all the booths and sample the wares but he'd paused long enough from that endeavor to speak to Connor. "I was up at the front of the festivities so I didn't actually see the vehicle myself. I just heard it was a beat-up green VW with out-of-state plates."

"That's right." Connor kept an eye on the crowd. There were displays highlighting all the town's major institutions—from the college to the hospital to the library. The chamber of commerce had the biggest display area, reminding visitors of the upcoming Rhubarb Festival in early June.

"Was the driver drunk?" the mayor asked. "Stoned? Senile?"

"None of the above. She just made a wrong turn."

"I'll say she did. So what did you do about it?"

"Gave her a warning and welcomed her to Hopeful," Connor said. "She's the new librarian in town."

The mayor snorted in disapproval. Connor wasn't sure if it was directed at him, the library, or the librarian.

"What's her name?"

"Ms. Johnson. Marissa Johnson."

Mayor Bedford's eyes widened. "Hold on. I know her father. He's a history professor at the college. Professor Bennett. Johnson must be her married name. I heard through the grapevine that she got divorced." The mayor shook his head. "So Marissa Bennett is back in town. How about that?"

Shit. Now Connor knew why she'd looked like she wanted to cut his heart out. He'd known her as Rissa Bennett. *Known* her in the biblical sense of the word.

She'd been a virgin—not that she'd warned him about that. No, he'd only discovered that fact when it was too late to turn back.

There were a lot of things he'd have done differently with Rissa if he could. But he knew too damn well there were no do-overs in life.

If there were, then maybe he could have saved Hosea Williams, one of the troubled kids he'd tried to mentor back in Chicago, instead of the eleven-year-old getting killed in a drive-by shooting. Hosea's death had spurred Connor on to do even more to save kids, some as young as seven and eight who got into trouble with gangs and drugs. Over time, he became burned out by all the failures, including his own.

The anniversary of Hosea's death was coming up but that was no excuse to wallow.

He certainly wasn't the only cop to be haunted by something gone deadly wrong. Back in Chicago, his own older brother Logan had been consumed by nightmares resulting from the death of his cop partner.

Cops don't dwell. They move on. Emotions were a weakness not a strength. They prevented you from doing your job. They'd driven Connor from the big city here to Hopeful, where he had a better chance of making a difference.

And now Rissa was back in Hopeful. She represented another black mark against his soul.

"You attended Midwest College briefly, didn't you?" the mayor asked.

"Freshman year."

"Did you know Professor Bennett?"

"I'd heard about him but I didn't have any of his classes."

Connor had had his daughter instead.

Not that he'd initially made the connection between Rissa and the history professor.

Hell, that had been ten long years ago. You'd think Rissa would have gotten over her anger by now. *Marissa*, he corrected himself. She'd gotten married. And divorced. Maybe she just hated all men at the moment.

No, she hated him.

"Good thing you didn't give her a ticket then," the mayor said.

"What?"

"She's a local. Her mom is on at least three civic committees, including the Women's Club."

"I met her mom today. She wasn't pleased that I'd pulled her daughter over."

"I'm surprised you haven't met her before."

"I don't have a lot of interaction with the Women's Club. I've seen her around town from time to time but . . . Anyway, that's not important."

"Yes it is. Trust me, if you piss off Linda Bennett, you're up to your armpits in alligators."

"She'll get over it."

"Normally she might. But she's not herself lately." The mayor lowered his voice. "She's at that age. You know."

Connor stared at him blankly.

"You know." The mayor ran a finger around his collar. "You've got a mother."

"Yeah, so?"

"Isn't your mother going through that?"

"Through what?"

"The change," the mayor whispered.

Connor couldn't believe he was actually having a discussion about menopause with the mayor. To make matters worse, he'd brought Connor's mother into the conversation. Connor eyed the other man over the rims of his sunglasses. "You're kidding, right?"

"I'd never kid about the change. I remember when my wife was going through that." Mayor Bedford shook his head and nervously fingered his red vest. "I wasn't sure I'd live through it. I wasn't sure she would, either. Nothing I said was right. Nothing I did was right. She even complained that I was breathing too loudly. Give me a break. How can you breathe too loudly?"

"Must have been rough for you," Connor said.

"You have no idea."

Connor preferred keeping it that way.

"And the crying. It never stopped. I take that back. Crying then yelling then crying again then yelling again. A vicious cycle." The mayor shuddered before sighing in relief. "Thankfully she came out the other side and we both survived. We've been married forty years."

"That's quite an accomplishment." Connor couldn't

imagine being married at all and for sure couldn't imagine being with the same person for forty years. He knew people did it. A few people. *Very* few.

His own parents had gotten divorced when he was a kid. His mom still harbored anger against his dad and had for nearly twenty years. He supposed the fact that Marissa was still angry with him after a mere ten years wasn't that hard to imagine.

He shouldn't have dumped her the way he had. He hadn't set out to hurt her.

Now he knew why he'd been intrigued by her. Connor's earlier feeling that life was going to get more interesting with Marissa's arrival had been an accurate assessment. He had yet to decide if it was going to get interesting in a good or a bad way. Given their history, the odds favored bad. Only time would tell. Meanwhile, Connor had a job to do.

• • •

Marissa's sister, Jess, hadn't been in the house two minutes before she started making trouble—deliberately or not. Five years younger, she'd perfected the art of pushing her big sister's buttons. She had their father's coloring—light golden-brown hair and big green eyes. "I heard about your splashy arrival. Everybody's talking about it. Did you think the parade was thrown for your homecoming or something?" Jess mocked.

"What parade?" their dad asked absently, his mind still clearly on the book on his iPad he'd just set down.

"The Founders' Day Parade was today," Jess replied. "For some reason your firstborn child here"—she pointed to Marissa—"decided to crash the parade."

"I made a wrong turn, that's all." Marissa was beginning to think this entire moving-back-home thing had been a giant mistake. Not that she'd had many other options, as she kept reminding herself. She'd had zero other options.

"Talk about messing up a first impression." Jess shook her head.

"First impression? This is my hometown."

"And you haven't been back much in ten years. Now we're supposed to welcome you with open arms? I mean, of course *I* do because you're my sister, but the rest of the town might think you're a screw-up."

"Gee thanks, Jess. Way to make me feel good," Marissa retorted.

"You know what I mean."

No, she didn't. That was part of the problem with her relationship with Jess. Marissa could never be sure what her sister meant. She sensed some resentment coming from Jess, but she had no idea why her sister would resent her coming home. Was it some kind of prodigal son or in this case daughter thing?

"Hey Daddy." Jess bent down to kiss their father's cheek. "Whatcha grilling tonight?"

"Steaks," he said.

Jess pouted. "You know I'm a vegetarian now."

Their dad frowned. "I thought you gave that up?"

"No, I used to be vegan but that didn't work for me."

"I'm sure we've got some veggie kabobs," he said.

Marissa stared at her dad and tried not to feel rejected because he had yet to really even acknowledge her presence. He'd nodded at her when he'd come onto the deck out back where they'd all gathered. But he hadn't actually spoken to her yet.

As if reading her mind, Jess said, "So, Daddy, what do you think of Marissa moving back home?"

Jess was the only one who still called their father "Daddy," as if to accentuate the fact that she was Daddy's little girl. Which made Marissa what? The other daughter? The one who messed up?

"My moving in is only temporary," Marissa quickly said.

"Hmm," her dad said.

What the hell was that supposed to mean? Marissa was rapidly reaching the end of her patience here. She glanced over at her mom and saw the expression of anger on her flushed face.

"Tell your daughter that you're glad she's here," she ordered her husband.

He blinked, apparently surprised by his spouse's irritation. "Of course I'm glad. Why wouldn't I be?"

"Because she crashed the parade," Jess suggested before laughing. "I'm just teasing. You know that, sis. Here, I'll even share my beer with you."

"No, thanks."

Jess appeared hurt by her refusal. "Fine. Be that way."

"I just don't feel like a beer right now," Marissa said and then wanted to kick herself for the apologetic sound of her voice. Her sister was the one who should be apologizing for being mean.

"Of course Marissa doesn't want a beer because she'd rather have her favorite lemonade I made for her," her mom said. "Here, have a nice big glass."

The lemonade cooled Marissa off.

"So, Mom, have you gone to that menopause support group yet?" Jess asked.

"Connie and I are going tomorrow night."

Connie Delgado and Marissa's mom had been best friends since kindergarten. They'd grown up together, got married and had kids, and now shared menopause together. Marissa wondered what it must be like to have a relationship over so many years. She hadn't kept up with any of her school friends. They'd just drifted apart after she'd left Hopeful.

As if to make up for her earlier snarky comments, Jess was on her best behavior for the rest of the evening. Marissa actually enjoyed sharing childhood memories of catching fireflies in a bottle on a warm summer evening or camping in a tent in the backyard with Jess, who had been afraid of polar bears attacking her.

By the time Jess left, Marissa shared a genuine sisterly hug with her. Their dad had yet to really become engaged in the conversation. He'd smiled during their reminisces but hadn't really contributed much beyond an occasional "Hmm."

Upstairs in her bedroom, Marissa sat curled up on her bed facing the window. Lightning flashed, warning of an approaching storm. She checked her Black-Berry for the latest weather update. No watches or warnings.

How prophetic was it that it was storming on her first night home? She sat there and watched it come closer, the flashes becoming zigzags across the night sky. The thunder swelled, beating down her defenses as tears slowly rolled down her face like the rain rolling down the windowpane.

Her emotions were a brittle jumble. She hugged her pillow the way she'd hugged Bosco during the tornado. The way she'd hugged her first love, Connor, the way she'd hugged her husband. What did that say about her, that everything she'd hugged and loved was gone?

Okay, she hadn't read any self-help divorce book that talked about comparing the men in your life to your pets, so that probably wasn't a helpful path to traverse. And she still had her family, after all. She'd loved and hugged them and they weren't gone. They were here.

Her strength was fragile but it would grow. She flinched as a clap of thunder rattled the windows.

There was a knock on her door. "Are you okay?" her mom asked as she entered the room.

"I don't know," she admitted, the tears falling easily now.

"Oh, hon." Her mom sat beside her and moved the pillow aside so she could hug her daughter.

"I still can't process it all," Marissa admitted on a sob. "The thing is, I was so clueless about Brad that I had no time to prepare. It came out of the blue, like that tornado."

"Oh, baby." Her mom stroked her hair like she had when Marissa was little. "I'm so sorry you have to go through this. But things will get better. I promise."

Marissa wished she could believe that.

• • •

Connor sipped his morning cup of coffee as he stared out the window of his apartment very early Sunday morning. The sun was barely up. Things were quiet. The neighborhood was still asleep.

Then he saw her. Marissa. Walking down the sidewalk. She wasn't jogging or running. Just walking. Not even power walking with that weird arm swinging thing going on.

She was wearing a blue T-shirt and conservative shorts. No Daisy Dukes for her. He should have just let her walk on by. He told himself that all the way outside.

She turned to confront him before he could say a word. "Is there some law against taking a morning walk?"

"Hey." He held up his hands in mocking surrender. "Chill out . . . Rissa."

Chapter Three

. . . .

"**What** did you say?" Marissa demanded. Connor was sans sunglasses this morning and she could see his face clearly, especially his hard-to-define eyes.

"You heard me."

"You know who I am?"

"Marissa Johnson, formerly known as Rissa Bennett."

And he'd known her too damn well, kissing every inch of her body. Doing things with his lips and mouth she'd never experienced before . . . or since. "Why didn't you say anything before?" she said.

"What did you expect me to say?"

"Nothing." He'd said nothing when he'd dumped her all those years ago. She was foolish to think he'd explain now. Not that she cared.

"I'm just guessing here, but you seem to be pretty pissed off at me still," he said.

"Ya think?"

"That was a long time ago. I mean, it's not like I ruined you for life or anything. You moved on. Got married."

"To a guy who cheated on me." Marissa hated that she'd said the words out loud.

"I heard you were divorced."

"Is that why you came out here this morning? To hassle me about being divorced?"

"Why would I do that?"

"Why should you care, you mean? You're right. I'm sure you haven't thought of me once in the past ten years. I know I haven't thought of you."

"Really."

There was no question mark at the end of his one-word comment. Instead he'd infused it with the silent observation *I think you're lying.*

"Yes, really. You don't believe me?" She was tired of people picking on her, starting with her sister last night and now her first lover this morning.

Connor shrugged. "Like I said, you seem pissed."

"I am."

"At me."

"Bingo."

"Why be angry with me if you haven't thought of me in ten years?"

"Because seeing you again reminds me of what a rat bastard you were."

Connor wasn't expecting her to call him out on his behavior although he should have, given the way he'd been pushing her buttons. What was wrong with him? Why was he looking for trouble?

Before he could say another word, she jogged off,

clearly in a hurry to get away from his rat bastard self. Could he blame her? Not really. There was little he could do to explain his behavior because he knew that no explanation would be good enough.

He kept watching her as she moved down the block. He remembered her telling him that she'd been a band geek in high school and hadn't made the track team. What instrument had she played? The flute? No, it was the clarinet. She'd laughed and told him she didn't play it well. Something to do with her lips on the instrument. He definitely recalled how that particular conversation had ended. They'd had sex.

Connor hadn't wanted a serious relationship. His first love had broken his heart after he'd followed her all the way here to Hopeful and Midwest College. Rissa had been his rebound girl. He'd had no idea she was a virgin.

To this day he couldn't say if he'd loved Rissa back then. Had he told her those words? He wasn't sure anymore. So much had happened in his life since then.

Hell, he'd only been nineteen at the time. Young, cocky and so damn positive he was invincible.

He knew better now. Knew that bad things happened to good people. That sometimes he couldn't protect those he'd been assigned to serve and protect. He couldn't always right the world's wrongs. Hell, he couldn't even right one city neighborhood's wrongs.

He hadn't been strong enough or smart enough or tough enough. Something was lacking in him. Not guilt, though. He had plenty of that to go around.

He hadn't been the first Chicago cop to burn out and move on. He was the first in his family though, and that was a big burden to carry. Although she missed having him nearby, his mom had been okay with the fact that he'd chosen to return to Hopeful instead of stay on in Chicago.

Connor suspected his dad, a career cop, thought he was a coward although he'd never said the word aloud. On his darkest nights, Connor heard the word in his head again and again. He should have stayed and fought. That's what Doyle men did. They stayed and they fought.

Not that his dad had ever fought to keep his marriage alive. Any of them. He'd been too busy being a cop. There hadn't been room for anything else, other than his addiction to alcohol.

His dad had eventually hit rock bottom and gone to an AA meeting. He'd been sober for over six years now. But he was still a cop through and through. That hadn't changed. Being a police officer was his first priority.

Connor was the same. His older brother Logan got that even though he teased him about being a cop in a podunk town.

On his good days, Connor told himself he'd come to Hopeful to find something—to make a difference—not to run from something. On his bad days, those words did little to stop the guilt that was like an explosive device in his gut.

Marissa had been the first to gently accuse him of using humor as a shield to hide his feelings. Several other women had made the same accusation in the intervening years but Marissa had been the first. She'd been pretty damn smart for her age.

She was obviously still pretty damn smart if she was a librarian. The dark circles he'd seen under her eyes indicated that she was having a hard time, which made him feel like even more of a bastard. He hadn't come outside to hassle her.

So why did you do it, Doyle? he asked himself.

Hell if he knew. He had a lot to figure out where Rissa . . . Marissa was concerned.

• • •

Monday morning, Marissa pulled her lame lime-green VW into a spot in the employees-only section of the library's parking lot. Not wanting to be late, she'd given herself plenty of time. She'd also changed her clothes several times, not that she'd had that many clothes with her. She certainly couldn't afford to buy anything new. She was lucky to have some classic pieces that she could mix and match to make them look different. And her collection of silver jewelry usually lifted her spirits. Today she'd chosen the oval dangle moonstone earrings and matching pendant. Her sky-blue top and black pants were also confidence boosters. Usually. On most days. But then, today wasn't like most days.

Today was her first day on the job. A new job that she couldn't afford to screw up. She had to make up for her disastrous first impression at the parade. Her first objective today was to apologize to her boss.

Roz Jorgen was waiting for Marissa. "Come in." She motioned her forward into her office and cleared a chair for Marissa.

"I'm so sorry," Marissa said before she even sat down. "I didn't mean to make a scene in the parade and ruin things."

"You didn't ruin anything."

"I certainly don't want to do anything that might

reflect badly on the library. I'm not a rowdy person," she assured her new boss. "Really I'm not."

"Despite the Green Day song blaring out of your car?"

"That's from a CD I burned with some of my favorite songs but sometimes I can't get the darn CD player to turn off."

"Sounds like the radio in Bumblebee." At Marissa's confused look, Roz added, "You know, the yellow car in the Transformer movies. My grandson is a big fan."

"Right." Marissa was nervous or she would have made the connection herself. At her previous job as Young Adult librarian she had a lot of interaction with teens and preteens who quizzed her on everything from which guy Katniss should choose in the Hunger Games trilogy to who Bella should choose in the Twilight saga. "Anyway, I'm sorry my wrong turn landed me in the middle of the parade."

"You certainly know how to make an entrance," Roz said.

"That wasn't my intention. Far from it."

"It certainly upped the interest in our new librarian. I suspect a number of our patrons will be stopping by today to check you out. No pun intended."

Marissa tried not to slide down in her chair like she did in high school algebra class so the teacher wouldn't call on her. She so did not want the spotlight on her right now.

You can't afford to be fragile, she sternly told herself. *You need to be as tough as nails.*

"I've got your paperwork here to fill out. Once you're done with that, I'll show you around and introduce you to our staff."

Marissa opened her Got Books tote bag real wide so she could find a pen, dislodging the brown paper bag containing her lunch.

"The staff room is through there," Roz said pointing to a door that opened off her office. "You can put your lunch in the fridge. There's also a large table where you can complete your paperwork."

"Right. Thanks." Marissa left the office, trying not to feel like the biggest geek to ever walk the planet. She was so nervous. One of her friends from her last job had called it geek sweats. She'd really loved the people she'd worked with there.

"You'll like the people here, too," she quietly murmured under her breath.

Apparently not quietly enough however as someone behind her replied, "Some of them, anyway."

Marissa swiveled to face her, her face turning red. "I didn't realize . . ."

"Don't sweat it." The newcomer held out her hand. "I'm Jill Harris. Head of the circulation department. That's what it says on my business card but around here we have to be the jack or jill of all trades, pun intended."

"Understood. I'm Marissa Bennett."

"I figured. I recognized you."

"From the parade? I can explain that."

"I wasn't referring to the parade. I wasn't there. But you and I were in the same French class together in high school."

"Oh. I'm sorry I didn't recognize you."

"That's okay. I was about ninety pounds heavier then and single. My maiden surname was Naponetti. I married Dane Harris four years ago. He was in band with you. Anyway, it's nice to see you again after all these years."

"Yes, same here."

Noting the paper bag Marissa held in her hand, Jill said, "Be sure to write your name on your lunch bag and water bottles before putting them in the staff fridge. Otherwise things will disappear. We have an unknown fridge Nazi here. I have yet to figure out who it is, but I will."

"Thanks for the heads-up."

"I'll let you work on that paperwork. See you later."

Marissa obediently took Jill's advice regarding her lunch bag before storing it and focusing on the paperwork portion of her employment. It seemed to take her forever to get it done and she felt self-conscious about that. Was her boss timing her, comparing her to other employees who'd filled out the forms?

Okay, she had to stop this tsunami of self-doubt or she'd drive herself and everyone else crazy. Afraid of being overheard talking to herself again, Marissa kept her pep talk silent and succinct. *Shake off the stress and get moving.*

• • •

Marissa did manage to shake off the stress at work but it hit her again once she walked into her childhood home and found her dad sitting in the living room, his attention focused on the pyramids displayed on the high-def flat-screen TV. She paused in the doorway, hovering there like a nervous hummingbird, waiting for him to notice her. She moved closer so she was in his line of vision without totally blocking the screen.

"Dad!" She practically shouted. She didn't mean to speak so loudly but she was getting more agitated and aggravated by the second.

He nodded but kept watching his program.

She felt like such a failure. There were only a few people on the face of the earth who could make her feel that way. Her dad was one of them. She'd married another.

Both men loved her in their own way. Or so they'd claimed at one time.

Wait, had her dad ever said that he loved her? Maybe when she was too little to remember. But not lately. Not for a very, very long time. A decade or two at least.

Okay, she was not going to stand here and be ignored. She really should just go upstairs with a carton of coffee ice cream and eat her sorrows away. But that smacked of giving up and she'd had it with doing that.

"What are you watching?" she asked.

"A documentary."

"About?"

"Egypt."

He looked so intent that she had to ask, "What are you thinking?"

"That the Silver Pharoah aka Psusennes actually did relocate Rameses' lost city."

Great. She was thinking about her dad and wondering what made him tick and he was thinking about ancient Egypt. That figured. No wonder she had issues.

Her dad went into how the Nile River had often changed course over the past several thousand years, making it hard to locate the lost city. She tried to outwardly politely listen but inside her resentment was growing. Her dad knew more about the Egyptian pharaohs than he did about her own life.

She told herself it was childish to be jealous of her dad's passion for ancient history. And had she not been feeling so vulnerable she would have agreed with her logical inner self. But as it was, her emotions were naked and exposed.

She didn't even know how to describe what she was experiencing because she'd never been like this before. Never been such a mess of anxiety, panic, depression, and despair. The self-help books she'd read said those reactions were all normal during and after a divorce.

At least she and Brad hadn't had any kids. The thought flashed into her head as she searched for some kind of silver lining.

"What do you think?" her dad surprised her by asking. In fact, she was so stunned she momentarily couldn't even frame an answer.

Then he added, "Don't you agree that the Silver Pharaoh must have found Rameses' fabled lost city?"

"You're the only one who thinks about things like that," her mom said as she entered the room.

"That's not true. We talk about it on my Facebook page with a lot of people who either agree or disagree with me on this issue."

"Do you have a Facebook page?" her mom asked her.

Marissa shook her head. "Not personally, no. I did work on the one for my former library."

"You should get one," her mom said. "You never know who might look you up. Just the other day I got a friend request from a guy I knew in college. In fact, when your dad and I broke up, Jay and I went out together."

Marissa's eyes widened. "You and Dad broke up?"

"Several times. Even then it wasn't easy to get his attention. So I'd break up with him and date someone else."

"But she always came back to me," her dad said.

"Don't sound so proud of yourself." Her mom shot him a look. "As I recall, you were the one who'd beg for me to come back."

Marissa knew that Brad had not begged to come back to her. Instead he'd tried to blame her, telling her that if she'd been better in bed he wouldn't have had to go looking elsewhere for satisfaction.

Cheating on her was a deal breaker. She'd told him that before he asked her to marry him and afterward. He'd sworn that it would never happen. But it had. In their bed.

Marissa lost a part of herself that day. The part that believed in happy endings and forever.

"I never knew that you and Dad had trouble," she said.

"We always have trouble," her mom said.

"But you never fight."

"It takes two to fight and your father doesn't always reside on this planet. Isn't that right, honey?"

"Hmm?" Her dad had that glazed look that said he was no longer following the conversation. It was a look he wore frequently.

"See what I mean?" Her mom rolled her eyes. "So how did your first day at work go?" she asked Marissa.

"It went well. I got the fridge rules for the staff room, which is always an important thing in a new job. And I met the rest of the staff. Everyone was very nice to me."

"And why shouldn't they be? You're a nice girl."

"I'm not a girl anymore, Mom. I haven't been for a long time now. I'm almost thirty."

"You don't have to get huffy."

Marissa immediately felt guilty even though she didn't think her voice had sounded anything but polite. "I wasn't . . . I . . ."

"I'm having a bad hormone day!" her mom said. "Dinner is in five minutes. If you both aren't seated at the table by then, you're not eating."

"She's not kidding." Her dad checked his watch. "It takes two minutes to get from here to the dining room. I've timed it."

Marissa barely had time for a quick stop in the powder room to wash her hands before rushing to her seat.

Her mom nodded her approval before glaring at her spouse, who came ambling in as if he had all the time in the world.

It was like watching a pair of adolescents pushing the envelope to see how far they could go before some adult stepped in and stopped the lunacy. Unfortunately, Marissa was in no shape to act that role. Instead she ate as fast as she could and excused herself, citing exhaustion from a bad night's sleep the previous night.

Alone in her room, she shut the door on her parents' issues. But that just allowed the memories of her own failed marriage to wash over her.

She closed her eyes and saw herself on her wedding day in white satin. Her father had given her away. Her mother had been teary-eyed. And Marissa had been so full of hope and happiness.

Then she saw Brad in bed with his assistant, the other woman's long red hair spread over Marissa's pillowcase, her burgundy nails digging into Marissa's husband's back.

In the beginning Brad had been remorseful. He'd

sworn it was a onetime thing. He'd even cried. That stage hadn't lasted long, however.

When Marissa hadn't given in, he'd quickly moved on, trying to use logic. Men weren't meant to be monogamous. According to Brad, the sociologists all said so. Marissa was a librarian, he'd said. She should know these things.

She only knew that he'd crushed her and left her broken.

When Brad's version of logic failed to impress her, he moved on to his angry defiant phase. He admitted he'd lied when he'd said he'd only slept with the other woman once.

Marissa replayed their last phone conversation in her head. "Why in our bed?" The words had been torn from her throat.

"It was the closest," he'd said bluntly. "Usually we did it at her place or in my office after hours. Why does it matter where we did it? Are you saying you wouldn't be divorcing me if you'd walked in on us in my office instead of in our bed?"

His voice had been filled with such vile disrespect and fury that she'd hung up on him and hadn't spoken directly to him since then. Her attorney had said to let her handle things, so Marissa had. She'd also changed her cell phone number.

She wished she could change her past as easily.

• • •

Marissa spent the next two weeks checking the local listings for available apartments. There was nothing in her price range. The places near the college were highly desirable by students who didn't want to live in the dorms.

There were a few sublets for the summer but they were in buildings so rowdy that the partying started early and never seemed to end. Marissa knew this because the beer cans were already flying between balconies when she arrived at nine in the morning. Most of the students left for the summer but enough stayed to make things noisy.

She was running out of hope of ever leaving her parents' house when she finally came across a promising possibility. The ad listed it as a one-bedroom apartment in a quiet and secure building.

She called and spoke to the building manager, Sally Parelli, who sounded very nice. It wasn't a huge complex. There were only sixteen apartments in the building.

She made an appointment to see the place first thing the next morning before work. It was plain and basic, with a small kitchen but a walk-in closet in the bedroom. And it faced west. Plus, the rent was reasonable.

"I'll take it," she immediately said.

She filled out the renter information form and promised to stop by after work to sign a lease—providing her references checked out. "Which I'm sure they will," Sally said. "Your dad has been a professor at the college for as long as I can remember. Everyone knows him."

Did they really? Because despite living at home for a few weeks, Marissa had yet to feel like she knew him. She knew things *about* him, sure. Like the fact that he loved quoting Terry Pratchett's novels. But that was different than really knowing him.

She was no Pollyanna. She realized that lots of parents didn't tell their kids that they were proud of them.

Her work with young adults had told her that. Many came from single-parent households where the struggle to get from paycheck to paycheck took every ounce of energy the family had.

"Your mom and I share the same hairdresser," Sally was saying. "And the same manicurist at Liz's Nails."

Marissa hid her hands in her tote bag as she dug for her car keys. She hadn't had a manicure in more than a year. When it came down to a choice between food and good nails, she'd gone with food. Her sister, Jess, would most likely have gone with the good nails option. Just one of many ways they were different.

"Plus you're working at the library here now," Sally said. "Your boss, Roz, and I are in the same book club group. We're also in the same knitter's group. Do you knit?"

"No. I've done some crocheting but that's about it."

"You should try knitting. It's not that hard. Anyway, I'm sure everything will check out. And I'm willing to have you pay the deposit over the next few weeks."

"I really appreciate that."

"Hey, I went through a divorce myself a number of years ago. I know how hellish it can be."

Marissa just nodded.

"I still get angry about it sometimes," Sally admitted. "When I do, I put on that Carrie Underwood song 'Before He Cheats' and dance. It makes me feel better. You might want to try that when you move in."

"I don't play my music loud," Marissa assured her. "I usually listen with headphones."

Sally laughed. "I never thought you'd be rowdy."

"I'm not."

"I believe you."

"I'll be back later today to sign the lease."

"That's fine. Unless you want to sign it now?"

"Really?"

"I'm a good judge of character and as I said, I know your parents. You're a local." Sally nodded. "I don't need to check your references any more than that. If you want to sign the lease now . . ."

"I do."

Marissa didn't even read it before signing, she was in such a hurry to get things finalized. Finally a place where she could put her own things and not live in days gone by.

"Great." Sally added her signature on both copies and gave Marissa her lease while keeping the other for herself. "It's a safe building." Sally said. "You couldn't find a more secure place because the sheriff lives here. Next door to you, in fact."

Marissa's stomach dropped. "The sheriff?"

Sally nodded. "Connor Doyle."

For a second, Marissa wanted to grab that lease back and rip it in shreds. How was she going to manage having Connor as her neighbor? She should have recognized the building from that Sunday morning when she'd been out walking and he'd confronted her, but she hadn't. After all, he'd appeared out of nowhere and she'd walked away. It never occurred to her that he might have an apartment right here.

Sally said, "The college kids aren't eager to live near the local law for some reason. But you're different. I'll bet it will make you sleep easier at night."

Marissa seriously doubted that.

Chapter Four

. . . .

"Are you okay?" Sally put a hand on Marissa's arm. "You've gone all pale."

"I'm okay."

"Do you need a glass of water or something?"

Marissa shook her head.

"Look, here he comes now," Sally said.

Marissa didn't have time to run for it. Besides, that would be the cowardly thing to do. Appealing but cowardly.

"Good morning, ladies." Connor was irritatingly cheerful.

Marissa hadn't seen him much since that early morning when he'd called her Rissa. She'd welcomed the break from his company in the interval but she'd always been on her guard against running into him. One time she'd waited in her car when she'd seen him walk into the Kroger until he came out a short time later. Luckily, no one had knocked on her car window the way they had a few days later in the library parking lot.

"Having car trouble?" Roz had asked.

"No." Marissa had started the rust-bucket VW, where- upon the sound of Copper's "Heartbreak Lullaby" began to blare out of the demented sound system. She'd turned the demon lime car off again. "It won't even let me eject the darn CD."

"I know a good mechanic if you want to get that fixed," Roz had told her.

Marissa had copied down the info even though she knew she couldn't afford to pay a mechanic. First she had to get an apartment.

And now here she was, with her lease in her hand and her nemesis a few feet away.

"You're just in time to meet your new neighbor," Sally said. "Connor Doyle, meet Marissa Bennett."

"We've met," Connor said.

Marissa didn't know which would be worse—him saying they'd been a couple a decade ago or him saying he'd pulled her over for being in the parade. She should have known he wouldn't elaborate. Maybe he was hop- ing she'd jump to fill in the silence and stick her foot in her mouth. Not gonna happen. She was learning when to keep her mouth shut and this was one of those occa- sions.

"Well, that's great then. You two already know each other." Sally reached for the vibrating cell phone at her waist. "Sorry, I have to take this. Excuse me for a mo- ment." She moved away, leaving them alone in the foyer between the four upper apartments.

"So we're going to be neighbors, huh?" Connor

grinned at her as if able to read her tumultuous thoughts. "I'm guessing by the panicked look on your face that you didn't know I lived in this building."

"I'm not panicked."

"No?"

"No." She was, of course, but she'd rather eat bugs than admit that to him. "Everything is not always about you."

"Fair enough." He shoved his aviator-style sunglasses on top of his head so he could fix her with a don't-lie-to-me stare. "So what were you thinking about to make you look so panicked?"

"My thoughts are my own."

His grin widened. "That's the first time you really sounded like a librarian. All prim and proper."

"Librarians are not all prim and proper any more than cops are all boorish buffoons."

"Just me, huh?"

"What?"

"You're calling me a boorish buffoon."

"That's not what I said."

"Of course not. But it *is* what you meant, right?"

"I refuse to answer that question on the grounds that I might incriminate myself."

"Was that ex-husband of yours a lawyer or some-thing?"

"Or something," she muttered. Brad was actually in middle management at a telecom company but he had plenty of lawyer friends.

"Did you pick up a lot of legalese from him?"

"I learned a lot from him. Some of it good. Most of it very bad."

"I'm sorry to hear that."

"Are you?" she said. "Why?"

"What are you insinuating now?" Connor demanded. "That I want bad things to happen to you? I don't. Why would I?"

"Not bad things, no. You're indifferent," she said. "You could care less, so why pretend otherwise? It's too late to pretend to be polite."

"Hey, I am very polite. Ask anybody."

"I don't have to ask anybody. I already know from my own experience with you that you're not polite or even nice, because someone with either of those sterling character traits wouldn't have done to me what you did."

"So basically you're telling me that I suck."

"That would be a pretty accurate assessment, yes."

"That was a long time ago. I could have changed."

"I doubt that." She went on the offensive. "Why do you care what I think about you?"

"Who says I do?" he countered.

Marissa bit her tongue and mentally reviewed her options. Could she ask Sally to tear up the lease she'd just signed a few minutes ago? She'd have to have a reason. Cold feet? She certainly couldn't tell her new landlady the truth.

"Don't let me scare you away," Connor said.

His words were a challenge she couldn't resist. "You couldn't scare me away if you tried."

"Oh, I probably could. But I don't plan on trying, so you can relax."

Right. As if she could ever relax around him. There was no way she could afford to let her guard down. She had to stay alert, stay aware and stay away.

Well, that last one was going to be more difficult given the fact that he lived next door, but she'd manage it somehow. Because that's what she did. She managed. She coped. And, yes, she cried. But only between coping and managing, and only for short periods of time and in total privacy.

Actually those crying jags had gotten shorter but it was getting harder and harder to keep them that way, given the stress of living with her parents. Maybe if her self-esteem hadn't already been in the basement she wouldn't have been as bothered by the situation at home as she was.

But it was what it was. Her entire life lately was what it was. It certainly wasn't what she'd planned or dreamed or hoped for.

"You somehow don't look reassured by my words," Connor said.

"I wasn't thinking about you."

"Weren't you?"

"No. As I said before, the world doesn't revolve around you."

"That's good to know."

"You should also know that I have no intention of changing any of my plans because of you." She discounted the one Kroger parking lot incident. "This was my hometown long before you ever showed up and it will continue to be my hometown long after you leave."

"What makes you think I'm leaving anytime soon?"

"I didn't say it would be soon. But that is what you do. You leave. You move on."

"So did you. You left and moved on."

Yes and look how well that turned out, she thought to herself.

"Just so you know, I don't plan on leaving Hopeful anytime soon," Connor said. "What about you?"

"I just got here and already you're trying to get rid of me?"

"I don't want to get rid of you. Far from it." He deliberately eyed her from head to toe. "You liven the place up."

"Are you saying Hopeful is boring?"

"No."

"Then why does it need livening up?"

"I didn't say it *needed* livening up. I said that you liven the place up. Two different things."

"I'm done trying to decipher your words. I have to get to work."

"Me, too." With a sweep of his hand, he indicated that she should go first. "After you."

Was he? Was he "after" her? Trying to get her interested in him again? Because there was no way she was going to do that. He could tease and tempt her all he wanted. He could bat those memorable eyes at her and flash his bad-boy grin and she would remain immune.

She had to if she wanted to survive.

• • •

By the time Connor arrived at police headquarters, word had already gotten out about his new neighbor. "Hey, I heard the new librarian in town just moved in your building."

The comment came from his administrative assistant, Ruby Mae Rivers, otherwise known as the department's version of *TMZ* without the videos of the stars. But her contacts made her a woman constantly in the know about everything there was to know.

Ruby Mae's short salt-and-pepper hair never changed from day to day. Nor did her raspy voice. In her mid-fifties, she was a mother of five and grandmother of ten.

She ruled them, and the people in the department, with an iron fist.

"News travels fast," Connor said as he poured himself a cup of coffee. Some of the employees got their daily dose of caffeine from the Cups Cafe but not him. He liked his coffee hot and strong. None of that fancy frappucino shit for him. His family already didn't approve of him working in a small town. If he started lining up for fancy coffee, they'd be sure to disown him. He wasn't sure how they'd know, but somehow they would.

Sort of the way his mom could always tell when Connor and Logan were roughhousing in the living room, using her pillows as footballs to launch across the room, occasionally knocking over lamps and smashing them.

Growing up, Connor had spent time split between two worlds. The one his mom and grandmother created, and the more dysfunctional one his dad had.

"The mayor wants to see you ASAP," Ruby Mae said.

Connor thumbed through his messages. "Anything going on that I should know about?"

"Not really. The hottest news is about you and your new neighbor."

"What's hot about that?"

"I just meant it's the latest news." Ruby Mae shuddered as he took a gulp of his coffee. "I don't know how you can drink that dredge."

"My granddad used to tell me that cop coffee put hair on your chest."

Ruby Mae's laugh was as deep as her voice. "A good reason for me to avoid it. How's your granddad doing?"

"He's doing great. In his mid-seventies and as ornery as ever."

"I suppose you're going to say that's because of the cop coffee."

"Nah. It's because of good genes."

"Oh."

"And cop coffee."

She returned his grin before reminding him, "The mayor is waiting."

The village hall municipal offices took up the other half of the building.

"You wanted to see me?" Connor said.

"Yes. Thanks for coming." The mayor indicated Connor should take a seat across from his massive desk. "I spent the morning with the school board and administration regarding your at-risk youth program."

"What about it?"

"They want you to work with another program. You know, sort of join forces."

"What other program?"

"One suggested by Marissa Bennett. Apparently she had a lot of experience with young adults in her previous library job."

Connor was really pissed off. This program was special to him. He didn't need Marissa messing it up for him. "What does she plan on doing? Having them read a bunch of books to turn them around?"

"She wrote up a proposal for the board." Mayor Bedford handed it to him. "I suggest you read it and then the two of you should work together to make the new program work."

"There was nothing wrong with the old program. With *my* program."

"Nothing is so perfect that it can't use a little improvement. Why don't you go on over to the library now and meet with Marissa?"

He'd rather poke bamboo shoots beneath his fingernails. "I have a prior engagement."

"Oh, right. You've got that presentation at the Hopeful Meadows Senior Center today. What's the topic again?"

"Avoiding scams and identity theft."

"Right. My aunt Gert is a resident there. She's really looking forward to the presentation. Well, you'll have to schedule your meeting with Marissa for another time then."

"Yeah."

"The sooner you two get together, the better."

Connor had no intention of getting together with Marissa. He'd done that once back in college and it hadn't worked out well.

"I hope you don't take this as an insult against all the work you've been doing in the outreach programs," the mayor said. "Two heads are better than one."

Connor doubted that. Especially when one of those heads belonged to Marissa. He didn't think clearly when he was around her.

Connor arrived at the senior center in a bad mood that got worse when the conversation immediately turned to his private life. He started his presentation professionally enough with the line, "I'll be giving you some tips to help you avoid scams and ID theft issues."

The mayor's aunt Gert interrupted him "I heard that you and the new librarian are moving in together."

"You heard wrong."

"Is that why she was driving in the parade?" Gert continued. "Was she trying to get your attention?"

"No," Connor said. "She just made a mistake."

"Trying to get your attention is a mistake?"

"She doesn't want my attention."

Gert frowned. "Why not? You're a good-looking fellow. She's single now that she dumped that no-good husband of hers. What's the problem? It's not like there are a lot of choices for a divorced woman."

"Maybe she's looking for a younger man," the woman sitting beside her piped up with. "One of those hottie college boys."

"Why would she want a boy when she can have a man?" Gert retorted.

"You know they say a male's sexual peak occurs when he's eighteen and then it's all downhill after that. Is that true?" Both women looked at Connor for an answer.

He gritted his teeth so hard his jaw hurt. "If you don't have any questions about scams and ID theft, I'm leaving."

"You've scared him," the woman beside Gert scolded her.

"He's a cop. He used to work in Chicago. I doubt he scares easily. Isn't that right, Sheriff?"

It was at moments like this that Connor wished he'd stayed in Chicago.

• • •

"How does it feel to be back home again?" Roz asked Marissa once the two of them were seated in Roz's office later that afternoon, "Are you settling in okay?"

Marissa nodded. "I just signed the lease on an apartment today."

"I know. Sally called and told me."

"Right."

"Small towns."

"I know." Which had made it difficult keeping her relationship with Connor secret all those years ago. Now she was so glad that no one else knew about their history.

"I wanted to talk to you about that proposal you had regarding young adults at risk in our community. The school board reviewed it at their meeting and they've given it the green light."

Marissa blinked. "I can't believe they moved that fast. I thought it would take months and months."

"Karen Griffith, the school guidance counselor spoke very highly of your plan. She was behind you one hundred and twenty percent. But there is one small catch. You'll have to work with Connor Doyle and the program he already has in place."

"Argh."

"Excuse me?"

"Nothing. I . . . umm . . . I just had something stuck in my throat. What do you mean, work with Connor?"

"The board wants you both to integrate your programs together."

"I'm not sure that's a good idea." Actually Marissa was positive it was the worst idea since NBC put Jay Leno where they did before returning him to the *The Tonight Show.*

"Well, the library budget certainly doesn't have any funds to do this on our own," Roz said. "We have to work with the school district and the mayor's office. That's where the funding is coming from. And their decision is that you and Connor have to make it work. Unless you don't think that's possible for some reason?"

What could she say—that he'd been her first lover and then dumped her? That he was a thorn in her side? That she was still battered and bruised from her divorce, still grieving the loss of her marriage and the vows she'd made? That working with Connor when she was still so vulnerable was emotionally dangerous for her? Of course she couldn't say any of that.

"Is there a problem?" Roz asked.

"I didn't anticipate that my program would be mixed with someone else's."

"I understand."

"The two programs are not similar. I did study his program before coming up with my own."

"I know you did. In an ideal world, you'd both be able to do your own thing. But that just isn't possible in this economy. And with these conditions, more kids than ever are at risk. You two will just have to suck it up and do your best. Can you do that?"

Marissa nodded, trying to look confident even as a little voice in her head was shouting "Danger Ahead!"

"Good." Roz smiled and turned her attention to a pile of papers on her desk. "I'm glad we got that settled."

Marissa knew when she'd been dismissed. She headed out of the office, her mind swirling with any number of ways this entire project could go wrong.

She ruthlessly cut those doomsday thoughts off at the knees. She could do this. She'd just bragged to Connor that she wasn't going to change any of her plans because of him. This was her chance to prove that. Or it was her chance to get rid of him . . .

No, she knew he'd never surrender his program and let her begin hers instead. She'd have to collaborate. And if she was being honest, he'd had some good results with his ideas. Not great, but good.

She was determined to be professional enough to work with him, no matter how difficult that might be. She could and *would* do this. She had no choice.

Chapter Five

· · · · · · · · · · ·

The minute Connor walked in the library, he was confronted by an angry female glaring at him. He'd just left a senior center full of angry females. He didn't need more aggravation.

"You keep doing that and you'll get wrinkles," he said.

She glared harder and growled, "I hate you."

Hearing laughter behind him, Connor turned to find Marissa standing there with a smile on her face. "Charming the ladies, are you?"

The five-year-old little girl who'd proclaimed her hatred for him stomped off to where her mother stood beside the circulation desk, horrified by her child's behavior.

"I'm sorry, Sheriff," the mom said in a harried voice. "She's having a bad day today."

He smiled. "No need to apologize. Bad days happen to all of us at one time or another."

He sure as hell was having one today. He refused to let that get him down. He could handle bad days with one arm tied behind his back. He couldn't handle the memories of the kids back in Chicago that he hadn't been able to save. Especially Hosea.

Connor clamped that line of thought shut and focused his attention on Marissa. "I assume you heard about the plan to merge our programs."

She nodded.

"So how do we get out of this? I'm open to suggestions."

"What do you mean, 'get out of this'?" She frowned. "There is no getting out of it."

"I don't need you butting into my program."

"Ditto."

"So how do we fix this? How about you let me keep doing what I'm doing and just make a show on the surface of being involved," he said.

"You are delusional."

"I didn't expect you to agree. Not right off the bat. But once you've interacted with these kids you'll back off."

"What makes you think that?" She didn't bother telling him she'd already met a half-dozen kids and had enlisted their input in her program. She sensed from the way that Connor had marched into the library that he was carrying a chip on his shoulder the size of a boulder.

"You're a librarian."

"Your point being?"

"These kids are tough. You're not going to turn them around by sticking a bunch of books in their hands.

What are you going to do, have them read Dickens or Shakespeare?"

"Shakespeare knew a thing or two about gang violence. The Capulets versus the Montagues. And don't try telling me we don't have gangs in Hopeful. Gangs are everywhere."

"I know how to reach these kids. You don't."

"How do you know?" she countered.

"You have no experience."

"Yes, I do. At my former library I created a number of programs for at-risk teens."

His expression clearly indicated he wasn't the least bit impressed by her statement.

"If there's no way out and we're forced to work together then we need to set some ground rules."

"I agree," she said. "I've already made up a list." She led him to the reference desk, where she'd left her file, and opened it up. "Here."

"No." Connor refused to take the pages she handed him. "You don't get to make up the list. That's my job. I do that."

Marissa pointed to the paper. "See rule number one. It says I make up the list."

"That's wrong."

"I suggest you direct your attention to rule number two. When you don't agree with me, you may say so but not by stating I'm wrong or stupid or any other derogatory comments."

"Telling you that you're wrong is not derogatory," he said. "It's simply a stating of fact."

"No, it's not a fact. It's merely your opinion." Seeing the attention they were garnering, she said, "I suggest that we continue this discussion in one of the empty conference rooms."

"How about your office?"

"I don't have an office. I have a small cubicle, where we can be overheard." At times it felt more like a partitioned prairie dog enclosure where every so often people popped their heads up to see over the wall.

"A conference room then."

As they entered the room, she realized it was in effect a glass fishbowl that provided little privacy aside from preventing them from being overheard because the door closed. Anyone walking by would see them talking.

Which was okay. There was no problem with that. She had to get out of the mind-set she had from her time dating him in high school when her parents had warned her about the dangers of going out with a college boy.

The warnings had started from her mother the instant Marissa turned thirteen. The idea had no appeal to her at that age. But when she'd first met Connor at the pizza place, she'd instantly felt the connection. A glance from him meant more that she could have imagined.

She'd worked hard to keep their time together a secret from her friends and family. Even her co-workers didn't realize that things had turned intimate with Connor. Marissa had really gotten into the whole secret rendezvous thing.

But those days were long over and she needed to remind herself of that fact. "If this is going to work we need to pool our resources," she told Connor in a very professional voice.

"Or you could just step aside and let me do my work as I've been doing for several years now," he suggested.

"I've been working with at-risk kids for a number of years as well."

"Doing what? Telling them to read a book?"

Anger crept into her voice. "You are so full of it! Why are you so threatened?"

He stared at her in disbelief. "Me? Threatened? By you?"

She nodded.

"That's funny. But I don't have time for humor."

"Your sense of humor used to be one of your strong suits."

"That was a long time ago," he said flatly.

"I asked around. People still think you have a good sense of humor and a commonsense attitude."

"See? That's what I'm saying. I have common sense."

"You just said you don't have time for humor."

"I take this part of my job seriously."

"So do I." She paused to give him an I'm-not-backing-down look. "That's something we can agree on. We both take working with at-risk kids seriously."

"Yeah but our approaches are totally different."

"You believe in tough love "

"I believe in showing them that the risks they take now have consequences. For example, they try huffing and they could die. The very first time. The kids don't get the potential risks, including brain damage and death. Huffing is breathing fumes from household products to get high," he added for her benefit.

"I know what huffing is. One in five kids will abuse inhalants by the eighth grade. The library is working with local schools and high schools to educate students and parents about the signs and dangers of inhalant abuse."

"Great. You keep working on that and stay out of my way."

"I wish I could stay out of your way and that you'd stay out of mine. But we're stuck here so we have to make do. Getting back to the rules, number three is important. Before I introduce you to my group of kids, I want your assurance that you are not going to intimidate them."

He crossed his arms across his chest and just glared at her.

"Yes, that's exactly what I'm talking about. That look. Don't use it on them."

"It's very effective," he growled.

"That voice doesn't work either."

"What are you talking about? It works damn fine."

"I want them to know we care what happens to them."

"I want more than that. I want *them* to care what happens to them."

"Well, of course I want that too," she countered angrily. "But that's not going to happen by scaring them."

"Sure it will."

"There are more effective ways to reach kids," she said.

"Yeah, right. With books?"

"You have an attitude problem!"

"So what are you going to do about it?" he drawled. "Have me journal my feelings? Hug a teddy bear?"

"What a great idea." She noticed a bear in the corner left over from a children's program discussion they'd had earlier in the day. "Here you go." She went over to grab it before handing it to him. "Hug it."

"Is that a dare?"

"Absolutely. I dare you to hug that bear."

He took it from her, twisted its arm and tossed it back.

"You call that a hug?" she scoffed.

"I don't do my best work with teddy bears."

"That's obvious."

"You already know from our time together how I hug," he said.

"That topic of discussion is off limits."

"So is me hugging a teddy bear where anyone can see."

"What are you afraid of?" she said.

"Not teddy bears, that's for damn sure."

"I think you'll learn a lot from observing the group's interaction."

"I plan on doing more that just observing."

"Then we have a problem," she said.

"You're just now noticing that?"

No, she'd known she'd have a problem with him the second she identified him at the traffic stop. But she didn't think she'd ever have to work this closely with him. Maybe she should have thought of that when she'd sent in that grant program request. Usually it took months and months or even a year or longer for something like that to get going. How was she supposed to guess that it would be approved so quickly or that it would come with strings tying her to Connor?

No, she couldn't have anticipated that. The question now was how was she going to work with him?

"Have you read the grant program proposal that I wrote up?" she asked.

"No."

"Then I suggest you do so. I read your previous year's

proposal. If you have a new one, I'd be more than happy to read it."

"Why bother? We both know that you won't approve of it."

"I might surprise you."

"You already have," he said.

His look was no longer intimidating but it made her heart thump nervously. The kids weren't the only ones at risk with this project. So was she. Big-time.

• • •

Marissa first met fifteen-year-old Jose Martinez her second day on the job. "So you're the one who punked the parade," he'd said. "You don't look like a troublemaker."

She'd been able to tell by the way he'd said it and by the way he was dressed that he considered himself to be a troublemaker.

"Nice T-shirt," she'd said.

He'd appeared surprised by her comment.

"Are they characters from a graphic novel?" she'd asked.

"Yeah. From *my* graphic novel."

"You did the artwork?"

He'd nodded defiantly.

"You're good. We're starting a teen group." She had yet to come up with a catchy name for it. "Our first program is going to focus on graphic novels. You should come Wednesday after school." She'd handed him a flyer she'd done up earlier that day.

He'd reluctantly taken it before walking away.

"You should stay away from that one," an older man had come up beside her to say. "I'm Chester Flint, by the way. President of the library board. Since you're new around here, you don't know that Jose has spent time in juvenile hall for spray-painting graffiti like he wears on his T-shirts."

"He's got talent."

Chester had looked at her as if she were a few pancakes short of a stack. "Talent? His only talent is for getting into trouble. We don't want his type here."

"'His type'? You mean because he's Hispanic?"

"I am not a racist. And I'm offended by your inference that I am."

Nice going, she'd told herself. Only on the job two days and already you're in a fight with the president of the library board. Not smart. "I'm sorry. I didn't mean to offend you."

He'd looked down his nose at her. "You'd do well to watch your step."

She'd nodded her agreement at his words. "I'm still learning the ropes here."

He'd relaxed his posture. "In time you'll understand what is expected of you." He'd nodded at her before walking away.

Marissa hadn't given up on the idea, however, and Jose did show up. The rest of the group had been recommended to attend by Karen Griffith, the high school counselor who'd called Marissa smart and perky. "These kids are at risk and I think you can help them," Karen had said in a phone conversation.

Marissa's interaction with the group of six was the catalyst for her writing the grant proposal for the program. They'd bonded in the ensuing month. She didn't plan on allowing Connor to speak to them before preparing them for his arrival and attitude. Which is why she didn't tell Connor about the meeting later that afternoon.

Red Fred was the first to arrive as always. His red hair and freckles along with his gangly awkwardness made him the butt of bullying. He considered himself a social outcast and a loner.

Jose was next to arrive. "Hey, dude, I got your T-shirt," he told Red Fred. He handed over a black T-shirt with the same graphic novel character on his own.

Molly and Tasmyn came in together. Both girls were thirteen and had self-esteem issues—Molly because of her weight and Tasmyn because of the birthmark on her face. Both had single moms struggling to make ends meet.

Nadine and Spider were the latecomers as always. The two self-proclaimed computer geeks excelled at technology but lacked interactive social skills.

They all considered themselves outcasts and loners. Marissa considered each of them to be special in unique ways.

It was rewarding to see the way the kids were slowly forming ties with each other. It wasn't always a smooth ride and there were times when she wished she could stop at a bar on the way home. But the bottom line was that she welcomed the chance to focus on someone else's issues for a change. She'd already grown tired of her own angst and drama. She'd come to care for them all over the past few weeks and she was protective of them.

Which was why when Connor showed up thirty minutes later, she tried to waylay him. She might as well have tried stopping a train.

The kids all stared at him with distrust. They knew who he was.

"What's he doing here?" Jose asked on their behalf.

Marissa could read Connor's mind and suspected he was about to say he was there to kick some ass. But he surprised her by nodding at Jose and saying, "Nice shirt."

Jose was not that easily impressed. He made no verbal reply but his body language said it all as he stood there with his arms crossed and his chin lifted up as if preparing for battle.

Marissa had to think fast. "Sheriff Doyle is here to talk about criminal minds in reality as opposed to fiction."

Nice save, she told herself.

What a liar, his look told her.

But he didn't contradict her.

"I didn't know we were having a speaker," Spider said.

"I wasn't sure his schedule would allow him to participate," Marissa said.

"Criminal minds start out young," Connor said. "What makes some people take the wrong path? A lot of different things."

"They have deceptive minds." Marissa gave him a telling look, accusing him of that symptom.

"Not just men," he said, returning her look. "Women, too."

"Are you two . . . like a couple or something?" Spider asked.

"Of course not," Marissa said. "We're just two authority figures expressing our opinions."

"She's expressing her opinion," Connor said. "I'm stating fact."

"That's not true."

His glare warned her not to contradict him.

"They seem to have authority issues of their own," Spider told Nadine, who nodded her agreement and kept texting.

"What are you doing?" Connor demanded.

"Tweeting that you guys are having an argument at the library," Nadine said.

"Put that away," he growled. "No tweeting at these meetings."

"Hey, it's a free country," Nadine said.

"At our first meeting, we all agreed to no tweeting, remember?" Marissa said.

"Whatever." Nadine tossed her smartphone onto the table in disgust. "I'll just tweet it later."

"This is our safe zone," Marissa said. "What's said here, stays here."

"Like Vegas." Red Fred spoke for the first time.

"If it was like Vegas, then gambling and prostitution would be legal," Spider said.

"Prostitution is legal in some parts of the State of Nevada but not in Las Vegas," Connor said.

"How do you know?" Nadine demanded, clearly still peeved with him for preventing her tweets.

"It's my job to know these things," Connor said.

"My mom and me lived in Vegas for a while." Tasmyn pulled the strands of her hair over half her face to hide her scar, something she did when she was nervous.

"Have you ever dissected a criminal's brain?" Red Fred asked Connor.

"That's forensics," Spider said. "He's a small-town sheriff."

"We're not that small a town," Red Fred said. "And he used to work in Chicago."

"No, I don't dissect brains," Connor said.

"See, I told you." Spider jabbed Red Fred with his elbow.

"That would actually be the coroner or medical examiner's job if it was necessary during an autopsy," Connor said.

"Have you ever been to an autopsy? They show them on TV all the time," Spider said.

The only reason Marissa noted the rapid change in Connor's expression was because she was paying very close attention, trying to anticipate what he'd do or say. Something dark and pain-filled flashed there for a second before it was replaced with hard-edged authority.

"We're getting away from the topic here," he said.

"No, we're not," Spider said. "The topic is criminal minds. Dead or alive."

"Cyborgs are into mind control. The Borg drill through your eye to your brain," Red Fred said.

"There are no Borgs in Hopeful," Connor said.

"That you know about," Red Fred said.

Marissa could see the wheels falling off the wagon so she stepped in. "Profilers at the FBI study what makes a criminal mind work. How they think. Law enforcement uses what they've learned to try and analyze behaviors." She was just piecing together bits of crime TV shows she'd seen, but she thought it sounded reasonable so far. A little incoherent perhaps but fairly reasonable. Or so she hoped.

"You're a LEO, aren't you?" Spider asked Connor.

"I don't think his astrological sign is relevant," Marissa said. Omitting the fact that she knew he was a Scorpio.

"LEO is an acronym for Law Enforcement Officer," Spider said.

"It refers to any individual sworn in to enforce the law as a federal agent, state trooper, sheriff deputy or police officer," Connor said.

"Air marshals and border patrol agents are also included. So are ATF, FBI and ICE special agents." Spider held up his smartphone with its Internet connection. "See? By the way, the sheriff's department is susceptible to being hacked. I just thought you might like to know that."

"We've got top-notched security," Connor began when Spider interrupted him.

"Not top-notched enough. I'm not saying I've actually hacked into the system, but I'm not saying I haven't."

"Same here," Nadine said. "Does that mean we have criminal minds?"

"No, it means the Borg want to hire you," Connor said. "Resistance is futile."

Marissa recognized the *Star Trek* catchphrase. She also recognized the way Connor glanced at her, telling her that her resistance would be futile.

No problem. She ate futile for breakfast along with her Frosted Mini-Wheats. Connor might have the group laughing now, but she wasn't going to let down her guard. Resistance wasn't futile, it was required or Connor would roll right over her.

Okay, the intimate scene that momentarily flashed through her mind was not acceptable. She needed to be thinking of tanks and steamrollers, not his naked body rolling over hers amid satin sheets . . . or high-thread count Pima cotton sheets.

Marissa ruthlessly booted the renegade thought out of her mind and focused on the goal here—the kids. Her problems weren't relevant.

Watching the group relax now that Connor had broken the ice, Marissa felt a tiny glimmer of hope that this project might work out after all . . . providing she kept her eye on the prize and off Connor.

Chapter Six

. . . .

"Today is Saturday. Moving day. Eat up." Her mom added another pile of scrambled eggs to Marissa's plate. "You're going to need your strength."

"I can't eat that much."

"Why not?" Her mom plunked the serving dish on the table and placed a hand to Marissa's forehead. "Are you sick? Maybe you should wait to move."

"I'm not sick," Marissa said. "It's just that this is enough breakfast for an army."

"We *are* an army. An army of helpers ready for the move. Isn't that right, George?"

"Mmmm." He didn't look up from his iPad, where he was reading something he obviously found so intriguing that he couldn't even put it down for a second to hold a conversation.

"I can't believe how attached you are to that thing,"

her mother said. "I would have thought you'd stick to books instead of embracing the new technology."

"If I was that backward thinking, I'd be reading papyrus and hieroglyphics instead of words on paper," he said.

"You *do* read hieroglyphics," Marissa said. "You just read them on your iPad."

"True." He smiled at her briefly before returning his attention to what he was reading.

Marissa had been living at home for more than a month now and this was the first time her dad had really smiled at her as if he'd seen her. She'd gotten a few absent-minded smiles aimed in her general direction and usually requested beforehand by her mom. But none of those had been real. At least they hadn't felt that way to Marissa.

All the self-help books talked about the important influence fathers had on their daughters' self-esteem. Volumes had been written about the dynamics. A dad's attention was always listed as a critical factor. So what did the lack of his attention mean?

Marissa lacked the emotional energy to figure it all out at the moment. She just wanted to move on. Move out and move on.

She wanted to be her own woman. Her own person. Not someone's daughter or sister or ex-wife.

Of course, that was impossible. She was what she was—daughter, sister, ex-wife, ex-lover. But she was much more than that. She just wasn't sure exactly what yet.

"What are you all doing sitting around?" Jess demanded as she entered the dining room. "We need to get a move on, people."

"But we're still eating," Linda protested. "Sit down and join us."

Jess sat down and looked around. "Do you have any pancakes?"

"No, but I could make you some. Marissa, would you like pancakes, too?"

"No, thanks." Marissa already didn't know how she was going to eat all the food on plate as it was. "I thought you were in a hurry, Jess?"

Jess shrugged and sank onto a dining room chair. "I've always got time for Mom's pancakes." She kicked off her sequined flip-flops and curled one leg beneath her before swiping some scrambled eggs from Marissa's plate like she had so many times when they were kids.

"The food is always better on my side of the plate," Marissa said, quoting Jess's favorite line when sneaking food from her. "Still?"

"Sometimes." Jess returned the fork she'd snatched. "You're my big sister. It's your job to look after me. Just as it's my job to help you on moving day by providing the muscle." The doorbell rang. "That must be them now."

"Should I make more pancakes?" Linda called out from the kitchen.

Jess snatched another forkful of fluffy scrambled eggs before jumping up and racing to the front door in her bare feet. Jess never walked if she could run. She'd been that way since she'd taken her first steps.

Marissa was the opposite. From a very young age, she'd been sure and steady. She'd never taken the same fall twice. She'd learned from her mistakes and didn't repeat them.

Moments later Jess led a trio of hotties into the dining room. "Help has arrived!" she cheerfully announced.

"Meet the Roberts brothers—Mike, Tim and Jason." She pointed to each one as she said their names. "Pull up a seat, guys. Pancakes are on the way."

"I'm going to go help Mom," Marissa said.

"Can I have the rest of your eggs?" Jess asked for permission but she'd already taken the seat Marissa had just vacated and had the fork halfway to her mouth.

"Knock yourself out," Marissa said.

As Marissa left the dining room she wondered if her dad even noticed that there were three newcomers at the table or if he was so engrossed in his iPad that he was clueless. She paused on the threshold to the kitchen. "Dad, we have company."

"They're not company, they're friends," Jess said. "Don't bother Daddy. He's rereading one of Terry Pratchett's books. He does that every Saturday morning. Which one is it today, Daddy?"

"*Pyramids.*"

Jess patted his arm affectionately, "One of his faves."

Marissa attributed the strange twinge in her chest to heartburn from eating a rushed breakfast. It certainly wasn't caused by the closeness her sister and father shared. Resenting that would be petty.

"Want me to make up another batch of pancake batter?" Marissa asked her mom after entering the kitchen.

"I'll do that if you'll watch these cooking and turn them before they burn."

"Okay." Marissa moved over to the stove.

"Then you can go tidy up."

" 'Tidy up'?" Marissa repeated with a frown.

"I'm not saying there's anything wrong with the way you look."

"Good."

"It's just that you look cuter when you don't have your hair scraped back in a ponytail. And that T-shirt is older than I am."

"Not true. And this is perfect attire for moving day. I sold all my sequined dresses on eBay to pay the bills."

Her mom sniffed back the sudden onslaught of tears. "I feel like such a failure."

Marissa was stunned. What had she said to set off her mom this time? Sometimes it was like dealing with the hormonal adolescents in her teen group. She never knew when they or her mom would go off on a bit of a rant.

"If I was a better mom you wouldn't have had to sell your clothes on eBay."

Marissa hugged her, taking care with the spatula she held in her hand. "You're a great mom. The divorce was the reason I had financial trouble. Nothing to do with you."

"Of course it had something to do with me. Everything you do has something to do with me. You're my daughter."

"Mom, I'm an adult. My mistakes are my own."

"I just hate that you've had to go through all the trauma that you've had to deal with for the past few months. I really thought your marriage would work out."

"Yeah, me too." Marissa returned her attention to the pancakes.

"Well, just because that one didn't succeed doesn't mean you shouldn't get back on the horse and try again." Her mom paused to pull the collar of her pink shirt away from her neck. "Is it hot in here or is it just me?"

"It is a little warm."

"I hate these hot flashes," her mom growled. "My face turns so red that I look like a tomato."

"How is that menopause support group you and Connie have been attending?"

"They've given me some good ideas. We all have become very familiar with our freezers." Her mom opened it and fanned the chilled air toward her flushed face. "Ah . . . that feels so good." She removed something from the freezer and stuck it into her cleavage.

"What are you doing?"

"A little trick I learned from the Hot Ladies. That's what the group is called."

"And they taught you to slip an ice cube down your shirtfront?"

"That would melt too fast and be messy. No, they told me about these cooler thingies. They're really gel eye masks but you pop them in the freezer for a bit to get them nice and cold and then you stick them in your bra. They fit there perfectly. It's an accessory that every Menopause Barbie should have."

"Just like every Iron Chef Barbie should be able to do this." Marissa expertly flipped the pancakes.

"Good job," her mom said.

"I learned from the best."

Her mom smiled at her and then out of the blue said, "You really should go to the divorce support group meeting."

"I don't have time," Marissa said.

"You told me you'd try to go and it's been over a month since then. Promise me after you move you'll go."

"Fine. I promise."

A few minutes later Marissa carried a platter full of pancakes to the dining room and the ravenous Roberts brothers. It took another two plattersfull to satisfy their appetite.

Marissa had prepared a written plan for the move. She didn't have much furniture, only the things from her old bedroom. Her mom had found some extra stuff in the basement—a comfy but worn chair and love seat along with an end table and a few lamps.

Marissa's ex had taken half the furniture from their house and Marissa had sold the rest. She told herself that it was for the best. This way she had no bad memories from that period in her life. Yes this furniture was old but it had no connection to her ex.

The Roberts brothers made fast work of shifting the furniture up and down stairs and into the small U-Haul truck that she'd rented. Her father's contribution was to drive the truck.

Marissa followed in her lame VW. Snow Patrol's "Open Your Eyes" blared from the car speakers. She slowed the car when she spotted an oval dining table and four matching wooden chairs alongside the curb with a sign that read FREE. She didn't have a dining table or chairs.

Stopping, she hopped out of the car to check them out.

Her mother, driving behind her in her white Toyota Avalon, instantly pulled up next to her. "What are you doing?"

"Checking out this table," Marissa said. "It looks to be in good shape."

"We are not picking up furniture from the curb."

"Why not?"

"We are not that bad off."

"I am."

"Get back in your car," she ordered Marissa. "Right now!" Her voice bordered on hysteria, signaling a full-blown meltdown would occur any instant if Marissa did not obey.

So she reluctantly turned away and climbed back in her Kermit the Frog car. Some things just weren't worth the battle to get them.

· · ·

Connor sat in the sheriff department's SUV and watched Marissa and her mom at the other end of the block. He wasn't stalking them. He was on patrol doing cop stuff. He'd heard today was moving day. Not that Marissa had told him.

Since that meeting with the teens, she'd been more close-mouthed than a CIA operative. Connor hadn't tried to interrogate her. He'd had been too busy. He'd arranged to have his IT security rep speak to Spider and Nadine about possible holes in the department's fire-walls and computer security. He already knew the two-some were suspects in a hacking incident into the high school records in order to change some grades, but there was insufficient proof to do anything about that case. He didn't intend to let his department's records be at risk. Keep your friends close, possible hackers closer.

His thoughts were interrupted by the sound of the dispatcher over the police radio. "Sheriff. Mrs. Craig at 4136 Chestnut Street is reporting a suspicious vehicle parked at the end of her block. It's a white SUV with writing on the side, but she can't find her glasses to read what it says."

Connor sighed. "That's me. I'm parked here. Tell her not to worry."

"Okay."

A moment later the dispatcher was back. "Sheriff, Mrs. Craig wants to know why you're parked there so long. Is there drug activity on her block that she should know about? She said I should remind you that she is part of the Neighborhood Crime Busters group."

"There's nothing suspicious. No criminal activity." Aside from him wasting his time watching Marissa. That should be criminal. He'd been thinking about her . . . dreaming about her too much.

Starting the SUV, he made an illegal U-turn on the now-deserted street, which Mrs. Craig immediately reported in.

"Sheriff, Mrs. Craig says a light-colored SUV just made an illegal U-turn—"

Connor cut her off. "That was me. Don't you have any real crimes to report?"

"Hold on."

Connor drove through the neighborhood while he waited, returning the waves of the people he knew as he passed by. The entire waving thing reminded him of Marissa stuck in the parade and doing her royal wave. She had pretty hands. He wasn't usually a guy who noticed a woman's hands, other than to check for a wedding ring or a weapon. But he'd always liked Marissa's hands and he'd taught her to do some pretty wicked things with them. The memories took hold, making him almost drive through a stop sign.

"Sheriff, we have a call about possible vandalism on a car at 920 Euclid Avenue."

"Now we're talking."

The location was only a few blocks away. Connor arrived, lights flashing, to find one of Marissa's teens with several cans of spray paint aimed at a formerly white sedan. Jose didn't seem the least bit upset at Connor's arrival.

"Step away from the vehicle," Connor ordered him.

"I can't stop now. The paint will dry and ruin it."

"Step away from the vehicle," Connor barked, his voice edged with warning. "And set the cans on the ground."

Jose reluctantly obeyed. "You think I'm dumb enough to tag a car in the middle of the day?"

"I'm just checking out a call we got."

"From a neighbor nervous about the Latino kid, right?"

"From a neighbor nervous about someone's car being vandalized. Where's the vehicle's owner?"

"Inside changing his baby's shitty diaper. I got his permission to paint the car. He hired me to do the job. Go ask him."

"I will. You wait here."

Connor had the dispatcher run the license plate to confirm the name and address of the owner, who had no outstanding warrants or tickets and who also was not in the best of moods after his diaper duty.

Swearing vehemently under his breath, the guy almost smacked Connor in the face with the storm door as he rushed out of the house—one hand covering his nose while the other held a small garbage bag.

Cursing even louder now, Diaper Dad raced to the trash bin and threw the offensive bag inside before slamming the lid shut. "Talk about toxic waste," he muttered. He paused, seeming to notice Connor's presence for the first time. "Why are you here?"

"We got a call from a concerned neighbor."

"He thinks I'm vandalizing your car," Jose interrupted him to say.

"I told you to wait by the vehicle," Connor said.

"You gonna arrest me for disobeying orders?" Jose challenged him.

The vehicle's owner quickly spoke up. "After seeing his T-shirt designs, I asked Jose to give my car a custom paint job. I believe in supporting the arts and I've admired Jose's work for some time now."

"Are you using any gang tags on it?" Connor asked Jose.

"I make my own designs," Jose said proudly. "I don't need to copy no one else's."

The sound of a baby's angry crying sent Diaper Dad heading back inside. "Jose is just doing what I asked him to do," he yelled over his shoulder. "I hope that clears things up." The storm door slammed behind him.

Jose stood with his arms crossed against his chest and his chin jutting out as if daring Connor. "So, you gonna arrest me or not?"

"Not."

Jose tried not to show it, but his body relaxed slightly. "Library Lady will be pleased to hear that," Jose said. "I heard she moved in with you."

"Not *with* me," Connor corrected him. "Next door to me. Who told you?"

"I don't reveal my sources."

"Was it Flo at the post office?" She was in charge of all the change of address forms turned in.

Jose just shrugged.

"Your grandma and Flo are friends, huh?"

"You keep my grandma out of it." Jose's expression darkened. "Don't you hassle her."

"Calm down. I'm not going to hassle your grandma. I've got one of my own."

"One what?"

"A grandma."

Jose relaxed his fight-or-flight stance a little. "I bet she's not as tough as mine."

"I bet she is," Connor said.

"The Library Lady is tough, too. I know you don't think so."

"I never said that."

"I can tell these things. It's 'cause I'm an artist."

"Yeah, well it's 'cause I'm a cop that I have to check out reports of suspicious activity."

"Someone is always suspicious of me," Jose said. "Except for—"

"—the Library Lady," Connor filled in. "Yes, I know."

"You two have this thing going on."

"What thing?"

"This Edward-Bella thing. Or maybe it's a Jacob-Bella thing. Not that I read that crap. Too sappy for me."

"I thought the fight scenes were pretty intense."

Jose's dark eyes widened. "You read that book?"

Connor nodded. "I read the entire series. What? You don't think cops can read?"

"Not that stuff."

"Why not?"

"Does the Library Lady know you've read those books?" Jose asked.

"The subject hasn't come up."

"She might be impressed if she knew."

"I doubt it. She's not that easily impressed."

Jose gave him a shrewd look. "You know her pretty well, huh?"

Connor couldn't believe he was standing here talking about Marissa with this kid.

"I heard she was moving in today. Why aren't you helping her?" Jose said.

"Why aren't you?"

"Because I'm working."

"So am I," Connor said.

"Yeah. Hassling poor Latino kids trying to make a living." Jose's tone had gone from defensive to teasing.

"I was not hassling you. If anything, you've been hassling me about Marissa."

"You didn't seem to mind. I think you have a thing for the Library Lady."

"So you've already said." Connor gave him a warning look.

"Or maybe not," Jose said, hastily backing away. "I've got to get back to work."

"Yeah, me too," Connor said. He was glad he'd gotten the last word in, but he couldn't help wondering why that didn't make him feel as good as it should. The idea that a kid with a smart mouth and a creative flair had bested him smarted just a little. Or maybe it was the possibility that Jose was right and that Connor really did have a thing for the Library Lady.

• • •

"Why couldn't you get an apartment on the ground floor?" Jess demanded.

"Because there wasn't one available."

Jess paused inside the door to her apartment. "Are you sure it wasn't so you could move in next door to Sheriff Hottie?"

"You're kidding, right?" Marissa had worried that she might run into Connor while her things were being shifted from the U-haul truck to her new place but so far there had been no sign of him.

"Am I?" Jess set the box of kitchen stuff that their mom had donated to Marissa. Picking up one of the items, Jess said, "What are you going to do with a crepe maker?"

"Make crepes."

Jess dumped the item back in the box and picked up another. "Hey, you got the potato ricer? I wanted that."

"You hate to cook."

"So?"

"Fine. If you want it so badly you can have it."

"No." Jess set it on the kitchen counter. "Where are you going to eat? You don't have a table."

"I saw one on the way here that was free and looked to be in good shape with four matching chairs. I wanted to pick it up but Mom had a fit."

"I'm sure she did."

"Anyway . . . um . . . thank your friends again for all their help."

Jess checked her vibrating phone for a text. "I've got to go. Dad is returning the truck. All your stuff is moved in." Marissa followed her into the hallway. "Oh wait, there's still part of the bed here."

"That's okay. I can bring that in."

"I'm sorry the guys couldn't stay long enough to put the bed together for you."

"It's together. This is just the headboard that goes against the wall. No problem. You go on. I'll take care of this." Marissa gave her an awkward hug. "Thanks again."

Jess was gone a moment later.

Marissa eyed the headboard before trying to lift it on her own. Damn, it was much heavier than it looked.

Then she heard a familiar male cop voice ask, "Need help?"

Chapter Seven

. . . .

Marissa turned to face Connor. "No, thank you."

"Step aside." When she hesitated, he put his hands on her shoulders and gently moved her. Marissa instantly felt the impression of his fingers through her thin T-shirt. Unexpected flares of awareness hummed from her head to her toes. His touch was brief but created such a powerful reaction that Marissa didn't know what to do about it.

This was the first time Connor had touched her since she'd returned to Hopeful and he'd already released her from his hold physically. But emotionally she felt a connection that took her back to their days together. And that totally disconcerted her.

If she responded so intensely to a passing contact, she could only imagine what a more intimate exchange might be like. The chemistry that had burned so brightly all those years ago was still present for her. Which made Connor dangerous to her peace of mind.

"You can just leave it here," she said the instant he entered her apartment.

"You plan on sleeping in your hallway? Don't be silly." He carried the headboard to her bedroom. He slid it into place and eyed her entire bed. "Hey, I recognize this."

Connor remembered the bed from the one time that he'd stolen into her bedroom when her parents were out. He'd parked his car a block away.

"Your mom came home early and almost caught us. I had to crawl out your bedroom window and climb down that old oak tree."

"You don't remember me but you remember the bed?" she said. "That's just weird."

"I don't forget something like that."

"Like what?" *Like loving her? Like thinking she was "the one"?*

"Like almost getting caught by an angry parent," he said.

That figures. It was all about *him*. Not her. She refused to show how much that fact aggravated her. "I'm surprised. I would have thought it would have happened to you a lot in high school."

"All through high school, I went steady with Becka and her parents adored me. They were very liberal about house rules so there was no need to crawl out of windows and risk breaking my neck climbing down a huge tree."

"Isn't that just peachy for you." She quickly moved aside but tripped over a plastic box sitting on the floor. She ended up making a swan dive onto her mattress.

Since Connor reached out to grab her, she pulled him down with her. He rolled so he didn't squish her.

They faced each other. She was so close she could see all the hard-to-decipher colors in his eyes. At the moment they seemed more gray than green or blue. His eye color was as hard to pin down as the man himself.

Yet here she was, pressed against him. She could feel the beat of his heart against the palm of her hand braced on his chest. They were both wearing worn jeans but he looked much sexier in his than she did in hers.

At the moment, which seemed frozen in time, sex was all she could think about. She knew she should move but she couldn't seem to actually do it. Would kissing him be as good as she remembered? Did she dare find out?

No, she couldn't risk it. Not yet. Spurred by fear, she leapt off the bed as if catapulted.

"Sorry about that," she said, determined to sound nonchalant and blasé. "I didn't mean to squish you like a pancake."

He got to his feet much slower than she did. "No problem. You didn't squish me."

Of course there was a problem as far as Marissa was concerned. A huge gigantic problem. She was still attracted to Connor. She couldn't let him see that. So she calmly walked out of the bedroom instead of shoving him out the door like a frenzied maniac.

He looked around the living/dining area with its meager furnishings.

"So are the rest of your things in storage?" he said.

"What?"

He pointed behind her. "Your things."

"This is everything."

The surprised look on his face made her regret her

honesty. She didn't want his pity, which she feared would be his next expression. So she took preemptive action by saying, "I'm into minimalism."

"Even minimalists need a table to eat off of," he said.

"I'm having one delivered soon."

"I thought you said this was everything."

"Everything that I have right now. Tomorrow I'll have a table and chairs."

"If you say so."

"I do. And why do you care about my furniture, anyway? Are you Nate Berkus or something?"

"Who?"

"Never mind. Thanks for your help but I've got a lot of stuff to do." Now she did rush him to the door, careful not to slam it in his face but to act totally normal.

The second he was gone, she called her sister. "Meet me on Chestnut Street. We're getting that free dining table."

"You're in luck. I'm already on Chestnut Street. I was going to surprise you. I've already loaded the chairs." Jess drove a hybrid SUV.

"I'll be right there," Marissa said, grabbing her keys.

"No need. One of the Roberts brothers is helping me. Stay put. We'll bring the furniture later. Sometime tomorrow. We've got someplace else to be right now. "

"Okay. Thanks."

Marissa spent what was left of the day finding a place for her things. Since she had more space than things, that wasn't real hard. Still, she'd moved things around a few times until she got it the way she wanted. The bedside table on the right or the left? She moved it three times and still couldn't decide, distracted as she was by the memory of Connor sprawled beside her on the bed.

She made the bed with the new comforter set and sheets her mom had given her as a housewarming present. There. She eyed the results with approval. This was a bed Connor had never seen . . . and wasn't likely to anytime soon.

A short time later her nesting mode was interrupted by the sound of someone knocking at her door.

Thinking it must be her sister with the table and chairs, she opened it without checking. An Angelo's Pizza delivery teenager stood there. "I didn't order a pizza," she said.

"It's already paid for," he said.

"There must be some mistake."

"No mistake, ma'am." He handed her the pizza.

She took it while still protesting. "Who paid for it? Hold on." She grabbed her phone off the kitchen counter and speed dialed her mom. "Did you or Dad order a pizza for me?"

"No. But that was a good idea. Maybe your sister ordered it."

Marissa eyed the nervous delivery guy suspiciously. "Was it the sheriff? Did he pay for the pizza?"

"I'm not allowed to say, ma'am."

Okay that was the second time the teenager had called her "ma'am." Her glare broke down his resistance. "Yes, it was the sheriff." He took off before she could interrogate him further.

"Why would the sheriff order you a pizza?" Marissa's mom asked over the phone.

"Never mind. It's just a mistake," Marissa said. "I'll call you later."

Without waiting to consider the consequences, she

marched the few feet to his door and knocked. He opened the door, still wearing the dark blue T-shirt and worn jeans he'd had on earlier.

"I don't want your pity pizza." She shoved the box at him.

"Okay. Bad idea." Connor took the pizza and slammed the door in her face.

Marissa stood there a second, stunned. Then she *bammed* on his door.

The instant he opened it, she said, "Don't slam the door on me. That's rude."

"So is shoving a pizza in my face."

He was right. "It wasn't your face," she muttered.

"You know what I mean."

"I was angry."

"No kidding," he drawled. "Don't blame me for the crap your ex did to you."

His accusation stung. "I don't. I blame you for the crap *you* did to me."

"That was ten years ago. Get over it."

"I'm trying to."

"By shoving a pizza at me?"

"Yes."

"And how's that working for you?"

"It sucks," she admitted morosely. "Everything sucks. Except for the pizza. Does Angelo still make the best pizza ever?"

"You haven't tried it since you've been back?"

She shook her head. She didn't have extra funds for eating out. She'd applied every penny to getting a security deposit for an apartment. Her credit cards were maxed out so she couldn't get a cash advance. "I've been too busy," she said. "Anyway I'm sorry if I overreacted to the pizza thing. Have a good night." She turned and hurried toward the haven of her own place.

"Hold on a second." He put a hand on the box. "It's still warm. Will you have a hissy fit if I offer it to you?"

Her pride wouldn't allow her to take his generous offering. But her mouth was watering. She didn't have much food in the house yet. "That's okay. But thanks."

"You're sure?" He held it out enticingly.

She nodded but couldn't seem to move away. It's as if the smell of tomato sauce and cheese and basil had her mesmerized. She blamed it on the pizza, not on Connor.

"Have a slice," he said. "You know you want to."

"Maybe just one slice . . ."

"You can take it with you if you're afraid to come in."

"It's not a matter of being afraid."

"Right. Well, there is the matter of me having a dining table while you don't."

"Only until tomorrow."

"The pizza won't last that long. Come in and eat."

She was weak. She wanted pizza. Badly. Now. She stepped inside. "Just for a minute . . ."

She vowed she'd set a new record for "eat and run" even as she took a slice and the paper napkin he offered her. Then she had to sit down at his dining room table—a nice pine job that looked like it was handmade—because it was rude to stand there and eat like a feral rabbit. Not that rabbits ate pizza.

She could hear her mom saying "What? Were you raised by wolves? Take your elbows off the table. Close your mouth while chewing." Marissa had been all of five at the time. She liked to think she had better manners now.

She closed her eyes and briefly focused on the taste of the pizza. "No one makes a pizza like Angelo's," she said.

"Mmm." Apparently Connor's mom had taught him not to talk with his mouth full as well. A moment later he said, "Would you like a beer?"

She shook her head.

"I ran into Jose earlier today," Connor said, offering her another slice before taking a second for himself. Seeing her eyes widen, he added, "No, I did not arrest him, if that's what you're thinking."

She'd actually been thinking how sexy Connor's hands were but was not about to make that confession. Instead she kept chewing and enjoying. The thin crust was so crisp and there was something both spicy and sweet about the tomato sauce that made it unique and delicious.

"Apparently he was hired to spray-paint a guy's car."

Marissa nodded because her mouth was still full.

"So you knew about that?" Connor said,

She nodded again.

"You didn't think to share that info with me?"

She shook her head and kept chewing.

"Why not?"

She pointed to her mouth, indicating she was unable to reply at the moment.

"I'll wait," he said.

She swallowed and dabbed her mouth with the napkin.

"So?" he prompted her.

"Angelo's Pizza is even better than I remember."
Connor's touch was also better than she remembered.
What had they been talking about? Oh yeah. Jose. "I
didn't think you'd be interested in Jose's job."

"We're supposed to be working together on this
project."

"On Jose's artwork?"

"You know what I mean," he said.

"That was something he arranged outside of our
group."

Connor moved the pizza box closer to her, inviting
her to take another slice. She took it. Her willpower was
clearly nonexistent—at least where the pizza was
concerned.

"What else has he arranged outside of the group?"
Connor asked.

"What's with the interrogation?" she countered. At
this rate, this would be her last slice of pizza.

"I'm a cop. It's what I do."

"What made you leave Chicago and come back to
Hopeful?"

"Now who's conducting an interrogation?"

"It's just a simple question."

"No, it's not."

"Fine. Forget I asked." Marissa knew her voice
sounded huffy and she didn't care. "Thanks for the
pizza." She moved to stand up but his hand on her arm
stopped her. It also stopped her heart for a second. Again
with the humming from her head to her toe. What was
all that about?

"I didn't mean to bite your head off," he said gruffly.

Since she didn't expect him to apologize she had no
response for that.

Finally she said, "If you don't want to talk about it . . ."

"I was ready for a change," he said.

She sensed there was a lot more to it than that but didn't press him. At least she didn't mean to press him. But the words tumbled out of her mouth anyway. "Was it a woman?"

He glared at her. "No, it wasn't a woman."

"Okay."

"It was work stuff, okay?"

"Okay. I can tell it's a touchy subject with you."

"I am not touchy. Touchy is for wimps."

"Right. God forbid you should be a wimp or be touchy or actually have some emotions."

"Hey, I have emotions. Too many damn emotions sometimes." His voice turned dark and rough.

She saw the pain flash in his eyes and felt guilty for bringing up something that was so difficult for him. "I'm sorry."

He regained control of his expression "You're sorry for what?"

She could tell he didn't want her referring to the reasons for his departure from Chicago again so she tried to lighten the situation a little. "Sorry I gave you a hard time about the pizza. Angelo's is indeed awesome."

"We had some good times back then, working there."

"And eating there," she said. "I think we tried every possible combination on the menu no matter how outlandish. Pineapple and spinach."

"Pineapple, spinach and shrimp."

"That was pretty good actually," she said. "It's when we added broccoli to that mix that things went terribly wrong."

He laughed. "That was bad. Very bad."

She shared a smile with him. It had been so long since she'd had a fun moment like this. She'd forgotten how wonderful it could feel. Or how addictive it could be.

Her eyes met his and she couldn't look away. She felt like a teenager all over again, caught up in a crush, so wild about the guy in front of her that she couldn't even think straight.

She wasn't that girl anymore but there was still a bit of her left inside Marissa. Enough to make her breathless. Enough to make her yearn for something more.

She nervously licked her lips.

His gaze shifted to her mouth. Was he going to kiss her? Would she let him? Yes, yes . . . no, no. No, she really shouldn't.

She moved back and almost slipped from her chair. "I should be going."

"Okay." He followed her to the door. "Here, let me." He leaned around her to open it for her, his arm brushing against her body, his warm breath stirring her hair.

She was momentarily trapped in the seductive cage of his arms before he stepped back. The door was open now. She really should make a break for it before she gave in to the wildly inappropriate thoughts racing through her mind.

"Hey, I've got your table," Jess said, making Marissa jump.

The spell was broken. For that's what it truly felt like, as if Marissa had been caught up in some kind of enchanted moment. The problem with those kinds of moments is that they weren't real. And they didn't last.

Getting free furniture was real.

"Need my help?" Connor asked as he had earlier.

Marissa noted the way he eyed her sister.

"No, I'm good," Jess said. "Tim is doing the heavy lifting."

The young hottie came up with stairs with a toothpaste-ad perfect smile. "Where do you want this?"

Marissa hurried inside her apartment to show him the empty dining area. The table came apart, with the legs separate from the top. Tim made fast work of putting it all together while Jess lingered in the hallway with Connor.

"Jess, I need your help in here," Marissa called out.

Her sister came inside. Tim had gone down to bring up the chairs. "We should really be helping Tim carry those," Marissa said.

"He likes doing things for me."

"I'm sure he didn't like the way you were flirting with my neighbor."

"What were you and Sheriff Hottie up to?"

"Nothing."

"Fine. Be that way. I can't stay and talk anyway."

"I thought you and Tim had to be someplace."

"We did. And now we're off somewhere else. Wait until Mom hears about your hanging out with your sexy neighbor."

"Do not tell her." Marissa added a warning look that should have worked but didn't. Damn. It used to work when they were kids. Life was so much more complicated now.

Now Jess was into bargaining for her silence. Come to think of it, she'd done that when they were kids, too. "I won't tell her if you go to that divorce support group meeting Mom keeps going on about," Jess said. "I'm tired of Mom bugging me to bug you."

"I'll go this week."

"You better."

"And you better keep your mouth shut."

Jess smiled and made a zipping motion across her lips.

• • •

Marissa was not looking forward to attending the divorce support group tonight but she had no choice. Not only had she made that bargain with her sister but her mother had continued nagging Marissa all week about going to the meeting. Attending tonight seemed like the lesser of two evils. At least Jess seemed to have kept her promise and not told their mom about Marissa being in Connor's apartment.

Marissa walked into the crowded room on the second floor of the Hopeful Park District building and selected one of the few empty chairs from the semi-circle. She liked it because it was closest to the door. The Park District offered its meeting rooms to a number of support groups in the evenings as well as classes like Cooking for One or Clearing Clutter. She'd rather be in one of those classes instead of where she was, but she'd promised to attend so here she was, feeling nervous and vulnerable.

As Marissa took her seat, several women turned to look at her.

Marissa only recognized one of them—Flo from the post office. Flo was not someone you would ever overlook. Her oversized glasses with the bold black frames were guaranteed to ensure she stood out in a crowd. Her long hair was dyed vivid black and always held back in her trademark ponytail. She hadn't changed her hairstyle or glasses since Marissa was in high school.

"Welcome. We're glad you've joined us," Flo said. "Would you like some coffee and cookies?"

"Thanks." As she helped herself to the offered goodies, Marissa worried that she might be turning into one of those people who couldn't turn down free food.

"Okay then, let's get started," Flo said.

Marissa hurried back to her chair. They went around the room saying their names so fast that Marissa couldn't keep up with them. Was the woman to her left named Amy or Sammy?

"We have a new visitor tonight." Flo nodded at Marissa. "Do you want to introduce yourself and tell us about yourself?"

She'd rather eat ground glass but had little choice other than to reply. "My name is Marissa." She hadn't considered the possibility that she'd have to do much talking tonight, not right off the bat. She wasn't comfortable baring her soul to strangers. She also worried she might have bits of dried fruit stuck in her teeth from the oatmeal raisin cookie she'd eaten. "And um . . . I'm just here to listen and observe."

The group gave her a collective frown.

"I'm divorced," she hurriedly added in case they thought she was crashing their meeting for the food and drink.

"Her mom warned me that she could be shy," Flo said. "So I'll introduce her. Marissa Bennett is a local girl who left home to go off to college. She met a man she thought was her Prince Charming. They got married, but one day she came home to find her s.o.b. of a husband was in bed with another woman."

"That's almost as bad as me discovering my ex had two mistresses," a pretty woman with short dark short hair said. She looked like she'd be more at home in an episode of *Real Housewives of Atlanta* than in Hopeful, Ohio.

"But having him clear out your bank account and take off to the Cayman Islands is even worse," another woman said.

"Ladies, it's not a competition," Flo said.

"If it was, I'd win for worst divorce," the woman to Marissa's right maintained.

"At least you were married for a dozen years," Flo said. "Poor Marissa here couldn't even hack it for a year."

Their eyes widened.

"You were married less than a year?" the woman on Marissa's left asked in amazement.

"She signed the divorce papers on their one-year wedding anniversary," Flo replied on Marissa's behalf.

"That's rough," Atlanta Housewife admitted. "Did you at least get a good settlement?"

"She had to come back home and move in with her parents," Flo said. "Do you think she'd do that if she got a good settlement?"

"I have my own place now," Marissa said.

"She moved into my building," Flo said.

Great. Marissa didn't realize that Flo lived there, too.

"That's a very safe place," Atlanta Housewife said. "The sheriff lives there."

"I know." Marissa wondered when the situation had gotten so totally out of her control. Probably the minute she'd walked in the door. No, it was when Flo had spoken for her. Marissa chastised herself for not taking control then. And for not paying attention when they'd done the speed roll call. But she could fix that if she took immediate action. "I'm sorry. I was so nervous that I didn't catch everyone's name. Could you please start over and introduce yourselves again?"

And bingo, that's all it took for them to beam at her and start talking all at once. Marissa couldn't keep up but at least the spotlight was off her for a while. Across the room Marissa caught the empathetic look of a young woman close to her own age. Her name was Deb Kirsch and as the evening progressed, she was the one person who made Marissa feel like she'd found someone with a similar viewpoint.

●   ●   ●

Connor had heard that Marissa was attending a divorce support group meeting tonight. It was hard to keep secrets in a small town. Hard but not impossible.

No one knew the exact details of his reasons for leaving Chicago. They figured city life had burned him out and who wouldn't prefer a great town like Hopeful to gritty Chicago.

Connor had almost been tempted to confide in Marissa and that surprised him. So did the other ways in which she tempted him. Being in bed with her made him hard. He wanted her . . . bad. One of his few nights off and here he was, home alone lusting after the girl next door. The sexy hot librarian next door.

His X-rated thoughts were interrupted by the sound of his phone. He could tell by the ringtone that it was his mom.

"You're not calling me while you're driving, are you?" Connor said.

"No. You know I signed Oprah's No Phone Zone Pledge. I'm calling you from a parking lot and the car is turned off."

"Everything okay?"

"Fine."

"How are you and GM enjoying Hershey, Pennsylvania?" Connor always called his grandmother "GM."

"Oh, we're done with Hershey. We're here."

"Here, where?"

"Here in Hopeful. We're about five minutes away from your place. See you soon."

Chapter Eight

. . . .

"Wait!" Connor said frantically.

"Whatever you want to say, you can tell us when we see you in a few minutes," his mom said.

He scrambled for an excuse. "I'm working,"

"No, you're not. We called the department first to find out. Bye."

Connor groaned. Why hadn't they given him a heads-up? He didn't consider phoning him five minutes before arriving enough of a warning.

He supposed it was better than just showing up on his doorstep. Speaking of his doorstep, he heard voices outside a few minutes later. He opened it to find Marissa standing there with his mother and grandmother.

"Your nice neighbor Marissa let us in and helped us carry our bags," his mom said.

"Give me that," he said. His hand brushed hers as he took the bag from her.

He could tell by the way her face flushed that she was as aware of his touch as he was of hers.

"Enjoy your visit," Marissa said as she hurriedly dug her key to her own apartment out of her purse and dove inside. Not really, but she sure seemed in a rush to him.

Had his relatives said something to Marissa to spook her? Or was that brief touch they'd just shared the reason for her quick exit?

He switched his attention from Marissa to his mom and grandmother, ushering them into his place. He was still a little freaked by their sudden appearance which is why he blurted out, "How long are you staying?"

His mother gave him a reprimanding look. "We just got here."

"It's just . . . I wasn't expecting you," he said.

"We wanted to surprise you."

"Mission accomplished," he said.

"We're heard about the Rhubarb Festival they do here. Sounds like fun."

"But that's not for several days."

GM narrowed her eyes at him. "Is that a problem? Are you expecting other visitors?"

"No," he said. "I only have a small apartment."

"The apartment I had in Warsaw when I was your age was small. This is twice as large. Three times. Is this attitude of yours because of the girl next door? Your new neighbor?" Not giving him a chance to reply, she continued, "She seems nice. You should date her. You're not getting any younger, you know."

His grandmother was aging him by the second.

Connor put his arm around her and teased her. "You know I'm not the marrying kind."

"Pshaw." She smacked him. "You're no bargain, but I'm sure we can find someone to put up with you."

"Gee, thanks."

"You would prefer we think you are God's gift to women?" she countered.

"Yeah."

"Fine." She patted his arm. "You are a gift to women but you still need to settle down with one of them. And the one next door looks nice."

"You met her and barely exchanged two words," he said.

"I have a sixth sense about these things." His grandmother fixed him with her laser-like stare. "What do you know about her?"

"She's the town librarian."

"Ah, this is good." His grandmother nodded her approval. "This is good, yes, Wanda?"

"Yes, that is good," his mom agreed, opening his fridge and staring at the pitiful contents in dismay. "You need a keeper, Connor."

"I wasn't expecting company."

His mother straightened and glared at him. "We are *family.* Not company."

"Right."

"It's a good thing we brought food," she said.

They always brought food. Delicious hearty food. But today they hadn't traveled from their brick bungalow on the South Side of Chicago where they could cook up a storm. Today they'd traveled from Hershey. "Did you bring chocolate?" he asked.

"Of course. But tell us about your neighbor. You never mentioned you had a pretty librarian living next door."

"She only recently moved in," he said.

"How recently?" his mom asked.

That was the first of what felt like a thousand questions. His relatives' inquisition tactics would make the most seasoned cop proud and the hardest criminal crack.

Connor kept his responses vague. He'd been an undercover cop. He knew how to lie. How to deceive. How to keep his cool.

But it was harder than he expected.

Later that evening, Connor was out on his balcony, his back to his apartment as he spoke into his cell phone.

"What's with the whispering, bro?" his older brother Logan asked.

"Mom and GM are here," Connor said. "Without warning. Staying until the weekend. It's only Tuesday. We're talking days."

"Damn. That's deserving of a 911 call."

"What am I going to do with them?"

"Hell if I know."

"Stop laughing," Connor growled. "This isn't funny."

"Not to you maybe. Are you afraid they're gonna turn your man cave into a mom cave?"

"I don't have a man cave," Connor said. "And stop laughing."

"Why should I? You always laugh when *I'm* in trouble."

"That's not true," Connor denied. "Only when you're in relationship trouble."

"Bingo."

"And not during your divorce."

"Damn straight."

"How long did it take you to get over that situation?" Connor said.

"You mean walking in and finding my wife in bed with an EMT?"

"Yeah that."

"Why do you want to know?" Logan asked suspiciously. "Did your girlfriend cheat on you?"

"I'm between relationships at the moment," Connor said.

"Did *you* cheat on someone?"

"No. I'm asking on behalf of a friend."

"A friend, huh? Likely story."

"It's the truth," Connor said.

"Yeah right."

"So how long did it take?"

"I can't put a time limit on it. Everyone is different. Is that friend you're asking for a male or female?" Logan asked.

"A female."

"Well, hell. That changes everything," Logan said. "You know how women are."

"Yeah."

"So who is she?" Logan demanded.

"Nobody."

"I thought you said she was a friend."

"I was just curious, that's all," Connor said.

"About a woman who is just a friend?"

"What?" Connor countered. "You don't think men and women can be just friends?"

"Sure. I'm friends with Delgado, my partner. We work well together."

"That's just peachy for you both," Connor said sarcastically. His brother was not supplying much moral support here.

"But you are different."

"No, I'm not. I've been friends with plenty of women."

"Yeah, you have," Logan agreed. "But you haven't been curious about them or their recovery from a bad situation. Makes me wonder what your real motive is."

"Put your detective hat away and focus on how I'm supposed to deal with Mom and GM," Connor said.

"Hey, you're the one who brought up this mystery woman."

"I got her a pizza to make her feel better and she shoved it in my face," Connor said abruptly.

Logan laughed. "I would have loved to see that. I like this woman already. What's her name?"

"None of your damn business."

"That's a strange name. But hey, her mom must have had her reasons for calling her that."

"Very funny," Connor growled.

"Yeah, you are. Gotta go."

His brother hung up before Connor could protest. Swearing under his breath, he turned to find Marissa on her balcony, a few feet away. It was just past twilight but there was enough residual light from inside that he could see the grin on her face.

"How much of that did you hear?" Connor demanded.

"Enough."

"How much is enough?"

"Put your detective hat away," she retorted.

"What are you doing out here?" his mother demanded after opening the sliding glass door. She turned to face

Marissa. "Oh, you're having a secret rendezvous with Marissa."

"Who is having a secret rendezvous?" his grand-mother demanded as she joined them. "Ah . . ." She said it with all-knowing wisdom. "You two don't have to meet in secret like this. Marissa, come on over. We'll have some coffee and talk."

"I can't," Marissa said.

"Of course you can. I insist. Tell her." His grand-mother smacked his arm.

"Tell her what?"

"He's pouting because we broke into your rendez-vous," his mother said.

"Does he pout a lot?" Marissa asked.

He could tell she was having entirely too much fun with his obvious discomfort.

"Come over and I'll tell you," he countered, daring her to say yes.

"I don't want to intrude," Marissa said.

"You won't be," his mother assured her. "But you will hurt my feelings if you refuse my invitation."

Damn. Connor knew Marissa was too polite to say no. His mom knew that, too, which is why she'd worded it that way. She always told him he got his smarts from her and not his father.

His mom sent him into the kitchen to make coffee, saying she couldn't deal with his antiquated coffeemaker. When she'd checked out the contents of his fridge, she'd also checked out the small appliances.

Meanwhile, she set out chocolate she'd bought in Hershey before opening the door for Marissa.

"Welcome. Thank you for coming. We didn't make

formal introductions before. My name is Wanda and my mother's name is Sophie."

"You can call me Grandma Sophie," the older woman said.

Wanda pointed to the plate of chocolate. "We just came from Hershey, Pennsylvania. Have you ever been there?"

"No."

"Sit, sit." His mom pulled out a chair for her. The instant she was seated, the questions began.

"So tell us about yourself, Marissa," his mom said.

"You don't have to do that," he hurriedly told Marissa.

His mom glared at him. "Then we'll just tell you about Connor instead."

"She's not interested."

"How do you know?"

Connor shoved a hand through his hair. "I know, okay?"

"Tell us about your parents, Marissa. Do they live nearby?"

"Yes, they live here in Hopeful. I grew up here. My dad is a history professor at the local college. My mom worked as a part-time bookkeeper while I was growing up but she quit so she could take my sister to school swim meets."

"Is your sister older or younger?"

"Younger."

"Any more siblings?"

"No that's it."

"Does she live here in Hopeful, too?"

Marissa nodded.

"It must be nice living so close to your family." She sent Connor a telling look, the kind of guilt-inducing stare that only a mother could perfect. "It's so hard when your child lives so far away. We live in Chicago, where Connor grew up."

"Logan still lives in Chicago," he said.

"Is it wrong to want all my sons at the table for Sunday dinners as we did for all those years?" his mother demanded.

Not wrong, he thought to himself. But not realistic either. "I live closer to you than Aidan does. Hopeful is closer to Chicago than Seattle."

Marissa had to resist smiling at Connor's discomfiture. She hadn't wanted to come over and planned on making a quick excuse and departing, but she had to admit that seeing him getting the third degree by his mom made her feel good. Let him see how it felt to be the one under the microscope for a change. She decided to stay and enjoy the show.

"I'm sure being so far away must be very hard on you," she told his mom, clearly indicating that she sided with her in the discussion.

"It is."

"You must miss him terribly."

"I do."

"And a son should really look after his mother, right?" Marissa said.

"Absolutely. That's how I raised him. That's how I raised all three of my sons. It wasn't easy being a single mom."

"I'm sure it wasn't."

"And they weren't the easiest boys to handle."

"I can only imagine," Marissa said.

"I don't know if you realize how stubborn Connor can be."

"Actually, I have noticed that."

"He got that trait from his father. All my sons did."

"I'm sure that made raising them even more challenging," Marissa said.

"It did. I did the best I could," his mom said.

"I'm sure you did."

"Hey, we didn't turn out that bad," Connor said defensively. "Most moms would be proud to have three police officers in the family."

"I wanted you to be a doctor," his mom said. "I wanted you all to be doctors. But did you listen to me? No, of course not. Instead you follow in your father's footsteps."

"I'm sure Marissa doesn't want to hear all this," he said.

"Sure I do. Go on," she encouraged his mother.

"I gave all my sons St. Michael the Archangel medallions. St. Michael is the patron saint of the police," his mom said.

"I didn't know that," Marissa said.

"What do you know about Polish chocolate?" his grandmother asked her.

"Not much," Marissa admitted.

"Mom, you know that the Belgians and Swiss are better known for their chocolate than Poland," Connor's mother said.

Their quibbling continued, allowing Connor to sidle closer to Marissa and whisper, "Quick, make a break for it while you can."

She stared at him in confusion.

He tilted his head toward the door. "Save yourself."

Marissa might have been able to do that had she not

cracked up instead, drawing his family's attention away from chocolate and back to her.

"What's so funny?" his mother asked. "Was Connor telling you a joke? He's really good at that."

"Maybe he was whispering sweet nothings in her ear," his grandmother said.

"He's really good at that, too," his mom said. "He's a real ladies' man."

Connor rolled his eyes.

"His brother Logan does that eye roll thing, too," his mom said. "Not that I let them get away with that when they were younger. It was a sign of disrespect and I wouldn't stand for that."

"Me neither," his grandmother said.

"But now that he's over thirty I let him get away with the eye roll every now and again," his mom said.

"What was he like when he was younger?" Marissa asked.

"He was a very good baby. Smiled all the time. Let me show you."

"No, Mom . . ." Connor said.

But it was too late. His mother had already reached into her huge bag and pulled out the small photo book she brought with her everywhere.

"I have one of these for each of my three sons," she said proudly. "Of course, there are much larger albums at home but these are my compact traveling ones. As you can tell from Connor's baby picture, he was so cute. And here he is at two years old. Cuter still."

"And naked," Marissa said.

"He didn't like wearing clothes much at that age," his mom said. "He loved his cowboy boots though."

Connor didn't have to see the photo to know which one it was. He was wearing bright red cowboy boots and a cowboy hat but that was it.

Marissa shot him a mocking look.

He fired back with a don't-mess-with-me glare but it had little effect on her.

"Maybe Connor wanted to be a sheriff at an early age," Marissa said. "Thankfully he no longer goes around naked."

"How do you know?" he said.

"I meant in public," she said.

He could see his mom's matchmaking antenna going up again. "Does that mean you've seen Connor naked in private?" she asked Marissa.

Connor watched Marissa blush and squelched any temptation to leap in to save her. She'd been baiting him. She deserved whatever she got.

She had seen him naked in private just as he'd seen her naked. Sure it had been years ago but it wasn't a memory he'd forgotten. He could tell by the look on her face that she hadn't forgotten either. But she lied. Not very well, but she gave it her best shot.

"No, of course not," Marissa said.

His grandmother leapt to Marissa's defense. "Of course she hasn't seen him naked. What kind of question is that to ask the poor girl? First you insult Polish chocolate and now this. I raised you better than that, Wanda."

Their good-hearted squabbling started again, giving Connor the chance to pull Marissa aside. "Ready to make your escape now?"

Marissa nodded and edged closer to the front door only to open it and almost bump into her own mom.

Chapter Nine

. . . .

"Mom! What are you doing here? How did you know where I was?" Marissa said.

"Your neighbor across the hall told me. Your father has a faculty meeting tonight and is working late so I brought you a casserole for dinner." She held it up.

The squabbling between Connor's mom and grandmother stopped as they immediately joined Marissa in the threshold.

"Connor said the same thing to us when we got here," his mom said. "Not about your husband's meeting. He said 'What are you doing here?'" She shook her head in disapproval. "It's enough to make a mom feel unwelcome. Come in, come in. We're so glad to meet you. I'm Connor's mother and this is his grandmother Sophie."

Marissa's mom looked around in confusion. "Am I interrupting something?"

"We should go so Connor and his family can visit together," Marissa said.

"What's in the casserole?" Wanda asked.

"Beef stew," Marissa's mom said. "It's my specialty."

"It's one of mine, too," Wanda said. "Do you add beer?"

Marissa's mom nodded. "It's one of my secret ingredients."

"Mine, too," his mom said.

"Would you like a taste?" Marissa's mom asked. "I made enough for an army."

"Great. Come on in." Wanda pulled her farther into Connor's apartment. "The more the merrier."

As the women headed for the kitchen, Marissa stared after them in dismay.

"Not as funny now that *your* mom is involved, huh?" Connor drawled.

"She doesn't keep my baby pictures in her purse," Marissa said.

"That's a shame. Did you feel a little bit guilty lying to my family about seeing me naked?"

"Quiet." She put her fingers to his lips.

To her surprise, he nibbled on them, his tongue darting out to caress the ultra-sensitive skin between her index and middle finger. She froze. She should have yanked her hand away as if she'd mistakenly touched a hot stove. She did do that eventually but by then he'd nibbled and tongued a bit more, rattling her completely.

His knowing smile helped her regain her composure. She refused to let him get an upper hand here. Speaking of hands, her fingers continued to hum and tingle. Which was ridiculous. Was she so desperate that the merest touch set her off? Or was it his touch and only his that did it?

Whatever the reason, it couldn't happen again. No one could say that she was a woman who did not learn from her past mistakes. She wasn't about to allow Connor to become a present—or future—mistake.

She'd already been down that road with him once before. Granted, it had been a long time ago but apparently her body had no trouble remembering.

Did he remember how powerful their chemistry was? Or was he merely getting a kick out of pushing her buttons?

Connor's mom returned from the kitchen to jab a stack of plates at his chest. "Set the table," she ordered him.

Marissa smiled. It was so nice to see someone bossing Connor around for a change instead of it being the other way around.

Her smile faded as her mom handed her the silverware. "Here. Help Connor," she ordered.

Now he was the one smiling as she reluctantly joined him at the dining table.

"Seems we both have bossy mothers," he said.

Marissa remained quiet.

"The fork goes above the plate," he told her, moving it.

Something about the way he said that made her want to stab him with the utensil.

She recognized that it was an over-the-top reaction and she didn't act on it but she'd felt it nonetheless. Just as she could still feel the tip of his tongue on her skin.

Three forks slipped from her grasp and clattered to the table.

"Everything okay out there?" his mom called out from the kitchen.

"Just peachy," he called back. "I was just telling Marissa to put the fork above the plate."

"You should let her put it where she wants to," his mother scolded from the other room.

Connor gave Marissa a look that reflected both humor and heat. "If I let you do that," he murmured, "you'd stab me with it, wouldn't you?"

"Of course not," Marissa said. "I would never do anything so rude. Unlike some people."

"I only stabbed someone with a fork once and I was five."

"You were six," his mother said as she brought in a tray filled with glasses of ice water. "And your brother Logan needed stitches."

"He started it."

His mom rolled her eyes.

"I saw that," Connor said. "I thought you didn't like eye rolls."

"Not when they are directed at me," his mom said. "Luckily we brought some food with us since we suspected that Connor would not have much."

"If you'd told me you were coming . . ."

She waved his words away. "We have a loaf of marble rye bread from a wonderful little bakery we found on the way here from Pennsylvania. The bakery also sold butter, which we knew you wouldn't have."

His grandmother brought the bread and butter while Marissa's mom brought the large casserole dish to the table. Connor gathered two more chairs and held them for each woman, starting with his grandmother. Marissa didn't wait for him to get to her. She could seat herself. But she noted his old-world courtesy.

"Marissa told us she grew up here in Hopeful," Connor's mom said. "It must be nice having all your children nearby." She bestowed another reproachful maternal look upon Connor.

Marissa's ex didn't get along with his own family at all. They barely spoke at the wedding, which should have been a big red flag.

She couldn't imagine Brad putting up with what Connor had today. Her ex would have gotten angry and stormed out. He certainly wouldn't give his mom a Cary Grant charming smile before scooting her chair in for her.

Hindsight was 20/20.

"Marissa only recently returned back home," her mother said. "So I know what it feels like to have your child far away. She moved to New York."

"You poor thing." His mom patted her mom's arm in commiseration.

"She's back now and that's all that's important. My Marissa has always been a good girl. I never had any trouble with her growing up. Well, there was one brief period during her senior year in high school when she dyed her hair black and called herself Rissa."

"But Marissa is such a lovely name," Wanda said.

"I know."

Luckily, her mom didn't know that Rissa the Rebel had hooked up with college hunk Connor.

"Connor went through a similar period," Wanda said.

"Really? Did he dye his hair and change his name?" Marissa's mom said.

"No," Wanda said. "He followed his high school

sweetheart here to Hopeful to go to college, abandoning his family and his career path of being a doctor."

"I never wanted to be a doctor," Connor protested.

"How do you know if you didn't even try?" his mother countered.

"I wanted Marissa to try out for the Rhubarb Queen but she wouldn't even consider it. As a former winner of the title myself, it meant a great deal to me."

"We're staying for the Rhubarb Festival," Wanda said.

"That's great." Marissa's mom beamed. "You'll love it. They have bake sales and songs and music and of course the beauty pageant."

"Why didn't you want to try out to be a Rhubarb Queen?" Wanda asked Marissa. "That sounds like fun."

Connor's look said *It's not so much fun when you're the center of maternal inquisitions, is it?*

"I wouldn't have been good at it," Marissa said. "I'm not a beauty queen kind of person."

"She always had her nose stuck in some book. Just like her father." Her mom shook her head.

"But Marissa, you are pretty," Wanda said.

"She was a late bloomer," her mom admitted. "Her sister, Jess, was Rhubarb Queen her sophomore year in high school. She didn't rebel the way Marissa did."

"She's the pretty sister," Marissa said.

"Don't be that way," her mother said. "I never said Jess was the pretty one or that you were the smart one. Both of you are pretty and smart. My younger daughter got her undergraduate degree in philosophy. She's working in the college admissions office while she decides what subject she wants to focus on for her master's degree. Marissa got her master's degree in library science and works at the public library in town."

"Did she go to college here?" Wanda asked.

"Her father and I wanted her to but she decided to go to Ohio State instead."

"Connor decided to come back to Chicago after his freshman year at college here."

"You're lucky he came back."

"Luck had nothing to do with it," his mom said.

Marissa waited, wondering if there had been a family emergency of some kind that had forced him back home. But no, that would have been too easy.

"Connor and his high school sweetheart broke up," his mom continued, "so there was no reason for him to stay here. She went on to marry a doctor, by the way."

"So you've told me numerous times," Connor said. "The stew is great, Mrs. Bennett."

"Call me Linda," Marissa's mom said.

Marissa knew what she wanted to call Connor. She wanted to call him every lousy name in the book. He'd told his family there was no reason to stay in Hopeful? As if his time with her was worthless. Meaningless.

Connor suddenly caught her eye and shook his head. For some reason she got the impression that he was trying to tell her something. Was he afraid she'd lunge across the table and spear him with her fork? No, there was something else besides warning in those hard to decipher eyes of his. It was almost as if he was sending her a visual apology.

His grandmother abruptly turned the conversation onto one of her favorite subjects—her homeland of Poland.

"Are you familiar with the music of Chopin?" the older woman asked Marissa.

"I love his piano concertos," Marissa said.

"They're much better than the medieval madrigals my husband is always listening to," Marissa's mom said.

"Did you know that Chopin's heart is buried in the Church of the Holy Cross in Warsaw?" Grandma Sophie said.

"No, I didn't know that," Marissa said.

"We Poles wanted Pope John Paul II's heart to be buried in Poland but the Vatican said no and buried him in St. Peter's Basilica. You know he was Polish, yes?"

Marissa nodded.

"He was born in Krakow and was our Pope for twenty-six years." Grandma Sophie made the sign of the cross. "He is revered in Poland. Are you Catholic, Marissa?"

Connor interceded. "Enough with the Polish Inquisition."

"I was merely asking a question, but if it is too personal, I apologize," Grandma Sophie said. "And I will end with one final brag. Poland was the first country in Europe to—"

"—have a written constitution," Connor completed.

"I'm not baking any kolachki for you," his grandmother said as she glared at him. "That will teach you to make fun of me. And no pierogies if you roll your eyes one more time. Now be nice or Marissa will never go out with you."

Marissa wanted to tell the older woman that she wouldn't go out with Connor but wisely kept that info to herself. His family might claim he got his stubbornness from his dad but Marissa thought that his mother and grandmother were pretty tough customers. But endearingly tough.

Marissa had grown up without any grandparents and there was just something about the twinkle in Grandma

Sophie's eyes, even when she was ticked off with her grandson, that made Marissa smile.

• • •

"Tell me again why you're hiding out at my place?" Kyle Sullivan aka Sully asked Connor the next evening.

"I'm not hiding out," Connor said. "Can't a guy crash at his buddy's house to watch a ball game without making a big deal about it?"

"Your mom and granny must be something else for you to be this desperate."

"Do not call her 'granny' to her face or she might drop-kick you. She has a temper. And they're trying to match-make."

"Is that all?" Sully scoffed. "Big deal."

"It *is* a big deal. You don't know what it's like."

"You poor momma's boy."

"A momma's boy mother doesn't want her son to marry. No woman is good enough. She wants to keep him to herself. That's not the case here."

"So your mom is trying to palm you off on someone else, huh? The sooner the better. And that scares you shitless."

"It does not."

"For a former undercover cop, you are such a bad liar." Sully took a swig of his beer. "So who's the woman they're trying to hook you up with? No, let me guess. The new librarian in town. Am I right?"

Connor made a growly grumbling noise, which his buddy took as an affirmative answer.

"I heard the two of you moved in together," Sully said.

"She lives in the same building, that's all."

Sully raised an eyebrow and his bottle of beer.

"Okay, so she's in the apartment next door," Connor admitted.

"That must be handy."

"Handy for what?"

"Hanky-panky, as your granny would say."

"Marissa is still recovering from her divorce," Connor said.

"That's good," Sully said. "Then she's not looking to settle down. You should be counting your blessings instead of complaining."

"How do you figure that?"

"Come on. A sexy librarian divorcee looking for a good time? What's not to like?"

"Who says she's sexy?"

"I've seen her around town," Sully said.

"Okay, then who says she's looking for a good time?"

"I do."

"Like you're an expert on the subject," Connor scoffed.

"I'm just saying . . ."

"You are so full of shit."

"What happened to 'full of shinola,' like your grand-dad says? Now there's a cool guy. I like Buddy. When is he coming to visit again?"

"I have all the family I can cope with at the moment. Besides, Gramps doesn't get along with my mom or GM."

Sully frowned. "Buddy doesn't get along with General Motors? He prefers Fords, does he?"

"No, that's my nickname for my grandmother. GM."

"Your family is twisted, man."

"No kidding," Connor said glumly.

"No worries." Sully punched Connor in the arm. "You can stay here as long as you want."

• • •

"What experience do you have with matchmaking mommas?" Marissa asked Deb as they sat in Cups Café sipping their iced coffees. This was the first time they'd gotten together since meeting at the divorce support group a few days ago.

While the college crowd gathered at the local Starbucks, Hopeful's full-time residents preferred the ambience and prices of the local business.

"Why? Are you looking to be matched up?" Deb asked.

"Not at all. But my mom has that gleam in her eye. I haven't even been divorced a year and already she's pushing me to get back out there and start dating."

"Just tell her that some of the self-help books say you should wait at least a year before reentering the dating world."

"She's not the only one bugging me about it. Someone at work tried to hook me up with their cousin who works at the hospital."

"I heard you and the sheriff were an item," Deb said.

"What?! That's not true. Who told you that?"

Deb shrugged. "It's just a rumor I heard floating around."

"Why would someone get that idea?"

"Because you live next to each other and you're both single and sparks fly when you're together."

"Those are argumentative sparks, not sexual sparks," Marissa said. "We have to work together on a special project. Neither one of us wants to but we don't really have a choice. We're sort of stuck with each other."

"Sounds like a relationship."

"A *working* relationship, maybe. But that's as far as it goes." Marissa took a sip of her iced coffee. "What is it about a divorced woman that makes everyone want to hook her up with someone?"

"I don't know. I do know that a lot of the couples who were friends before my divorce no longer invite me to their events," Deb said. "I tell myself it's because having me would make it an odd number of people to dinner. But it's almost like they're afraid that divorce is a contagious disease or something."

"I know what you mean." Marissa had had a similar experience when she was back in New York.

"It's like you become a social pariah," Deb continued. "My single girlfriends have been really supportive and they try to help but they don't really understand what it feels like. Yes, some of them have been dumped but it's not the same thing as ending a marriage, ending a promise, a declaration in front of your family, friends and in your church that this is going to last forever. That you and your spouse are going to do whatever it takes to make it work. The sense of failure is just so overwhelming. You've probably read the same self-help books I have. I know that divorce is a grieving process. That there are stages you have to progress through and that there is no one time schedule. Everyone progresses at their own speed and in their own way."

Marissa nodded. "Logically I know that. The thing with Brad is that he pursued me. I think I was a challenge to him. He really had to go after me because I wasn't convinced we'd be a good match. But he was relentless and charming. He'd do such sweet and romantic things. He could have gone after other women but he stuck with courting me. And that made me feel so special, so wanted. Those powerful, positive feelings drowned out my original doubt. Even so, something made me tell him that cheating was a deal-breaker for me. When he proposed to me, I made sure he understood that before I said yes."

"It seems to me that your inner radar was warning you even then that he was a cheater," Deb said.

"You're right. Most women don't say, *Yes, I'll marry you providing you honor our marriage vows and don't stray.*"

"True."

"I mean, logically, I know there is life after divorce. I know it's a matter of moving on, of being able to get rid of the baggage you're carrying."

"Everyone has baggage."

"Did you ever see that episode of the CBS sitcom *How I Met Your Mother* that showed the baggage the characters had and the baggage they were trying to figure out everyone else had? I lie awake at night wondering when I'm going to be able to get over it and throw the baggage away. Incinerate it. Ship it into outer space. Blow it up."

"I have those thoughts at night, too," Deb admitted. "Although it's usually about doing that to my husband, not to my emotional baggage."

"Was it an acrimonious divorce?" Marissa asked.

"I wouldn't be going to a support group if it wasn't. You know, I really envy people who are able to end things smoothly and calmly. Like your ex, my husband cheated. Unlike your situation, he did it more than once.

The first time he pleaded with me to take him back and I did. He was good for a while and then he cheated again. We separated and I almost took him back a third time. But the trust had been broken and I couldn't see it ever being repaired again. Not after the second occurrence. You know that saying, 'Ignore what a man says, pay attention to what he does'? My ex said all the right things but did all the wrong ones. It took forever for him to sign the divorce papers. It's like he saw that as a surrender, as if losing a marriage was a football game or something. That we were in overtime and if he just hung in there long enough he'd score a point and win."

"Did you have kids?" Marissa asked.

"No. That would have really made things even more difficult. My parents were divorced when I was a kid, and I swore to myself that I would never get a divorce."

"My parents have tried to be supportive. Well, my mom has. My dad is kind of oblivious to it all," Marissa said. "He hasn't said anything, but I feel like he's disappointed in me."

"Did he like your ex?"

Marissa shrugged. "He never said. He didn't say he didn't like him either."

"At least you're not running into your ex all the time."

Marissa wasn't running into Brad but she was running into and having to work with Connor a lot of the time. She was so afraid of letting down her guard around him. Okay, so the truth was that she wasn't just afraid, she was terrified with a generous amount of panic mixed in.

Her life would be so much simpler if he hadn't returned to Hopeful or if she hadn't. Or if her feelings for him and the chemistry between them had totally disappeared. But more and more, she found herself traveling into the world of what-if.

What if Connor hadn't deserted her a decade ago? What if they'd stayed together? Would they still be a couple? Could she have gone with him to Chicago to be a cop's wife? Could she have dealt with the constant danger to a big-city law enforcement officer? What if he'd stayed here in Hopeful and neither one of them had ever left? Would they have kids by now? In what-if land, there were millions of possible scenarios to explore.

"Do you ever wonder 'What if'?" Marissa asked Deb.

"Sometimes. What if he hadn't strayed? Yeah, I think about that a lot sometimes."

"Do you ever wonder what your life would be like if you'd married your first love or someone else instead of your ex?"

"Sure. Who doesn't? I've even looked them up online."

"Did you ever contact someone that way?"

"No," Deb said. "I don't have the nerve. Why? Have you done that? Contacted someone from your past to see if they're still available?"

"No," Marissa said. Which was true. She technically hadn't contacted Connor. He'd contacted her when he'd pulled her over during the parade. Fate had put them together. Neither one of them had taken measures to make that happen. In fact, they both had made moves to avoid such a thing happening. Although she'd done more than he had.

Connor seemed to take some pleasure in the fact that he could still get to her. Maybe that was just male ego. Not that Connor was pursuing her. Although there was that pity pizza . . . but that wasn't much, really. It's not like he was sending her dozens of roses like Brad had when he was courting her. Or sending sexy text messages.

No, Connor didn't make any of the obvious moves. Instead he'd just look at her. But the wow factor was increasing with every glance and every stare he sent her way.

She only had one first love in her life, and for good or bad that was Connor. That fact colored her reaction to him. To every look, every touch, every comment.

"I wish I could just tune it all out," Marissa muttered.

"Me, too," Deb said.

"I'm sorry for venting like that. I don't mean to sound like Wendy Whiner."

Deb smiled and pointed to herself. "Or even worse, Deb Downer?"

"No way. Not you. You're the only person I can really talk to about all this. You get it." Now what Marissa had to "get" was that wandering into what-if land carried its own dangers and was full of emotional land mines.

Chapter Ten

· · · · · · · · · · · ·

Dealing with teenagers was like herding cats . . . only worse. Days like today made Marissa doubt her own judgment in wanting to do more. Why couldn't she leave well enough alone? *Nooo.* She had to come up with a group to help teens.

The American Library Association had books and subcommittees on the subject of appealing to young adults. *Booklist* did special webinars about what they termed as Reluctant Readers. Marissa would add the words *Rebellious*, *Recalcitrant* and *Rowdy* to that description.

Today's drama involved the group's plans for the upcoming Rhubarb Festival this weekend.

"I still say that we should be auctioning off one of my apps instead of a T-shirt," Snake said.

"It's not just a T-shirt. It's a custom, one-of-a-kind

T-shirt," Jose said. "Your apps aren't custom. Anyone can download one for ninety-nine cents. The T-shirt I did is worth a lot more than that."

Snake was clearly not convinced. "Or so you say."

"You got a problem with that?" Jose said, going into defense mode.

"You all voted on this," Marissa reminded them.

"Red Fred does whatever Jose tells him," Snake said. "That's why he voted for the shirt. And the girls don't even know what an app is because they don't have smartphones."

"An app is an application," Tasmyn said, shoving her hair away from her face to glare at Snake. "Not everyone is rich enough to afford a smartphone."

"And I'd like to remind you that I'm a girl and I voted for the app," Nadine said.

Snake waved her words away. "I don't think of you as a girl."

Now Nadine joined Tasmyn and Molly in the glarefest.

"Tool." The normally low-key Molly threw the insult at him.

"You have to be popular with girls but hurt them before you can be a tool," Nadine said. "Outside of this group, Snake can't even talk to a girl."

"He used to be popular with us and he hurt us," Molly said "That means he qualifies."

"Trust me, he's no tool. He's not cool enough to be a tool," Jose said.

"It's not cool to be a tool," Nadine said.

"And it's not cool to insult people," Marissa pointed out. "Just because you don't agree with others, doesn't mean that you should insult them."

"Why not?" Red Fred said. "They do it on TV all the time. Especially on Fox News. And politicians do it, too. You should read some of the blogs out there."

"My mom says Fox doesn't really do news," Molly said.

"And my mom says Fox are the only ones who do the news," Red Fred stated.

Marissa wasn't about to let things go off into a political discussion of "red-" and "blue-" state moms. She had enough trouble as it was. "We don't insult others because it's rude. And insults lead to bullying, which will not be tolerated here and should not be tolerated anywhere."

"Right," Red Fred said. "We're all in this together. Just like on *Glee*."

"Except we don't sing or dance," Tasmyn said.

"And we don't have slushies thrown at us," Nadine said.

"I do," Red Fred said.

"You *used* to," Jose said. "But not since you started wearing the T-shirts I designed for you."

Red Fred nodded. "Right."

"So is the library gonna let us have a display for the shirt and the auction in their booth at the festival?" Jose asked.

"Rhubarb sucks," Red Fred said. Before Marissa could protest, he added, "No, really. Have you ever tasted it raw? It's really sour."

"Kinda like that library board dude who gives us the evil eye whenever he sees us," Jose said. "Especially me."

"He's like a hundred years old or something," Red Fred said.

"What are we going to do with the raffle money?" Tasmyn asked.

"We already decided we're going to give it to poor kids who can't read," Red Fred said.

"We're poor," Molly said.

"Yeah, but we can read," Jose said.

"I think we should give it to UNICEF," Snake said. "Doesn't Angelina Jolie do stuff for them?"

"You just picked them because of Jolie," Molly said.

"And you just picked that Humane Society because you wanted a signed picture of that dude from *The Vampire Diaries*," Snake countered.

"The St. Tammany Humane Society is Ian Somerhalder's favorite charity." Molly's voice was almost reverent as she said the star's name.

"Well, it's not *my* favorite charity," Snake said.

"They help pets in the Gulf area. Don't you want to help animals?" Molly said.

"Snake is worse than a tool," Tasmyn said. "You need an empathy app because you're missing that emotion."

"Emotion doesn't pay the bills," Snake said. "Apps do."

"And T-shirts," Jose said. "Hey, maybe you should do an app of a few of my designs. People could use it as a background to download on their phones."

"Now you're talking my language," Snake said. "And we'll split the profits sixty-forty with me getting sixty percent."

"Screw that. I get sixty percent," Jose said. "It was my idea and my art."

"It's my app," Snake pointed out.

"Fifty-fifty then. Final offer."

"Done."

Marissa had no sooner wrapped up that meeting than she had to work at the reference desk.

"I don't remember the name of the book but I

remember the cover," a patron told Marissa, who'd heard that comment more times than she could count.

"It had gears and man-titty," the patron said.

Marissa hadn't ever heard *that* description before.

"It had gears and a man's chest with his nipples kind of showing. Ring any bells?" the patron continued. "It was out in the past year or two. And the book was this size but not hardcover." She indicated a trade size.

"Do you remember anything about the author's name?" Marissa asked.

"It was unusual."

"What was the book about?"

"Victorian England."

"Let me see what I can find." Marissa went online to a romance reader's chat room she'd visited before. Sure enough, within minutes they'd given her the title and author. *The Iron Duke* by Meljean Brook. Marissa checked the library's holdings on the computer and went to retrieve it from the shelves. "Is this it?" she asked the patron.

"That's it." The woman grabbed the book. "I just remembered they called it steampunk romance. Anyway thanks for finding it for me."

Once the woman moved away, Roz approached the reference desk. "I'm impressed, too. I was passing by and heard her description. Gears and man-titty." Roz grinned. "Maybe I should recommend that for the book club that Sally and I are in."

"I don't know my landlady's reading tastes but I do know that she likes Carrie Underwood's songs," Marissa said.

Roz nodded. "She likes cranking up 'Before She Cheats' and dancing to it."

"She told me I should try doing that."

"And have you?"

Marissa shook her head. She didn't say that she didn't dance, even in private. She didn't exactly know why. She hadn't even danced at her own wedding. Something in her past prevented her but she had yet to figure out what it was. It couldn't have been anything good. And that was enough to make her not want to remember it. She had enough trauma and drama in her life. She didn't need to add more.

• • •

By the end of the day, Marissa was ready to go home and relax in a lovely bubble bath. But as she headed for the exit, Connor's mother and grandmother stopped her.

"Marissa!" his grandmother called out.

"Shh," Wanda said. "We're in a library. We're supposed to be quiet."

"I wasn't that loud," the older woman protested.

"Hello, ladies," Marissa said.

"I told you to call me Grandma Sophie," Connor's grandmother said.

"And you should call me Wanda," his mom said. "I hope you don't mind that we stopped by. We wanted to see where you work." They looked around expectantly.

Naturally Marissa had to give them a tour. It would be rude to say she was leaving when Wanda and Grandma Sophie had been kind to her. So she showed them the various departments—circulation, children's, adult, technical services.

"Where is your office?" Grandma Sophie asked.

"I don't have an office. I have a cubicle."

"My daughter-in-law Megan has a cubicle at her

branch of the Chicago Public Library," Wanda said. "She's a librarian, too."

"My grandsons seem to have a thing for librarians," Grandma Sophie said.

"There's really nothing to see in my cubicle," Marissa said. Actually there was too much to see. She'd decorated the tiny area with things meant to inspire her—from the Nathan Fillion READ poster to an amethyst geode to a King Tut bobblehead. "You've seen all the important things."

"Marissa," Roz said. "I thought you left. You've already worked a long day. Go on home."

Marissa made the introductions and they all chatted a few minutes before Roz returned to her office.

"We didn't mean to keep you," Wanda said. "Let us make it up to you by buying you a cup of coffee at that place across the street."

Once again Marissa didn't know how to say no. So she found herself sitting in the Cups Café with Connor's family, sipping coffee and eating a kolachki from the café's bakery section.

"It's not as good as mine," Grandma Sophie said. "I'm also famous for my pierogies. How about you, Marissa? Do you cook?"

"Some."

"What are your favorite dishes?"

"The easy ones. Comfort food. Beef stew. Chicken and dumplings."

"Comfort food is good," Wanda said.

Marissa didn't add that she hadn't had the time or energy to cook much for ages. Instead she relied on frozen dinners and fast-food takeout. She'd stopped at the local McDonald's so often she knew their Dollar Menu by heart.

"Dumplings are part of Polish comfort food," Grandma Sophie said. "Are you sure you're not part Polish?"

Marissa returned her smile. "Not as far as I know."

Grandma Sophie pointed to her PROUD TO BE POLISH T-shirt. "We come from a proud heritage. We can trace our roots back three centuries. We are third cousins to Casimir Pulaski. That's why Connor's middle name is Casimir. Pulaski fought alongside Americans during the Revolutionary War. He even saved the life of George Washington and dipped into his own personal money when finances were hard to keep things going. He was wounded in Savannah and was buried there. We celebrate Pulaski Day in Chicago the first Monday in March."

"Any excuse to close down the local government offices," Wanda said with a grin.

Grandma Sophie frowned at her. "Pulaski is honored because he is a hero. President Obama even signed a bill making Pulaski an honorary American citizen."

"It sure took them long enough," Wanda said.

Grandma Sophie shrugged. "Better late than never." She set down the rest of her kolachki. "If you're interested, Marissa, I can show you some of my recipes."

"That would be great." Marissa didn't want to be one of those women who only cooked for company and not for themselves. She wanted to be able to recapture the fun she used to have with her favorite recipes.

Wanda excused herself to use the ladies' room. When she returned she said, "Connor called and I told him we were with you. He said he needs to speak to you,

Marissa. He asked you to stay here to meet him in five minutes."

Marissa frowned. "Did he say what it was about?"

"No, he just said it was urgent."

Wanda and Grandma Sophie made their way out of the coffee shop, leaving Marissa sitting at the table alone, wondering what the heck Connor could need to speak to her about that would be so urgent. Connor joined her a few minutes later.

"What's up?" he said.

"Your grandmother offered to share some of her recipes with me."

He looked surprised. "She doesn't do that very often. I hope you were suitably impressed."

"I was." She took a quick sip of what little coffee remained in her cup. "So what was so urgent that you needed to speak with me?"

"I was about to ask you the same question."

"What do you mean?"

"I heard you needed to talk to me."

Marissa frowned. "Your mother told me the same thing about you."

Connor rolled his eyes. "The matchmakers are at work."

"You think they set this up?"

"Yes. Guilty as charged."

"Have they done this to you before?" she asked.

"No."

"Then what's motivating them now?"

"You are."

"Me?" She looked at him in astonishment. "What did I do?"

"Come on. You instigated them staying here, bragging about how great the Rhubarb Festival was."

"I did not. They already said they wanted to attend the festival."

"You could have told them it's a bust and not worth visiting."

"So could you," Marissa countered.

"That would have looked suspicious."

"So would my bad-mouthing the festival. My mother was right there, if you recall. As a former Rhubarb Queen, she was raving about the festival more than I was."

"I saw the look on your face," he said. "You were having a great time watching them needle me. Until the tables were turned and they focused on you. And now look where we are."

"We're at Cups Café," she said.

"Exactly. I don't usually come here."

"Why not? Don't tell me you prefer Starbucks?"

"I prefer my coffee black," he said.

"You can get that here."

"Forget the coffee. What are we going to do about this situation?"

"With your family, you mean?"

He nodded. "You led them on."

"I did no such thing."

"You met them here for coffee and a kolachki. Are you going to eat the rest of that?"

"Yes, and it's not as good as your grandmother's."

"How do you know?"

"She told me so," Marissa said.

"That figures. Her kolachkis are pretty incredible. So are her pierogies."

"So she also told me."

"What else did she tell you?"

"That your middle name is Casimir."

Connor looked around in discomfort. "Quiet."

"What's the problem?"

"That's top secret intel," he growled.

"Why are you so embarrassed? There are worse middle names."

"I'm not embarrassed."

She grinned. "You sure look embarrassed."

"It's the lighting in here."

"No, it's not. It's you."

He narrowed his eyes at her. She recognized the warning. She just chose to ignore it. "I think Connor Casimir Doyle has a certain ring to it. Wanda also told me that her sons seem to have a thing for librarians."

"Just because my brother married a librarian doesn't mean I'm going to do the same thing," Connor stated.

"Of course not. There's no way I'm interested in marriage again after the hell I just went through. No way!" Marissa matched his emphatic denial.

"So we're agreed then?"

"About marriage?"

"Yes."

"Absolutely," she said.

"But maybe it would be easier if we let my mom and grandmother believe that we're a couple."

"Whoa." She nearly choked on the last bit of her kolachki. "How do you figure that?"

"If we don't, they'll just keep putting us together. Who knows what they'll pull next."

"They seem like reasonable women to me."

"Trust me, they're not," Connor said.

"They're only going to be here a few more days."

"You have no idea the havoc they could wreak in that time."

"And you do?"

He nodded. "You bet I do."

"Come on. They're just a pair of women and you're a big strong cop. Don't tell me you can't handle them."

"Can you handle your family?"

"Sometimes."

"Yeah, well, sometimes I can handle mine, too. Just not now, apparently."

"What's different now?" she asked.

"You."

"I didn't do anything wrong."

"You had to tweak the tiger."

"They don't look like tigers to me," Marissa said.

"Little do you know."

"So you keep telling me. You know, I am not the Pollyanna you seem to think I am."

"Sure you are. A divorced Pollyanna but still, one wearing rose-colored glasses."

She glared at him. "You take that back."

"So you don't believe that people are basically good?"

"No," Marissa said. "Not everyone is good." Her ex certainly wasn't.

"But you think the kids in your group are good?"

"Of course. Don't you?"

He shrugged.

"Okay, I may be a bit of an optimist compared to you," she said. "But that's setting the bar pretty low. If you don't think the kids are good then why are you working so hard to help them?"

"Because they can be prevented from . . ."

"From what?" she interrupted him. "From making mistakes? They're going to make mistakes. We all make them and learn from them."

"What have you learned from your mistakes? That men aren't to be trusted?"

"Bingo."

"That's not true," he said. "Thinking that is a mistake and you'll just have to learn from it."

"Learn what?"

"That there is a guy you can trust," he said.

"You?" she said bluntly.

"I didn't say that."

"Of course you didn't. You speak in riddles." She gathered her purse and tote bag. "I'm tired. I'm going home."

"I heard we could be in for some big storms this evening," he warned her as she left.

Great. Just what she needed. More stress.

• • •

The weather gods granted Marissa with enough time to climb into her tub filled with citrusy bubbles and soak for a few minutes with her remaining bag of French fries in hand. She'd gone through the drive-through and made her selections and eaten most of them the minute she walked in the door. Time was of the essence if she wanted to beat the storm.

The distant rumbling of thunder made her feel so edgy she almost dropped a fry into the water. She finished the last one and crumpled the paper, tossing it toward the wastebasket near the sink.

"You go, girl!" she congratulated herself as she made the basket. Once she'd completed washing up, she carefully got out of the tub and dried herself off before wrapping a floral cotton robe around her body. The familiar feel of the soft material reassured her but a nearby flash of lightning had her nearly slipping on the damp bathroom floor.

She waited for the ensuing clap of thunder, which sounded like an explosion. She felt as if nature was declaring war on her. The threatening storm clouds had turned the early evening to premature darkness.

She tried to stay calm, brushing her teeth in an attempt to focus on normal everyday things. She had a weather radio set to turn on automatically if a watch or warning was issued. The sound of the automated voice startled her. "The National Weather Service has issued a Severe Thunderstorm Warning effective until eight thirty P.M." Their county was listed. "Cities in the line of this storm include Hopeful." She didn't hear the rest. She heard all she needed to know.

"Severe thunderstorms don't mean tornadoes," she told herself. The sound of her own voice was drowned out by increasing loud bangs of thunder.

Wait, some of those bangs were coming from her front door. Someone was knocking. She was so rattled she opened the door without looking through the security peephole first to see who it was.

"Are you okay?" Connor asked. "I know you don't like storms." When she didn't reply, he added, "Because of the tornado."

"That was a long time ago," she said.

"So storms no longer bother you?"

A nearby crack of thunder made her jump and contradicted her statement.

His smile told her he'd noticed.

"*You* bother me," she said.

"Oh yeah?" He was clearly pleased with her admission.

"Don't smirk at me. That's not a good thing."

"What's not a good thing? Storms or the fact that I bother you?"

"Either one of those."

"I wasn't smirking, by the way," he added.

"Right. I know a smirk when I see one. You also have a tendency to glower. Especially when you're around the kids."

"That's my cop face."

"It's not nice."

"It's not supposed to be."

With his declaration, the electricity went out. Somehow she ended up in his arms, her face turned up to his. The next thing she knew, he was kissing her.

Chapter Eleven

. . . .

Marissa closed her eyes and parted her lips. This was the guy who'd taught her how to French kiss and he was still a master. Not that he tugged her into the deep end of the sensual pool. He started out hot and gentle before progressing to hot and hungry.

Her sensual memory recalled his moves despite the long passage of time. Lightning flashed around her and the thunder mirrored the boom of her heart as his right hand moved from cupping her face to caressing her throat before lowering to slide beneath her robe and cup her bare breast.

It had been so long since she'd been kissed this way, touched this way. The last man to do so had been her husband. Her *ex*-husband. And he'd never really kissed her like this. He'd never touched her as if she were the most precious and sexy woman on the planet. He'd never made her feel treasured as well as desired.

Marissa needed this. And Connor was giving it to her. One kiss blended into several as he rhythmically brushed his thumb over her nipple. She was completely bare beneath the thin cotton of her robe. He had only to lower his hand over her hip to reach her feminine core. They were in the semi-darkness. What was to stop them?

Another bright flash of lightning brought with it a sliver of reality. Connor had come to check on her. His mother had probably sent him. That possibility was like a dash of cold water.

She broke away from him. "We can't do this." Her fingers shook as she refastened her robe.

"Why not?"

"Because your mother is next door. Your grandmother, too."

"So?"

"So this is too weird."

"Weird?" She could tell by the tone of his voice that he was clearly insulted.

They were interrupted by a knock on the door. "Are you two okay in there?" his mom loudly called out.

"We're fine," Connor answered.

"You said you were going to check on Marissa because she's scared of storms," his mom said.

"Maybe he just made up the scared thing," Grandma Sophie said loudly.

Connor turned to Marissa. "Okay, I can see your point now about the weird factor."

Marissa opened the door to his family. "Connor didn't make it up. Storms really do spook me." So did sexy cops who kissed better than any guy she'd ever locked lips with. At seventeen, she'd thought Connor was an awesome kisser and she realized that hadn't changed. It was a disturbingly exciting discovery.

"You were gone a long time, Connor." His mom aimed a compact flashlight in his face. "I always travel with one of these, but we were getting worried." Then she looked at Marissa, who was hurriedly checking her robe to make sure nothing was showing that shouldn't be.

"We were looking for a candle," he said.

"That was thoughtful of you," Grandma Sophie said.

The lights went on as abruptly as they'd gone out.

"It sounds like the worst of the storm has passed," Marissa said. "And the electricity is back on so I'll be fine, Connor."

"Don't take a bath while there's any lightning," Grandma Sophie said. "I had a friend back in Chicago who was electrocuted by taking a bath. Lightning hit her house and traveled through the metal pipes."

"Now you've given Marissa something else to spook her," his mom said with a chastising look.

"What? What's wrong with what I said?" Grandma Sophie demanded.

"I think we should leave Marissa in peace now," Connor said. He herded his relatives out.

"I just didn't want her to get electrocuted," Marissa heard Grandma Sophie say as they all headed to Connor's apartment. "Getting a shock like that would not be a good thing."

Marissa raised her index finger to her lips, which still vibrated from Connor's kiss. She was shocked at how much pleasure she'd gotten from the feel of his mouth on hers. Shocked and awed . . . and that wasn't necessarily always a good thing. Not in her current circumstances.

• • •

"I raised you to be thoughtful," Connor's mom told him once they were inside his apartment. "Not to make out with the nice girl next door."

"You've been trying to hook me up with her since the second you arrived," he said.

"No." She frowned her disapproval. "Not 'hook up.' You think I don't go online and read the blogs and stuff? I know what 'hook up' means these days. It means sex. Marissa is a good girl. She's not the kind you take advantage of. Not that you should take advantage of any woman. That's not what I meant." She paused. "Where was I?"

"You were telling Connor not to have sex with Marissa," his grandmother said.

His mom nodded. "Right."

"I don't believe this," Connor muttered. "I need a beer."

"You don't want to become dependent on alcohol," his mother said, trailing after him as he headed for the fridge. "That's a dangerous road. You saw what happened with your father. As the child of an alcoholic, you may be more prone to become one yourself, not to mention the fact that you're a cop like him."

"I'm *not* like him," Connor said. He'd heard this lecture a million times before.

"I only know that you were not over there looking for a candle. Unless Marissa stores them under her robe?"

He wore his cop face and his most intimidating glare but his mom didn't budge. So he tried logic. "The only thing Marissa and I have in common is that we are both anti-marriage."

"Meaning you want to have sex with her and not marry her?" Grandma Sophie smacked his arm. "You were raised better than that."

Connor didn't say that he'd already had sex with Marissa when he was a freshman in college. He didn't want to say anything. None of this was anyone's business but his.

"What have you got against marriage?" his mother demanded.

"The fact that it ends in divorce," he said.

"That is a problem," his grandmother conceded.

"Marissa is still recovering from her divorce." Connor said it as much as a reminder for himself as for his relatives.

"Then you need to go slow with her," his mom said.

Connor set his beer on the kitchen counter. "She's not interested."

"She looked interested to me," his mom said.

"Me, too," his grandmother agreed.

"I am not having this conversation with you two. End of discussion." He walked away and turned on the TV to a baseball game.

"If that's what you want . . . then fine," his mother noted. "End of that discussion for now. But please change the channel. I can't stand to watch the Cubs lose another game."

"Maybe they'll win."

"And maybe pigs can fly," she retorted.

"Actually, they can at the Rhubarb Festival. One of the booths has plastic toy pigs you can toss at a pile of empty cans to see how many you can knock down."

"Just one of the many things I'm looking forward to at the festival," his mom said.

Connor was looking forward to the time when the festival was over and his relatives would head back to Chicago. He loved them, but he loved them more when they weren't in his apartment grilling him about his sex life.

• • •

"Wouldn't it be nice if you met a nice guy here in Hopeful and the two of you settled down to raise a family?" Her mom voiced the comment out of the blue as she and Marissa ate a packed lunch on a picnic table at the compact Book Street Park located across the street from the library. Marissa was on her hour lunch break from work, where things were crazy as they all geared up for the library's participation in the Rhubarb Festival. The bottom line was that her mom's tempting promise of cold shrimp salad was too hard to resist.

"Where is this coming from?" Marissa said. "I thought you wanted to talk about the Rhubarb Festival tomorrow and Jess's birthday next week."

"I do. That doesn't mean I can't share my hopes and dreams for your future along with my salad."

"My hope and dream is to make it from paycheck to paycheck and to hopefully put a little away for emergencies," Marissa said.

"Or you could hook up with a nice guy and let him take care of you."

Marissa angrily jabbed a plastic fork into a plump shrimp. "The way Brad took care of me?"

"Obviously not. The sheriff is a nice guy. Granted, he wasn't all that polite when you first arrived but he seems to have gotten over that. I really enjoyed the time we spent at his place with his mom and grandma. They seemed to have raised him right."

Marissa stayed quiet. She should have said that she didn't need a man to take care of her but the truth was that when she was lying awake in the middle of the night worrying about bills and debts, a part of her did wish for a partner to help her through tough times. A little help and moral support would be so nice.

That's what she thought she'd have with Brad. Instead he'd left her empty and scared.

You're tough, she silently reminded herself. *You're better off depending on yourself. Then you won't be disappointed. If you wanted something done right, you had to do it yourself.* That applied to moral support, too. Easier said than done, though.

"Let's talk about Jess's birthday," Marissa said firmly. Anything was better than listening to her mom try to reunite Marissa with the guy who was Marissa's first love.

"I thought I'd make her favorite red velvet cake."

"Uh-huh." Marissa was already thinking about work, making a mental list of things to be done before tomorrow.

"And I got her a gift card from her favorite online store."

"Uh-huh."

"I also dumped your dad and had sex with Jon Bon Jovi."

Marissa almost choked on her salad but managed to keep a straight face. "How was it?"

Her mom threw a balled-up paper napkin at her. "You weren't paying attention to me. I get enough of that from your father. I don't need you taking a page out of his book. His ancient Egyptian book."

"I'm sorry." She squeezed her mom's hand.

"You were always more like him than me."

The accusation stung. "That's not true."

"You both stick your nose in a book and ignore the people around you."

"You mean that Jess is more like you. Outgoing and a former beauty queen."

"We share the honor of both being former Rhubarb Queens, that's true. I just wish . . ."

"What?"

"That you were happy," her mom said quietly.

"Yeah," Marissa said. "I wish that, too."

• • •

Connor glanced up from the paperwork he was dealing with on his desk to find Ruby Mae standing there with a look on her face that did not bode well for him.

He sighed and put down his pen. "What's my mother done now?"

"She and your grandmother are driving me nuts."

Welcome to the club, Connor wanted to say but didn't. "I thought I was being polite by offering to give them a tour of the facility here," Ruby Mae said.

"And?"

Ruby Mae stuttered and shook her head over her own inability to communicate her frustration with the situation.

That's when Connor knew it was really serious. Ruby Mae was *never* at a loss for words. He'd heard stories about her going back decades. Even during the disastrous tornado, which had struck her first year on the job, she'd been in total control throughout the chaotic after-math. Or so he'd heard and he believed. Nothing rattled her.

But then she'd never met "two Polish broads from Chicago," as his paternal grandfather Buddy referred to them. They were indeed a force of nature.

Connor immediately went into triage mode. "Was any blood spilled? Any bones broken? Anyone seriously hurt?"

Ruby Mae shook her head. "Nothing like that. Not that I wasn't tempted."

"Where are they now?" he asked.

"Talking with the mayor."

"Why? What did my mom do wrong?"

"Where should I begin?" Ruby Mae sank into the visitor's chair across from him and briefly lowered her head to the edge of his desk before sitting up and glaring at him. "You should have warned me that they're dangerous."

"I wouldn't go quite that far."

"They wanted to look at our holding cells, so I showed them."

Connor could see where this was going. "Don't tell me you let them near the busted cell . . ."

"The one with the lock that doesn't work? Of course I warned them not to touch that door. But did they listen to me? Nooooo."

"So how did you get them out?"

"Who says I did?" Ruby Mae growled.

"You said they're talking to the mayor."

"That's right. They called him on their cell phone to complain about cuts in our budget that don't allow for the lock to be repaired. He came over to talk to them face to face. It was one of their demands."

"Their *demands*?"

"Your grandmother came up with most of them. Better coffee was one of her demands and I have to say I go along with that one," Ruby Mae admitted.

Connor closed his eyes and counted to ten.

"I don't suppose we could just leave them locked up now that the mayor knows where they are, huh?" Ruby Mae's raspy voice actually sounded a bit hopeful.

"I'm sorry they've disrupted things." He was prevented from saying more by the arrival of Mayor Bedford.

"You certainly do have a unique family," the mayor said.

Connor sighed. "Yes, I do."

"Don't worry. I called Digger Diehl. You know, the Drain Surgeon? Anyway, he's also a locksmith. He got them out."

"Too bad," Ruby Mae muttered.

"What?" the mayor asked.

"It's too bad they locked themselves in there. They don't follow orders very well." Rita Mae shot an it's-your-fault glare at Connor. "I specifically told them to avoid that cell."

"Anyway, all's well that ends well," the mayor said in that cheerfully hearty voice of his, the one Connor thought sounded like Santa Claus. "They told me how much they are looking forward to the town's Rhubarb Festival tomorrow." He puffed out his chest. "I may have bragged a bit about it."

"Where are my relatives now?" Connor asked.

"At Cups Café, having lunch."

Connor nodded. "I'll be back in a few minutes."

"Such a devoted family man," he heard the mayor say as Connor was leaving. "His grandmother told me how disappointed she is that he isn't married yet."

"She's going to be even more disappointed when he reads his stubborn granny the riot act," Ruby Mae said. "Talk about a train wreck."

• • •

Connor walked into Cups Café to find his mother and grandmother calmly sipping coffee and eating grilled cheese sandwiches.

He could tell by the way that everyone in the place turned their heads to stare at him that they all knew about his family getting locked in the holding cell. The owner was one of Ruby Mae's contacts. Or maybe his mother had filled in the large lunch crowd.

He yanked out an empty chair at their table.

"Connor." His mother gave him a radiant smile. "I'm so glad you could join us for lunch."

"Are you trying to get me fired and sent back to Chicago? Is that your plan?" he growled.

"Of course not."

He could tell by her expression that his mother was telling the truth. But he could also tell that, in her eyes, the idea had some merit. She just hadn't thought of it.

GM patted his hand. "You look like you're having a hard day. Want some of my sandwich?"

"No. I want you two to stay out of trouble. Do you think you can manage that?" He glared at them both.

They serenely smiled back at him.

"I have no idea what you're talking about," his grandmother said.

"Getting locked in that cell? Ring any bells?" he said. "Demanding to speak to the mayor?"

"He seems like a very nice man," his mom said.

"He's married," the woman at the next table leaned over to say.

Connor's glare extended to her now as well. "We're trying to have a private conversation here."

"Then you shouldn't have come to Cups," the woman said before returning her attention to the menu.

He didn't know who she was, but she was right. This wasn't the proper place to have this conversation. "I expect you both to return to my apartment when you are done here."

"We were just trying to be helpful." His mom gave him one of her trademark reproachful looks meant to instill guilt.

"Well, don't," he said.

"You weren't this crabby when you lived in Chicago."

"Yes, he was," GM said. "Sometimes."

"Gee, thanks," Connor said.

"You're welcome." She patted his hand again before holding up half of her grilled cheese sandwich. "Sure you don't want a bite?"

"No, thanks."

"Don't you worry. We'll cook you up something good for dinner," his grandmother said.

He just prayed they didn't cook up any more trouble.

• • •

"You owe me," Marissa told Connor that evening as he walked by the library booth she was setting up for the Rhubarb Festival the following morning.

"I do?"

She nodded. "You owe me *big-time*."

"How do you figure that?"

"Your mother and Spider got to talking in the library this morning and once she told him who she was, he talked her into setting up a Facebook account online using his laptop."

Connor swore under his breath.

"He told her how she could post photos for her family and everyone to see. She was about to pull out your baby brag book when I interceded."

"Tell me she didn't flash that photo around," Connor said.

"Did I hear you mention 'flash'?" Flo asked as she walked by.

Marissa had seen Flo earlier setting up the divorce support group's booth where they were selling home-made strawberry-rhubarb jam to raise funds. Their slogan was "We Help People out of a Jam."

"Are you talking about the Rhubarb Flasher?" Flo asked Connor. "Is he back?" She looked around nervously.

"No, he's not back," Connor reassured her.

"How can you be sure?"

"Because he's locked up in Statesville Prison in Illinois for unrelated charges."

"Thank heavens for that," Flo said. "Then I can look forward to a peaceful festival."

As soon as she left, Connor resumed his earlier conversation with Marissa. "So did Spider get my mom on Facebook?"

"No, I stopped them in time."

"How did you manage that?" he said.

"Do you mean how did I manage to do that with your

'Resistance Is Futile' mother? You have the same trait, you know. You also inherited her stubbornness."

"She claims I got that from my dad. You really did talk her out of it?"

"I took her aside and told her about the dangers involved with social networking. We talked about the predators and the security risks. And then I helped her set up an account."

"You *what*?"

"You heard me. But I did the privacy settings so the access was limited and we discussed inappropriate content and photos."

"Is *your* mom on Facebook?" he demanded.

"Yes. Both my parents are."

"Hi there," her mom said as she joined them. "I finished our Women's Club booth so I thought I'd stop by the library booth and see if you needed some help. But I see you've already got a nice strong man here to assist you." She gave an approving nod at Connor's presence.

"Connor isn't pleased that his mother just opened a Facebook account," Marissa said.

"Is this about the naked baby picture thing?" Marissa's mom asked. "Because if it is, I can assure you both that as moms it's our duty to embarrass our kids every chance we get." She laughed at their aghast expressions. "I'm only kidding. Geez, can't you guys take a joke? Oh, there's Connie. I've got to run. We're both judges in the Rhubarb Queen pageant tomorrow and there are still a few things to iron out yet."

Marissa looked at Connor. "I'm sure they'll behave."

"Your mom and Connie?"

"Your mom and my mom."

"I seriously doubt that," Connor said.

"But then my bud Connor was born a doubter." Marissa recognized the newcomer as Kyle Sullivan aka Sully. He'd recently spoken to her teen group about a day in the life of a firefighter. Sully was one of those guys who never met a woman he didn't like, who could have posted for a Hottie Firefighter calendar, and who had a self-confessed thing for Chicago-style hot dogs served at a place by the interstate. His blue eyes and sun-bleached light brown hair made him look like a bit of a beach bum. But she had the feeling that when that fire alarm bell rang, he was all business.

"This place is as crowded as Union Station in Chicago during rush hour," Connor grumbled.

"It's good to see you again, Marissa," Sully said with a grin.

"What do you mean *again*?" Connor demanded.

"We hooked up at the library," Sully said.

"Hooked up?" Connor was growling now.

Marissa couldn't help it. She was enjoying Sully's flirting and Connor's apparent jealousy. She could have explained that Sully was a guest speaker. She probably *should* have explained. But she didn't. Instead she grinned back at Sully, which didn't please Connor one bit.

"She doesn't need your help," Connor told Sully. "She's got me."

"Does she?" Sully said.

"She does." Connor stood there and crossed his arms as if daring Sully to proceed further.

"What if she doesn't want you?" Sully said.

Both men turned to confront her. She sighed. The flirting game was clearly over and pissing rights were about to begin. They'd just converted her into a prize to be won. Or territory to be fought over.

Which was ridiculous. She knew from word around town that the two men were good friends. They were both probably having fun at her expense.

That possibility irritated her. "Go away. I don't need or want either one of you. I'm doing just fine on my own."

"Translated, that means she wants you to go," Connor told Sully. "And me to stay."

"I think you've got that backward. She wants *you* to go and *me* to stay," Sully said.

"If you both insist on staying then I'm putting you to work," Marissa warned them. "The bunting needs to be hung from the top of the booth. The ladder is here." She pointed to the back of the booth.

"I'll do it," Sully quickly said, shedding his white T-shirt. "It's hot," he explained with a grin.

Since Connor was in uniform, he couldn't remove any articles of clothing. And when a moment later a resident from the Hopeful Meadows Senior Center asked for Connor's help setting up their booth, he was duty-bound to go. But the glare he sent Marissa over his shoulder told her that this wasn't over.

"He's a good guy," Sully told her.

Maybe, but was he the *right* guy for her? Marissa wished she knew the answer to that question.

Chapter Twelve

. . . .

"I was just wondering . . . does really size matter?" Connor's mom asked Marissa the next day.

Marissa almost spit out the rhubarb lemonade she was sipping. The Rhubarb Festival was in full swing here at Hopeful's lovely Centennial Park. Marissa had done her morning shift at the library booth without any hint of trouble, so she was completely unprepared for a question like the one that Wanda had just posed to her.

"In the contest for the best rhubarb leaf contest," the older woman clarified. "I was just wondering."

"Um, yes, I believe size matters as well as condition," Marissa said in her best librarian voice.

"That's good to know," Connor said, appearing out of nowhere as he so often did. "How about stamina? Is that a requirement as well?"

Marissa refused to blush. Since glaring at him hadn't

worked in the past, she tried something new. She decided to confront him. It didn't matter that he was in uniform and wearing those sexy cop sunglasses of his. It didn't matter that their kiss had been as incredible as she remembered. He wasn't going to intimate her. "Are you still talking about rhubarb?" she said.

He adjusted the sunglasses so he could eye her over the rim. "Of course."

"Then stamina doesn't matter. Not for rhubarb."

His grin told her he got what she meant. Now that she considered what she'd just said, she realized it could be misconstrued as flirting with him. She couldn't even remember the last time she'd flirted.

It felt surprisingly good.

What was wrong with her? She was standing here surrounded by Connor's mom and grandmother, who were both eyeing her as if sizing her up for birthing offspring. *Connor's* offspring.

"I've been collecting recipes. I had no idea that you could do so much with a fruit like rhubarb," Wanda said.

"Botanically speaking, rhubarb is a vegetable not a fruit," Marissa automatically said. "It's a relative of buckwheat."

"And Ohio is the buckwheat state," Wanda said.

"Actually we're the buck*eye* state," Connor said.

Wanda patted his cheek.

Connor had his sunglasses firmly back in place but Marissa was sure that behind them he was rolling his eyes.

Since she didn't know what to say next, she fell back on her standard patter for the event. "In seventeenth-century England, rhubarb sold for more than twice the price of opium."

"You mean it's a drug?" Wanda looked horrified at this possibility and glanced around at the surrounding booths as if she'd just walked into a huge pot party or a meth lab.

"No, it's not a drug," Marissa said. "It was just highly prized. You shouldn't eat the rhubarb leaves, though. They're toxic."

"Come on." Grandma Sophie tugged on Wanda's arm. "I don't want to miss the Rhubarb Rockers dancing in the band shell."

Their departure left Marissa alone with Connor. Yes, they were surrounded by hundreds of people in the park but in that moment if felt as if the two of them were the only ones in the world. She recognized that this was a dangerous feeling, so she quietly blurted out, "I do not want to talk about what happened between us."

"Neither do I. Wait, what do you mean by what happened between us?"

"That kiss the other night."

"Right. Well, I don't want to talk about it either."

"You never want to talk about anything," she muttered.

"And you do?"

"No."

"We're on the same page then." He leaned closer.

He wouldn't kiss her here in front of the entire town . . . would he? She certainly didn't want him to . . . did she?

"What are you two talking about so intently?" her mother asked as she joined them.

"Nothing," Marissa and Connor said in unison, leaning back so there was more space between them.

"I just wanted to let you know, Marissa, that the

Rhubarb Queen pageant will be beginning soon. I was hoping you'd come watch. Your sister is already in the audience." Her mom looked at her expectantly.

"I have to work at the library booth."

Her mom was not pleased with this news. "I thought you already did that this morning?"

"I did, but now I'm helping my group of teens," Marissa said.

"*Our* group of teens," Connor corrected her.

"You sound like a pair of proud parents," her mom said.

"No way. Not that I'm not proud of them, because I am. Jose designed the signs." Marissa pointed to the small corner of the booth that had been allotted for their use.

"I was counting on you coming to support me in my work as one of the judges. Especially given the fact that your father chose not to attend."

Her mother deliberately referred to him as Marissa's father and not her husband when she was aggravated with him, which seemed to be most of the time these days.

"Instead he's dressed like Indiana Jones next to some mummy at the college's booth," her mom said. "What does that have to do with rhubarb?"

"I'm not sure," Marissa admitted.

"He's never before acted with such disregard for my feelings. He knows how important this is, so he's always been in the audience in previous years. But now, when I need him most he abandons me for some mummy!"

"Do you want me to talk to him?" Marissa heard herself asking.

Her mother grabbed her hand in gratitude. "Would you? That would be great. I've got to get back." She rushed off as quickly as she'd arrived.

Marissa turned to Connor. "I don't suppose you could order my dad to step away from the mummy and head over to the pageant area, could you?"

"I'm afraid not. Looks like you've got some mummy issues to deal with."

She patted his cheek. "Hey, you've got mummy issues of your own."

His grin weakened her knees and left her feeling like she'd been hit by . . . well, hit by a sarcophagus. Her dad might be pleased by the analogy but Marissa wasn't. She wasn't supposed to feel this fluttering in her stomach.

She was too old for the sweaty-palms-dry-mouth sensations of a first crush. She shouldn't even be considering jumping Connor and having her way with him, not when she was standing here in front of the Hopeful Memorial Library booth surrounded by crowds of people.

She wanted to rip off those sunglasses of his, look into his gray-green-blue eyes and see if she could read his thoughts. Thoughts of *ripping* had her eyeing the very official-looking shirt of his uniform. There was a reason male strippers often wore cop uniforms.

Okay, she had to stop this. She should not be thinking of Connor as a male stripper. That was not a good thing. Well, yeah, it kind of was a good fantasy. A damn fine fantasy, in fact. But that's all it could be. A fantasy.

The reality was that she needed to step away from Connor and his sensual influence on her and head over to the booth where her father was hanging out with a mummy.

Marissa sighed.

"If you really need my help . . ." Connor began before she interrupted him.

"No, I can do this on my own," she said and meant it.

She couldn't afford to lean on him, not when doing so could end up with her flat on her face. No, she had to stand on her own two feet. And those feet needed to move her out of Connor's gravitational pull.

As it turned out, Connor was the one who left first, which aggravated her. She wished she could be the first one to walk away for a change.

• • •

"Nice hat, Dad," Marissa said. She'd finally found the booth where he was holding ancient Egyptian court.

"Thanks." He touched the brim. "I got it online."

"At IndianaJones.com?"

"Something like that."

"Mom's not happy that you're not going to see the pageant," Marissa said.

"Are you going?"

Marissa shook her head.

"Then she's not happy with you either," her dad said.

"I guess that's something you and I have in common," she said.

He just shrugged.

"It would mean a lot to her if you'd go," Marissa said.

"I've gone to that silly pageant for a quarter of a century. Just once, I want to do what *I* want to do."

Marissa pointed to the pyramid-shaped banner on the booth. "I didn't even know there was such a thing as a 'Pharaoh's Pals' group."

"This is our first year at the festival. I'm not real fond of the name of our group. It needs some tweaking yet."

"How are you tying the pharaohs in with rhubarb?"

"They're as old as rhubarb," he said. "The culinary use of rhubarb is relatively new, as you no doubt know.

That dates back to the eighteen hundreds. But the earliest medicinal use was about five thousand years ago in China. The pharaohs go back five thousand yeas as well. Granted, they didn't use rhubarb, but both rhubarb and the pharaohs share five thousand years of history. I know it's not the *same* history, but five thousand years is nothing to sneeze at."

"What about the history that you and Mom share?"

"The quarter century of going to that pageant with her? I've earned a year off. Why don't you go?"

"I'm working at the library booth," Marissa said.

"And I'm working here."

Marissa could tell that no amount of arguing was going to change her father's mind. And to think the day had started out so serenely. Earlier this morning, she'd walked to Centennial Park, cutting through Hopeful's Historic District with its Victorian homes and lush gardens. In May, the phlox had been out but currently the old-fashioned roses—the kind that smelled divine—were in full bloom. She'd actually paused to smell the roses.

And now here she was, at an impasse with both her parents.

She ran into Connor on her way back to the library's booth.

"No luck with your dad?" he said.

She shook her head. "He's very stubborn,"

"Parents are like that sometimes."

"Yes, but at least yours don't live here."

"True. And don't think I'm not thankful for that fact."

Marissa sighed. "After being gone all those years, I'm not used to being drawn into all their arguments and having them know everything I'm doing."

"At least your parents aren't trying to act as matchmakers."

"My mom is. My dad doesn't care."

"Count your blessings," Connor said. "When there are two of them, they double-team you."

"I guess."

"Here, this will cheer you up."

For the first time she noticed the small cardboard box in his hands. "What is it?"

"Rhubarb." He held up a bite-sized piece of stalk and dipped it into the tiny container in the corner of the box. "With honey. Hurry up and open wide."

She opened her mouth to say no but he'd already put the rhubarb in her mouth.

The combination of tart and sweet was unexpectedly good. She hadn't had this snack since she'd left Hopeful.

"Good, huh?" He leaned closer. "You've got some honey on your mouth."

He brushed his thumb over her bottom lip and then lifted it to his own mouth to suck the stickiness off.

Her earlier stripper fantasy about Connor returned with a vengeance. *Him, naked, pouring honey over her nude body and then sucking it off.* She felt her nipples tightening beneath her pale blue top.

Thank goodness the ruffles hid that fact from him. She looked down to make sure that was the case then nervously tucked a strand of her hair behind her hair, which set her moonstone dangle earrings moving.

"I like these." He reached out and gently set the piece of jewelry in motion again. "What is this?"

"Moonstone. Legend is that it brings emotional balance."

"Oh yeah? How's that working for you?"

"Not as well as I'd hoped," she muttered. Her hormones were running wild and screaming like banshees. *Sex. I want SEX. NOW.*

"I've got to get back to the library booth." She really meant she had to get away from him before she did something stupid.

"I'll come with you."

"No, don't."

"Okay." Again he was the one who turned and walked away, dammit. She was supposed to do that, not stand here with a container full of rhubarb and honey and a body zooming with unfulfilled sexual needs.

"I'm in trouble," Marissa told Deb a few hours later. The two of them had found a spot away from the crowd with some privacy to go with their slices of strawberry-rhubarb pie. Marissa was on break from her library booth duties.

"What's wrong?" Deb said with a concerned look on her face.

"Swear you won't tell a soul."

"I swear. What's going on? Is it your ex?"

"No."

"Does it have something to do with that matchmaking situation you talked about the last time we were together?"

"Yes. Connor kissed me," Marissa awkwardly blurted out.

"The sheriff?"

Marissa nodded.

"Wow," Deb said.

"Yeah. Double wow."

"By which I take it that you enjoyed the kiss?"

"He's a great kisser." Marissa almost added that he'd

always been a great kisser but stopped herself. She wasn't ready yet to confess her earlier relationship with Connor as her first lover.

"So what's the problem?" Deb asked.

"I shouldn't be having these feelings."

"What feelings?"

"The more time I spend with him, the more he tempts me," Marissa said, nervously fingering her dangle earrings.

"I see you're wearing moonstones. I like reading about gem lore. Legend has it that its supposed powers include reuniting lovers who have quarreled."

"I don't want to be reunited with my ex," Marissa said.

"Are you sure about that?"

Marissa nodded. "Moonstone is also supposed to bring emotional balance." She gently flicked her earrings. "It's not working."

"Wait, let's get back to Connor kissing you. When did this happen?"

"The other night. And no, it didn't get more serious than that." Well, it kind of had, given the fact that he'd undone her robe and cupped her naked breasts, but Marissa figured there was no need to go into details like that. They just got her all hot and bothered again.

"Are you falling for him?" Deb sounded concerned but not half as concerned as Marissa was.

"No. Absolutely not. It's just lust, not an emotional thing. Listen, to say that I'm gun-shy after my sham of a marriage is an understatement."

"Yet you and Connor shared a kiss."

"It was just lust," Marissa insisted.

"Do you want to kiss him again?"

"Yes, and that's a problem."

"If it's only lust, then maybe you should . . . you know . . . get it out of your system by sleeping with him."

Marissa already knew that having sex with Connor was not the cure for getting him out of her system. In fact, it just made her want him even more. That had been true a decade ago and she had the feeling it was just as true today.

• • •

"How's it going?" Connor asked the teens gathered at the library's booth.

Nadine looked up from her smartphone. "No one said I couldn't tweet from the booth," Nadine said, clearly still miffed about the tweet issue.

"That's not why I'm here," Connor said.

"If you're looking for Marissa, she's not here," Jose said.

"I'm not looking for her." Hell. He was but he wasn't admitting that.

Jose just looked at him as if he knew Connor was lying but he didn't confront him about it.

Too bad. Connor was itching for a fight. He got one from an unexpected source—the library board president.

"We need to talk," Chester Flint said, pulling him aside.

Connor shoved his sunglasses up onto his head in order to glare at the older man. He didn't appreciate being hauled around like a hogtied farm animal, and his look informed Chester of that fact.

"There's a problem," the older man said.

Connor's look said that the problem was Chester.

"This is turning into a big mess."

Connor nodded his agreement.

"I should have held my ground. A poetry jam was a stupid idea. But I didn't protest. I could have. I'm also president of the Rhubarb Festival planning committee as well as the library board. I should have said no. But I went along with it. And now we've got a problem," Chester said.

"What problem?"

"Those delinquents in the library booth. It's totally inappropriate to have them there."

"And why's that?" Connor's voice was laid-back but his expression was anything but.

"Because the one with the tattoo entered the poetry jam."

"You mean Jose?"

Chester shrugged. "I don't pay attention to their names."

"You should."

"You're right. I should pay attention so I can tell you all the things he's done wrong. And not just him. They're in it together. They are all a pack of trouble."

"How do you figure that?"

"Can't you see?" Chester's face was becoming increasingly flushed with anger. "They deliberately came up with this plan to discredit the entire festival."

"What plan?"

"To enter the poetry jam."

"There's no law against that."

"That kid with the tattoos . . . Jose. He won." Chester's voice reflected his outrage.

"There's no law against that either."

"There should be. You should have heard him."

"I wish I had," Connor said.

"I wish you had, too. Then you'd know why I'm so upset."

"You could just get to the point and tell me why you're so upset."

"His poem didn't even rhyme. Not only did he take the Lord's name in vain, but he was also disrespectful about the American flag and our country. Plus, he actually compared a rhubarb's stem to a part of the male anatomy."

"I'm not the poetry police," Connor said.

"But you are involved with this teen program. By having him in the library booth, you're sending the wrong kind of message to our community."

"And what message would that be?"

"That bad behavior is rewarded," Chester said.

"They haven't done anything bad."

"They have in my book. Maybe not yours. Not yet. But they will, you just wait and see." Chester made the dire prediction with utter certainty and then marched away.

Connor returned to the library booth to find Jose looking ready to do battle, as he often was. The arms-crossed-feet-planted-apart-tough-guy look was familiar to Connor, who'd used the same body language himself as had dozens of kids he'd dealt with back in Chicago.

"I guess the old guy wasn't happy about me winning that poetry jam instead of his granddaughter," the teen said.

"Jose deserved to win," Red Fred said.

"And you deserved to come in second and not third," Jose told his friend.

"That's right." Nadine turned her smartphone for them to see the screen. "I just tweeted that you were robbed."

Their conversation was interrupted by the arrival of Flo, who grabbed Connor's arm. "I just heard there was a robbery at the festival. I saw it on Twitter." She looked around nervously. "You don't think it was the Rhubarb Flasher, do you? You're sure he hasn't broken out of prison?"

"Why would a flasher want to steal an award?" Red Fred said.

"An *award* was stolen?" The news didn't calm Flo down too much. "Was it for biggest rhubarb leaf? Longest stem? Fattest stem?"

Before Connor could answer, Connor's landlady, Sally, joined Flo. "Did you hear about the kid who used the *p* word in the poetry jam?" She paused the moment she saw Jose. "Oh. You're the one."

Jose nodded.

"The *p* word?" Flo was confused. "You mean pie?"

"She means penis," Jose said proudly.

"Wait." Flo was confused. "We don't have a penis contest at this festival."

"He compared a rhubarb's stem to uh . . ." Sally tilted her head.

"Well, he's hardly the first one to do that," Flo said.

"Maybe not, but he's the first one to do it onstage."

"Do what onstage? You didn't drop your pants, did you?" Flo fixed Jose with the same icy glare of disapproval that Connor had seen her give anyone at the post office who tried to jump the line of waiting customers.

"No way," Jose said.

"I know your grandma," Flo reminded him.

He looked down. "I know," he muttered.

"His grandma will be proud," Nadine said. "Jose won first prize in the poetry jam."

"And then someone stole your award?" Clearly outraged, Flo turned to Connor. "Sheriff, what are you going to do about this?"

Connor didn't have a clue. He wished Marissa would show up so she could take over this circus and he could walk away. He knew she'd say he was good at walking away, and that might be true.

"Jose's award wasn't stolen," Connor said.

Flo frowned. "But I saw it on Twitter."

"Not everything you see on the Internet is true," Connor said,

"I know that. But Twitter is different."

"I'm the one who posted the tweet," Nadine said. "And I was referring to the fact that Red Fred should have won second place in the poetry jam instead of third."

"That's okay," Red Fred said. "Before he took off, my dad used to tell me that second place is another word for loser."

"No offense, but your daddy was full of horse manure," Flo said, her Appalachian heritage evident for the first time in her accent.

They all fell silent for a moment, as if collectively agreeing to her comment. The momentary lull was interrupted by Marissa's return.

"Did I miss anything?" Marissa said.

"Nah," Jose said. "It's all good."

But Connor wasn't sure his powerful attraction to Marissa was a good thing. Not a good thing at all. It had him feeling all messed up and out of control which raised a major red flag because as a cop he prided himself on being in control.

He'd lost it once back in Chicago and he wasn't about to let history repeat itself here in Hopeful even if this was a different scenario. So Connor did what he did best in emotional situations like this. He simply walked away.

Chapter Thirteen

. . . .

"I want to thank you all for coming to our support group meeting tonight," Flo said.

Marissa couldn't be sure, but it seemed to her that Flo was directing that comment directly at her. Had she somehow guessed that Marissa had been tempted to walk into the "Cooking for One" meeting in the neighboring room instead of coming tonight?

Marissa nervously fingered her silver-and-moonstone dragonfly dangle earrings as she took a seat. There was no sign of Deb, who had promised she'd be attending tonight and who had convinced her that she should give the group another try.

"Tonight we're going to be talking about dating after divorce," Flo said.

Marissa gulped. Had Deb told them about their conversation? Marissa had trusted her.

"Breathe," Deb whispered as she slipped into the chair next to her. "Don't panic. I didn't say a word."

"I'm bringing this up because I got invited out on a date," Flo said.

The other attendees all started murmuring.

Deb had filled her in regarding most of the members of the group, letting her know that the woman Marissa had labeled as someone who looked like they should be on that *Real Housewives of Atlanta* TV show was actually named Brenda.

"Who's the lucky man?" Brenda asked.

"It's Digger Diehl, the plumber," Flo said.

"Maybe you'll get a discount on any future repairs," Brenda said.

"I rent an apartment," Flo reminded her. "The landlord pays for the repairs."

Brenda frowned in confusion. "Then why are you going out with a plumber?"

"Plumbers make good money," Flo said.

"No one makes good money in this economy," Brenda said.

"Wall Street brokers do."

"Well, we don't have any of those here in Hopeful so I'm going out with Digger. Besides, I like him." Flo smiled at them all. "So I thought we could all share our dating experiences. How long did you wait after your divorce before you went out with someone else?"

"The instant the ink was dry on the divorce papers," Brenda said. "I had guys lined up."

"Let's go around the room," Flo suggested. "We'll start with you, Marissa."

"Me?" She looked around at their eager faces. "Why me?"

"Because you were seen being hand-fed by our sexy sheriff at the Rhubarb Festival the other day," Flo said. "Are you two dating?"

"No." She shook her head so vehemently she got a little dizzy. She was actually miffed that Connor had walked away from her yet again when she'd returned from her break to the library booth. He hadn't said a word of greeting or farewell. He'd just taken off.

"You can tell us, you know," Flo said. "We're discreet. Nothing leaves this room."

Deb came to her rescue. "I still haven't dated anyone," she said. "And it's been almost two years since my divorce. I've done some group activities, meet-and-greet sorts of things. But not a date. I'm not ready. And I haven't found anyone who makes me want to go out on a date."

"You get out of practice," another woman piped up to say. "I was married for fifteen years. I'd been off the dating market that long and my skills are rusty. Things have changed a lot."

"Several of the local churches offer group settings like Parents without Partners meetings," Brenda said. "I met some great guys there."

Flo frowned. "I thought you didn't have any kids."

"I don't. But that doesn't mean I don't want to date a guy who does have kids."

"Whatever you do, don't let things get too serious," another woman said. "Enjoy the rebound relationship but don't confuse it with love. Don't jump right from one man to another. You need some time on your own to get your head straight. That's my advice."

Flo nodded her agreement. "Let's face it, ladies, we all have baggage from our failed marriages."

"And it's hard to put yourself out there when you still feel like a failure," Deb said.

Surprisingly it was Brenda who said, "You need to improve your self-esteem yourself and not depend on a man to do it for you. Believe me, I've done that and it doesn't work. The man leaves and your self-esteem goes out the door with him. It totally tanks."

As others joined the discussion, Marissa realized that they all had different stories to tell about when they'd started dating again or if they even had or would in the future. There was no right or wrong answer. Which was too bad, because she'd sort of been hoping they'd provide her with a clear consensus. Instead, they left her as confused as before. But at least she wasn't alone in her confusion. They were all in the same boat.

• • •

Marissa planned to have coffee with Deb after the meeting but Deb said she was coming down with a cold and wanted to go home. So Marissa headed to her rusty lime VW in the parking lot before she realized that she was missing one of her dragonfly earrings. She remembered nervously tugging on it several times during the meeting and prayed it had fallen off in the meeting room.

She hurried back inside and raced up the stairs to the second floor. The room was empty but her earring was there. She was so relieved she almost cried. It was her all-time favorite piece of jewelry in her small collection.

She quickly put it back on, making sure the fastening was secure before heading out in the hallway.

Seeing Connor coming around the corner, she ducked into the elevator. She didn't feel up to talking to him right now.

He stopped the closing doors with his hand. "Hold on." He joined her in the elevator.

The doors slid shut and they were enclosed in the metal box. *No problem*, she told herself. *It will be on the first floor in a few seconds.*

"Why did you run away?" he said.

Instead of answering, she said, "What are you doing here?" She noticed he was in civilian clothes. The man was made to wear jeans and a blue chambray shirt. His eyes seemed more blue-gray than usual in the elevator's rather dim light.

A second later, the lights went out, leaving only an emergency bulb going as the elevator abruptly stopped. Marissa grabbed onto Connor to prevent herself from falling.

"What did you do?" she demanded.

"Nothing."

"You stopped the elevator."

"No, I didn't."

"Then what happened?"

"I suspect it's a power outage," he said.

She didn't realize she was still hanging on to him until that moment. She really should let him go and free herself. She could stand on her own two feet. She didn't need him—or any man—propping her up.

But damn, it felt good to have his hands resting on her waist. Her body sure wasn't suffering from any power outage as sexual electricity surged through her.

The last time there'd been a power outage, she'd been almost naked while he kissed her. "I'm okay," she said before he could ask.

"You feel better than just okay," he murmured.

Maybe her wild memory of their kiss the other night

had been a result of her heightened emotions due to the storm? Yes, that had to be it. And her emotions were once again heightened by the elevator stopping.

"Do you have claustrophobia?" He was so close his warm breath bounced off her mouth.

She didn't have claustrophobia. She had the hots for him. That's what was wrong with her.

He kissed her and she was a goner. She melted the instant his lips touched hers. He moved so she was backed up against the elevator wall, his body pressed against hers. His tongue tangled with hers and his hands slid beneath her sleeveless top. He stealthily undid her front-fastening bra, freeing her breasts to caress them with skillful care and fierce passion.

She liked it. She liked everything he was doing to her. No, not just liked. *Loved. Adored. Wanted more. Much more!*

Her body throbbed with pulsing need. So was his. Her thin cotton skirt did little to hide the feel of the bulge beneath of his jeans. The denim barrier was like a magnet, drawing her hand toward it. She tugged his shirt from his jeans and slid her fingers against his washboard stomach. She stood on tiptoes to better align herself to him, allowing her pelvis to rub against his.

One of his hands remained on her breast while his other lowered to cup her bottom. He inched her skirt up until his fingers were pressed against her bare thighs and her silky underwear.

She protested his other hand leaving her breast but only briefly as he used it to bend her knee and rest her leg against his, opening her to the feel of his fingers entering forbidden territory.

She threaded her fingers through his hair, guiding his

mouth to her breast where he stroked her nipple with his skillful tongue. She tilted her head back as he worked his magic on her, his fingers gliding inside her body to find the enticing wet warmth of her inner passageway. His movements set her on fire inside and out.

He began with an intimate butterfly-light probing before caressing her clit with his thumb while his fingers thrust her into a world of wild pleasure. The walls of her vagina clenched and vibrated with the force of her orgasm. She held on to Connor as she was consumed with surges of sexual energy that burned brightly.

He reluctantly removed his hand and his mouth from her body.

Marissa moaned her protest at his withdrawal.

"The lights are back on," he said gruffly. "The elevator is moving."

He smoothed her skirt back into place.

The elevator bumped to a gentle stop on the lobby level. Marissa returned to earth with the speed of a missile landing. Her body was still experiencing tiny aftershocks deep within her. She crossed her legs tightly, which only made the detonations deeper.

"Are you guys okay?" the building security guard asked as the elevator doors opened. "A building transformer blew but we finally got the backup generator going."

Marissa frantically looked around the elevator to see if it was equipped with surveillance cameras. Thank God it was not.

She should have checked that out much earlier, before Connor got beneath her skirt, and her guard, to send her shooting off to another universe.

"While you're here, Sheriff, I've got a question about the building's security," the security guard said.

Marissa saw her chance and she took it, heading straight for the nearest exit, her bra still unfastened.

"Wait," Connor called out but Marissa made a break for it, praying her demon car would start. It did, and then played "Crash and Burn" by Savage Garden.

"I know, I know," she told the car. "I get it, okay? I'm not going to crash and burn again."

•   •   •

"The fridge Nazi hits again," Jill dramatically exclaimed as Marissa walked into the staff room for her lunch break the next day.

"What happened?"

"He or she is getting bolder. They took my salad. I think they took your lunch too."

Marissa looked over her shoulder. Sure enough, there was no sign of her bagged lunch.

"It's one thing to throw away leftovers or confiscate someone else's water bottle, but this has gone too far."

"Do you have any idea who's doing this?" Marissa asked. She'd have to hit McDonalds on her lunch break now. Maybe she'd skip the double cheeseburger and just have several batches of fries. It was that kind of day. She hadn't gotten much sleep last night. Instead her body remained on heightened hormone alert, wanting more of the intense pleasure Connor had given her in that elevator.

"I don't know," Jill said. "Some of the other staff members think it might be someone outside of the library."

"Outside?"

"One of the kids in your teen group."

"This area is restricted to staff members only."

"Yes, but it's frequently not locked."

"The fridge Nazi was around before I started the teen group," Marissa said.

"True. You're right."

Marissa hated that her teens were automatically first on the suspicion list. Their meeting tonight was scheduled to be a wrap-up of their Rhubarb Festival fundraising event. Marissa had all the money locked in a cash box in her desk drawer. The total came to the grand amount of $140.99. It wasn't as much as Snake had hoped for but more than Tasmyn expected.

"I think you should all come with me when I present the check to the Literacy Group. We could take a picture and put it in the library newsletter."

"Can't we just mail the check?" Molly asked. "I don't like having my picture taken."

"Me either," Tasmyn said.

"I can Photoshop the picture and make us all look good," Nadine said.

Tasmyn and Molly didn't look completely convinced.

"You already have Jose's and Red Fred's photo for their awards at the Rhubarb Poetry Jam. Put that in the newsletter," Snake said.

"I plan to."

"Jose had to apologize to his grandma for taking the Lord's name in vain," Snake said. "She had a bad cold and couldn't come to the festival."

"It was her first time missing it," Jose said.

"But she was okay about the rest of your poetry?" Snake said.

Jose sidestepped the question by saying, "She was pleased that I won first prize. No one in my family has ever won a prize at anything before."

"Same here," Red Fred said.

"Was your mom pleased with your award?" Marissa asked.

Red Fred shrugged. "She didn't say."

"You told her, didn't you?"

He nodded. "She has a lot on her mind right now. There's talk that they might be laying people off and she's worried about losing her job."

"My mom is worried about her job, too," Molly said.

"I wish I could be like that guy who started Facebook," Snake said. "Then all your moms could come work for me and they wouldn't have to worry about money anymore."

"Yeah, that would be nice," Molly said. "I wish that could happen."

Marissa wished she could do more to help them all. They were just kids. They shouldn't have to worry like this. And some of them, like Tasmyn and Jose, also had to deal with moms who had drug addictions. Tasmyn was staying with an aunt who had four kids of her own while Jose, whose mom was incarcerated, was living with his grandmother.

All Marissa could do was be here for them, defend them and provide moral support and friendship. And chocolate. She passed around a bag of small chocolate Mars bars. "We need to celebrate."

"What are we celebrating?" Jose asked.

"Our success at our first festival," Marissa said.

"The Corn Festival is next month," Jose said.

"We'll make an even bigger splash there," Marissa predicted.

•   •   •

Marissa met her mom and sister in Book Park across from the library after work the next day. She found her mother spread-eagled on a huge blanket on the ground. Her sister joined Marissa and exclaimed, "Oh my God, Mom's collapsed!"

"I have not collapsed," their mother protested.

"Did you faint? Is it your heart?" Jess knelt and bent over to put her head on their mother's chest to listen for a heartbeat.

"That's not how you check a pulse." Marissa knelt on the blanket and put her fingers on her mom's wrist. "Stop smothering her, Jess."

"Relax, girls. I didn't faint and my heart is just fine."

"If you're fine why are you lying flat on the ground?" Marissa said.

"I'm not on the ground. I'm on a blanket that's on the ground. And I'm watching clouds." She tugged them both down to lie beside her. "No one has time for this anymore. They're all rushing around with headphones in their ears listening to their iPods or talking on their cell phones. No one stops to just be in the moment and enjoy the simple pleasures of watching clouds."

Although it was a little after five, there were still several hours of daylight left and plenty of cumulous clouds to view. Marissa knew she should be worried that someone from work would see her, but somehow she couldn't ruin the moment.

"We used to do this as kids," Marissa said.

"You need to do it as adults, too," her mom said. "Look

at that one." She pointed a little to her right. "See the way the sunlight is hitting it so brightly against the blue of the sky?"

"The one just below that looks like a penis," Jess said.

"Ladies," Connor said looking down on them. "Everything okay here?"

Marissa hadn't seen him since he'd given her an orgasm in the elevator forty-eight hours ago. She refused to sit up and let him know how much his arrival had thrown her.

"We're watching X-rated clouds," Jess said.

Seeing his suspicious frown, Marissa said, "No, we're not drunk or high. We're just living in the moment. It's a family thing."

"X-rated clouds are a family thing?" he asked.

"Yes," their mother said. "Do you have a problem with that?"

"No, no problem. Enjoy your family thing, ladies."

As he walked away, Jess said, "He has a nice ass."

Marissa was horrified, even if she agreed. "Shut up! He might hear you."

"So?"

"So . . ." Marissa turned to her mom. "I thought you called us here to talk about Jess's birthday party tomorrow?"

"I thought we'd start now with the cloud gazing. I think there's going to be a great sunset in an hour or two."

"It doesn't get dark until at least nine o'clock," Jess said.

"Do you have someplace else more important to be?" her mom said.

"As a matter of fact, I do," Jess said. "It's my birthday eve and the Roberts brothers are taking me out."

"Which one?"

Jess smiled proudly. "All three of them."

"What about your party tomorrow?" their mom asked.

"What about it?"

"You're still planning on coming, right?"

"Sure. But I may have to leave early."

"How early?"

"Eight," Jess said.

"But we're not even starting until seven."

"I'm good at eating and running," Jess said.

"Yeah, I know," Marissa said.

"You're just upset that I have a date and you don't," Jess said. "Unless you're bringing the hunky sheriff tomorrow night?"

"I thought it was only for family," Marissa said.

"You can bring a date if you want," Jess told Marissa. "Right, Mom?"

"Are the Roberts brothers coming to dinner? I have to buy more food if they are. Is the sheriff a big eater?" their mom asked Marissa.

"He's not coming," Marissa said.

"Did you even ask him?" Jess challenged Marissa.

"No."

"Wimp."

"Brat."

"Girls, please behave," their mom said. "Look, there's a cloud that looks like the peace sign. It's an omen that we all should get along."

"It looks more like a pitchfork to me," Jess said. "Or another penis."

"I give up," Marissa muttered, getting to her feet. "I'll see you tomorrow."

Marissa went home and ate a bowl of ramen noodles along with a salad. She'd just finished washing up the kitchen when Connor came knocking on her door. She knew it was him because this time she checked the peephole.

"Why did your mom just call and invite me to your sister's birthday party?" he said.

"What did you tell her?"

"That I'd get back to her."

"What'd you say that for?"

"Because I thought I'd check with you first," he said.

"You should have told her no."

"Why?"

"Is this your way of paying me back for spending time with your family?" Marissa demanded. "You're going to crash my sister's birthday party?"

"I was invited, so I wouldn't be crashing."

"You shouldn't be attending, either."

Connor said. "You know the more you tell me not to do something, the more it makes me want to do it. I'm just saying."

"And I'm just saying that I don't want you there."

"Why are you afraid of spending time with me? Is it because of what happened in the elevator?"

"Nothing happened."

"We almost had sex. You had an orgasm. In an elevator. I can refresh your memory, in case you forgot." He stepped closer.

She put her hand on his chest. Big mistake. She could feel the warmth of his skin beneath his shirt. Another chambray shirt like the one he'd worn and she'd unbuttoned in the elevator.

"That's not necessary," she said.

"So you do remember."

"Yes," she said. "And it's not going to happen again. Good night." She firmly closed the door on him and the temptation he provided.

•   •   •

Marissa's very first memory was of seeing her sister shortly after Jess was born. "You lucky girl," her mom had been telling her for nine months. "You're going to have a sister of your very own!"

"I don't want a sister," Marissa's five-year-old self said. "I want a Barbie."

"You can have both. If you're a good girl."

Marissa had been a good girl for the most part ever since then. Her sister, Jess, on the other hand, had always been hell on wheels. One of Jess's favorite activities as a toddler had been to put her arms around an eight-year-old Marissa and say "Love you!" right before yanking hard enough on Marissa's hair to bring tears to her eyes.

Jess was turning twenty-three today, and she still had a way of getting to Marissa with that combination of sisterly love and trouble.

It didn't help that Jess walked in the front door with a tiara on her head. "The birthday girl has arrived!" She struck a pose that would have done Heidi Klum proud. "Is that homemade red velvet cake I smell?"

"You know it is," Marissa said. "You made Mom make it."

"You are such a crab." Jess set her iPod in the speaker docking station in the living room. "I brought my own birthday playlist."

A second later, Katy Perry's "Firework" filled the room. "Come on." Jess grabbed Marissa's hand. "Dance."

Jess kicked off her sandals and jumped around the room, tugging Marissa with her. She finally noticed that Marissa wasn't showing an equal enthusiasm. "You call that dancing? You're barely moving your head."

Marissa yanked her hand away. "I don't like dancing."

"Everyone likes dancing."

"I don't."

"Since when?"

"Since as long as I can remember," Marissa said.

"Really?"

"Yeah, really."

"You'd think I'd have noticed that before," Jess said.

"You'd think." Marissa couldn't help the sarcasm the snuck into her voice.

"Maybe it's just the wrong song."

"It's not."

Jess ignored her and skipped ahead to the next tune, which was. Enrique Iglesias's "I Like It." "Is that better?" Jess asked even as she bopped around. "No? How about this one? Lady Gaga's 'Just Dance' makes everyone dance." Jess scooted around the room, tossing her hair, her hips, and lip-syncing with the song.

Marissa felt unexpected tears prickling her eyes. She wanted to dance, she really did want to join her sister. But something invisible yet incredibly powerful held her back. "I'm going to go check with Mom to see if she needs help in the kitchen," she said before making her escape.

The tears were a little harder to hold back when Marissa saw her mom boogying to the song in the kitchen. "The birthday girl must be here, huh?" Her mom waved her offset icing spatula in the air to the beat of the music.

"This one's for you, Mom," Jess shouted out before playing Bon Jovi's "It's My Life."

"The greatest band ever," Marissa's mom shouted back before punching her arms in the air and almost splattering the ceiling with cream cheese frosting.

"Give me that." Marissa took the spatula and started licking the frosting off it. She needed a sugar rush really badly.

"Why aren't you dancing?" her mom finally said after the song ended and Lady Gaga's "Bad Romance" came up next.

"That's the question, isn't it. Why can't I dance?"

"What do you mean?"

"Didn't you notice that I didn't even dance at my own wedding?" Marissa ate more frosting.

"You didn't?"

"No, Mom. I didn't."

"I guess I thought it was some sort of religious thing on Brad's part."

"No. It had nothing to do with him."

"Maybe you're just shy. Oh, there's the doorbell. Will you get that for me, please?" her mom said.

Marissa reluctantly set the now-licked-clean spatula in the dishwasher and headed to the front door, walking past her sister who was still dancing to "Bad Romance."

As if on cue, she opened the door to find Connor standing there with a huge grin on his face. "So you're a Lady Gaga fan, huh? Who'd have guessed it."

Chapter Fourteen

. . . .

"What are you doing here?" Marissa said.

"I was invited to your sister's birthday party, remember?" Connor said.

"And I told you not to come, remember?"

"I remember everything." The look he gave her set her entire body on fire. "Every touch, every kiss . . ."

"Shh." She put her hand to his lips and looked around nervously.

"What's the problem?" He spoke against her fingertips. "We're not teenagers anymore, trying to hide from your parents."

"Hide what from our parents?" Jess asked from behind them.

"Nothing," Marissa hurriedly said. "Connor was just leaving."

"Don't be silly," Jess said. "He just got here. Come on in."

"There's a police emergency he has to attend to," Marissa said. "Right?" She gave him the look.

He gave her the nice-try-but-no-cigar look in return. "Actually, the department can handle it on their own. They don't need me tonight." Now his eyes were traveling over her body, saying that *she* needed him tonight and *he* needed her.

"That's good to hear," Jess said.

Marissa didn't know if it was good or not. She only knew that her resistance to Connor's sex appeal was falling dangerously low. And he was wearing those damn jeans and chambray shirt again. Meanwhile, Lady Gaga sang on in the background about not wanting to be friends.

Jess pulled Connor into the living room and danced with him while Marissa stood by and watched. The man had moves. Damn, he could swivel his hips. You'd never know by looking at him now that he was a cop. He looked like a guy in one of those sexy jean ads. The man not only had moves, he had a damn good butt, too.

"Close your mouth, hon," her mom said as she joined her. "You'll catch flies."

Marissa pulled her mother back into the kitchen. "You shouldn't have invited him."

"Why not?"

"Because this is a family gathering."

"Jess has invited her guy friends. Why shouldn't I invite yours?"

"First off, Jess's friends aren't coming. Second, Connor is not my guy friend."

"He's a guy and he's your friend."

Marissa eyed her suspiciously. "Have you been talking to his mom?"

"Not since they left, but that reminds me that I do owe her a call."

Jess must have set her iPod on repeat because Katy Perry was singing "Firework" again.

Marissa wanted to stay in the kitchen and give her mom the many reasons why she shouldn't contact Connor's mom but she was more concerned with what Jess was doing with Connor in the other room.

She found him waiting for her by the living room entrance. "You stopped dancing," she said.

"This is more a girl song," he said before the music changed. "But this one by Enrique is better." He took her hand and tugged her to him so fast she almost bounced off his muscular body.

"I don't dance," she said in a panicky voice.

He put his hands on her hips. "Just move these."

"No, thank you." Marissa pushed his hands away even though they felt damn good on her body. She pulled her fuchsia ruffled top into a more demure neckline and smoothed her nervous fingers down the sides of her black capri pants.

"Librarians do dance, you know," Jess told her as she twirled on by. "Some even belly dance."

"This has nothing to do with my being a librarian," Marissa said.

"Then what does it have to do with?" Connor asked.

Afraid it would make her sound stupid, Marissa couldn't admit that she had no idea why she was so afraid to dance. Instead, she just shrugged.

"What's wrong?" her dad asked as he entered the living room. He squinted at Connor. "You look familiar. Were you in one of my classes last semester?"

"He's the town sheriff," Jess said.

"What did my students do now?" her dad said to Connor. "Did they tell you I'd bail them out of jail?

"The spring semester has been over for two weeks now, Dad," Marissa said. "Your students have all gone home."

"Good thing. I need to focus on my research on the family of the Silver Pharaoh during the summer break. Did you know that dancing was a common part of life in ancient Egypt? I suspect their music didn't sound like this, though."

"It probably didn't sound like your medieval madrigals either," Jess said as the next song came on. "It's *my* birthday, Daddy. That means *I* get to pick the music."

"And you picked Lady Gaga?" he said.

Marissa was as surprised as Jess that their father was able to identify the pop singer.

As if reading her mind, her dad said, "I may not be totally up on popular culture but you'd have to be locked in a sarcophagus not to know who Lady Gaga is."

"Right." Jess laughed and hugged him.

Marissa wished she could share her sister's free-spirited ability to express her emotions.

To her surprise, Connor took her hand and twined his fingers between hers. She didn't pull away but instead took comfort in his touch. She flashed a brief smile of gratitude his way and was rewarded with one of his wicked grins.

"I left something in the car," Connor said. "Marissa is going to come help me find it."

A second later, they were outside on the front porch. Her childhood home lacked just one architectural style and was instead a hodgepodge of styles from various historic eras, which greatly upset her father and amused her mother.

"It's a mutt of a house," her mom used to say when Marissa was a kid before fondly patting the column on the corner of the front porch.

"Who ever heard of putting an Arts and Crafts column on a Victorian-style house?" her dad would mutter.

She knew she was thinking about those memories to avoid focusing on Connor, who was still holding her hand. Not only that, he was brushing his thumb over the top of her hand. The soft caress sent her back to her high school days when holding his hand on her front porch would have let her parents know that she was seeing a forbidden boy.

Looking at him now, there was still a flash of forbidden in his eyes. He might represent law and order in his day job but now that he was off-duty, he represented wicked temptation. He projected power in a way he hadn't as a nineteen-year-old and that made him even sexier.

Like a fan at a rock concert, she leaned closer, drawn in.

He leaned forward, too. Was he going to kiss her? Right here on her parents' front porch?

So what if he did? She wasn't a teenager anymore. She was a free woman. Nervously licking her lips, she heard him groan before he finally did kiss her.

His lips had barely touched hers when they were interrupted.

"Hey, you two . . . Whoops." Her mom stood in the

front doorway grinning at them. "Sorry. I didn't mean to interrupt. Carry on." She shut the door.

Connor rested his forehead against Marissa's. "What is it with us and interrupting moms? I'm sensing a theme here."

Marissa was sensing that she was in deep trouble. What had they said at her divorce support group meeting the other night? *Enjoy the rebound relationship but don't confuse it with love.*

Could Marissa do that? Could she enjoy sex with Connor without falling in love with him? Was she in love with him now?

No, surely not. She was attracted to him, yes. And he seemed to be attracted to her as well.

But that didn't mean she loved him.

And it for sure didn't mean he loved her.

She half expected him to walk away but he didn't. Instead he leaned back and smiled at her. "I heard there's red velvet cake being offered tonight."

Marissa wondered if that was all that was being offered. His look told her he was wondering that, too. Was *she* on the menu? Dinner, red velvet cake and then a quick getaway for sex? Should she take a page out of Jess's book and eat and run?

She still hadn't decided after the vegetable stir-fry dinner. The conversation was sparse as everyone seemed content to focus on the yummy food.

Afterward, the red velvet cake was brought to the table with elaborate fanfare. Three candles were lit.

"Twenty-three candles wouldn't fit on the cake so I only did the most recent three," Marissa's mom said before proudly setting her masterpiece in front of Jess. "Remember, you have to make a wish before you blow them out. But first we have to sing you 'Happy Birthday.'"

Marissa had forgotten the family tradition. She hadn't been home for a birthday in a decade.

"Well, sing fast," Jess ordered. "The candles are melting."

"So am I," their mom said, waving her hand in front of her flushed face. "Hot flash!" She turned to confront her husband. "Did you turn off the air-conditioning?"

"No."

"Are you sure?"

"I think I'd remember if I did."

"I don't know about that. You forgot your wallet at home just yesterday."

"I was deep in thought—"

"About the Silver Pharaoh, I know," her mom said.

Jess clapped her hands to get their attention. "People, sing fast or I'm blowing these candles without you."

So they launched into the super-speedy version of "Happy Birthday." They'd barely finished the last "you" before Jess blew the stumpy candles out.

"You made a wish first, right?"

"I wished you'd get the song over with," Jess said.

"You know if you tell anyone your wish, then it won't come true."

"You know, the ancient Egyptians have some interesting superstitions . . ." her dad began when her mom interrupted him.

"Not now, please."

He frowned. "What? I was just going to—"

"Launch into another dissertation about ancient Egypt."

"Actually, a dissertation is usually a lengthy *written*

essay," he began when his wife once again interrupted him.

"Get your mind out of ancient Egypt and focus on the here and now." She jabbed her finger on the table, narrowly missing the plate that Jess was holding out for her with a slice of cake.

Marissa's dad tried again. "I just thought it would be interesting—"

Marissa's mom cut him off again. "Trust me, it's not."

"You don't even know what I was going to say."

"Yes, I do. After twenty-five years of marriage, I know. Let's not argue in front of the sheriff." She sent a pointed look at Connor.

"Why?" Marissa's father countered. "What's he going to do? Shoot us?"

Marissa wondered if Connor was tempted. What was a person to do when Parents Behaved Badly? This all seemed like a page from a reality show or something. A bad dream, perhaps.

"I'm unarmed at the moment," Connor said.

"Don't pick on him," Jess said. "It's just Daddy being Daddy."

"You always take his side," Marissa's mom said.

"Delicious cake," Marissa said, frantically trying to redirect the conversation. "Did you do something different with the recipe this year?"

It actually worked. "No, I used the same recipe. You just haven't had my red velvet cake for a while. Remember that cake with the pyramids on it for your eighth birthday?" Marissa's mom asked her.

"Why did you want a pyramid on your cake?" Jess asked.

"It was Dad's idea," Marissa said. She'd really wanted

a German chocolate cake but that request had gone unnoticed.

"We'll have to make one for you this year, Marissa," her mom said.

"No, that's okay," Marissa hurriedly said. Everyone at her birthday party had made fun of her for weeks afterward because of that cake.

"It'll be fun," her mom said,

No, it won't. Marissa wanted to say the words aloud but didn't want to hurt her mom's feelings. Since they'd had that cloud-gazing episode in the park yesterday, her mom had seemed calmer and happier. Until the flare-up with her dad today.

"I hate to eat and run," Jess said.

"Then don't," their mom said. "You haven't even finished your slice of cake. At least do that before you take off."

"Can I take some more slices with me to share with the Roberts brothers?"

"Sure. I'll package up the rest of the cake to take with you. But first you have to open your presents."

Marissa had gotten Jess an iTunes gift card.

"Thanks," Jess said before instantly turning to her next present.

"I brought flowers for you," Connor said. "I left them in the car."

"I thought you and Marissa already went outside to get what you left in the car."

"They got distracted," Marissa's mom said.

"Oh yeah?" Jess grinned. "Did you catch them making out on the front porch like a couple of teenagers?"

"My lips are sealed," their mom said.

"Were Marissa's lips sealed for the kiss?" Jess said.

Marissa jabbed her sister. "Jess! Shut up!"

Jess jabbed her right back like they'd done as kids. "You can't tell me to shut up on my birthday."

"Yes, I can."

"I'm gonna go get those flowers now," Connor said.

"You be sure to come back now," Marissa's mom said, sounding very Southern all of a sudden. "We certainly don't want to say or do anything to scare you away."

Marissa wanted to crawl under the table or race out the front door. Neither option was possible however. "Behave," she ordered her family.

"You behave," Jess said. "You're the one making out with the town sheriff on the front porch, where anyone could see you. Oh, those are lovely, Connor," Jess said as he returned to hand her a mixed bouquet of flowers in various shades of pink and purple.

"I'm glad you like them." He resumed his seat and smiled at Marissa.

While Jess focused on unwrapping her next present, Marissa leaned closer to Connor to whisper, "You should have made a break for it while you had the chance."

"I couldn't leave you behind," he said.

But of course he had left her behind a decade ago. Walked out on her.

Why couldn't she want to bed a guy without a history with her? Why did it have to be her first love?

Jess exclaimed her pleasure at the large gift card from her favorite online retailer as well as a one-gallon tin of her favorite Kernel Fabulous gourmet popcorn. "White Cheddar. My favorite!"

"I wasn't sure if it was this or the Caramel Combo you liked best," their mom said.

"Thanks, Mom." Jess stood to give her a hug before saying, "I hate to eat and run but I have to go."

"Let me pack up the cake for you to take with you. I'll just be a minute," their mom said.

The minute their mom was gone, Jess turned her attention to Connor. "So you and my sister were making out on the front porch, huh?"

"Do not answer that," Marissa warned him.

"You know, the rules of courtship and marriage in ancient Egypt are actually quite interesting," Marissa's dad said. "Unlike ancient Greece where women had few rights, in ancient Egypt women could marry for love, could own property and retain those property rights after marriage. She could even initiate a divorce. If the divorce was the man's idea, then he had to return her dowry if there was one and had to pay a fine."

"Those were the days," Marissa said.

"Not that all men obeyed those rules about paying the fine," her dad added before quickly closing his mouth when her mom returned to the room.

"There were deadbeats even back in those days," Jess said as she gathered up her birthday goodies and put them in a large shopping bag their mom provided.

"Who's a deadbeat?" Marissa's mom asked.

"Never mind," Jess said, kissing her on the cheek. "Thanks again for everything. You too, Marissa." Jess gave her a quick hug but broke it off before Marissa had time to hug her back. "And you, Connor." Jess's hug with Connor was longer.

Marissa could tell by the gleam in her younger sister's eyes that she was trying to push Marissa's buttons.

Marissa refused to let her.

Not tonight.

Tonight Marissa was going to take a page out of her sister's book and enjoy life without worrying about the consequences.

"We should be going as well," Marissa said.

"I understand. You two probably want to be alone." Her mom nodded her approval.

"Let me know if you'd like some more information about ancient Egyptian marriage," her dad said.

"Marriage is a four-letter word for me right now," Marissa firmly stated. "Been there, done that, not going to make that mistake again."

"But you'll get married again someday," her mom said. "Because marriage can be a good thing, right, Connor?"

"Why are you asking Connor?" Marissa said. "He's never been married."

Apparently fearing a discussion about matrimony, Connor took Marissa's arm and led her toward the front door and away from her prying family.

"I'll call you," her mom said.

It was only when Marissa was halfway out the door that she realized she hadn't hugged her parents good-bye. But they were already engaged in their now-customary bickering so she made her escape.

"Wise move," Connor said approvingly.

"I'm sorry about that."

"About what?"

"About my family," she said. "About the marriage thing."

"No problem."

"They don't usually argue like that. Well, they have since I've come back to Hopeful but I don't remember them doing that when we were growing up. I'm not sure what's going on with them."

"Are you still upset I came?"

"No." She trailed her fingertips along his cheek. "I'm glad you did."

Was she falling for Connor? If not, she was getting damn close. What did it mean that she was feeling equal parts panic and passion?

"I'll see you back at our place," he said, opening her car door for her.

She got in. Her demon car turned over right away and the song "Halfway Gone" by Lifehouse started playing.

She reached her apartment building by the time the song was done. The instant she parked she got a text message. Thinking it might be Connor, she checked only to find that it was from a coworker at her old library.

Ur ex married slut. Thought u'd want to no.

Marissa's mind went blank and her body went cold. It wasn't like she still loved her ex. Obviously he thought Marissa was easy to replace.

A knock on her window startled her.

"Everything okay?" Connor asked.

"Absolutely." She grabbed her purse and followed Connor upstairs.

She welcomed his kiss the instant she unlocked her door. It made her feel wanted and desired. Made her feel like she wasn't a failure as a woman.

Pulling him inside, she kept her mouth against his, murmuring her pleasure as he kicked the door shut with his foot and kept his attention totally focused on her. She heard the *thump* of her purse as she dropped it to the floor. He nudged the neckline on her fuchsia top out of his way so he could caress her through the silk of her bra.

Moments later, she helped him tug her top completely off. He quickly undid the buttons on his shirt and placed her hand on his bare chest. He back stepped her down the hallway toward her bedroom. She made no protest.

He shoved her capri pants off before helping her remove his jeans. He had to pause to kick off his shoes. And all the while they kept kissing. His tongue tussled with hers as he removed the phone she still held in her hand and tossed it onto the nightstand. He lowered her onto her bed and followed her, urging her body into the cradle of his hips.

She could feel his arousal through the thin cotton of their underwear. What was she doing? Could she have sex without love? Did she love him? What if he broke her heart? What if he slept with her and then dumped her?

Passion and panic. Panic and passion. Panic and *panic*.

Marissa couldn't breathe. She turned her head away, breaking off their kiss to gasp, "I'm sorry! I can't do this!"

Chapter Fifteen

. . . .

"What?" Connor's voice was unsteady as he hovered above her, his lower totally aroused body still pressed against hers.

"I'm sorry." The nervous words tumbled from Marissa's mouth. "I'm not ready. I thought I was, but I'm not."

"You sure seemed ready a second ago."

"I know."

"Then what happened?"

"I can't explain." She pushed him aside and scrambled off the bed.

"Yes, you can." Connor moved after her and in doing so, knocked her cell phone off the nightstand. As he picked it up, he saw a text still displayed on the screen. Marissa tried to grab it before he could read it but he held it over her head.

"So this was all about your ex getting married?" he

growled. "You get a text with the info and you suddenly want to get between the sheets with me?"

"No, it's not like that."

"Looks like that to me." He angrily tossed her phone onto the bed before grabbing his jeans and yanking them on.

"Let me explain."

"Don't bother." He reached for his shirt and shoes, not bothering to put them on.

"I didn't plan this."

"You could have fooled me. In fact, you did fool me. I thought you were into this . . ." He gestured toward her bed. "But it was all an act. Did you think sex with me would make your ex jealous? Was it your way of getting back at him? If he was going to be with someone else, then you were, too?"

"If that was the case then I would have jumped into bed with someone months ago."

"Maybe you were waiting for the right moment," he said.

"I thought this was the right moment . . ."

"But you were wrong. And so was I to think you were over that asshole you married."

"I *am* over him."

"Right. And that's why you climbed into bed with me before getting cold feet at the last second."

"This has nothing to do with him."

"That's a lie and you know it."

She shoved her hand through her hair. "Okay, so it does have something to do with him but not in the way you think." How could she explain her panic to him when she couldn't even really explain it to herself?

"I don't want to hear it." He headed out of the bedroom.

She trailed after him. "I'm sorry."

"Yeah, me, too."

He slammed her front door on his way out, emphasizing his anger and frustration. She didn't blame him. What was wrong with her? Was she ever going to regain her confidence or would she always be this mess of confusion? Had she simply tried to move too fast? Was that it? Did she merely need more time? Was Connor right when he accused her of jumping into bed with him because her ex had remarried?

Was she insulted that Brad had replaced her so easily? Was this all about proving that she was worthy of a man's attention?

Marissa didn't even realize she was crying until she tasted the saltiness of her tears on her lips . . . lips still swollen from the intense hunger of Connor's kiss.

She wished she could just jump into her car and run away from all this. But her rust bucket totally lime VW probably wouldn't make it very far and her problems were within her. Which meant she couldn't run from them.

She remembered one of the *Peanuts* cartoons on her old bedroom wall where Linus says, "No problem is so big or so complicated that it can't be run away from."

Too bad that wasn't really true.

• • •

"Thanks for meeting with me," Marissa told Deb as they sat together at Cups Café half an hour later. "I know it's kind of late."

"It's only nine thirty."

Marissa felt like she'd lived through three days' worth of issues in the past few hours. "I don't know where to start."

"Start wherever you want."

Marissa looked around. The café closed in an hour so there weren't many customers still hanging out.

"I can't dance," she said abruptly. "It's my sister's birthday today. And my ex just married the woman who broke up our marriage."

"Are those three things connected?"

"No. I don't think so. I mean, I don't know why I can't dance. It's not that I don't how. I have this weird panic that prevents me from dancing. Even when I'm alone I still can't do it. And I don't have a clue why. I don't have a clue about a lot of things. But I have lots of panic. Tons of it."

Deb patted her arm. "It will be okay."

"Will it? I'm not so sure." Marissa choked back a tiny sob. No way was she going to cry in Cups Café. Maybe meeting Deb in a public place had been a bad move. But Marissa had needed to escape from her apartment and Connor.

"Does the dancing thing have something to do with your sister's birthday?"

"I have no idea."

"How long have you felt that way?"

"As long as I can remember," Marissa said.

"As you know, I've read a lot of self-help books. Tons of them. This dancing phobia sounds like people who have the naked dream. They're at work, or at dinner, and suddenly realize they're naked. But it's not really about being naked. It's about a fear of exposing your worst weakness—the something you're ashamed of—the something you believe nobody could love you for . . . if they knew. Your fear of dancing could be the same thing." At Marissa's blank look, Deb added, "Or not. Never mind. Like I said, I'm a self-help junkie. Let's skip the dancing and deal with the ex."

"I shouldn't care and I don't. It's not like I still love him or anything. But the news just made me feel like such a failure."

Deb nodded her understanding. "Like you were rejected all over again."

"Is it supposed to be this difficult?"

"I don't know if it's supposed to or not, but it just is. Especially when one spouse cheats on the other. It's hard to trust again. You get gun-shy."

"I've made a mess of things," Marissa said.

"Because you got divorced?"

Marissa shook her head. She was once again at a loss for words. She was too ashamed to admit she'd gotten cold feet about having sex with Connor tonight.

"Don't be so hard on yourself," Deb said. "Starting over is tough."

"Yeah, it is. I feel like such a wimp for not being able to cope better," Marissa admitted. "It feels like I'm constantly screwing up."

"Why do you say that?"

Marissa shrugged.

"You're not the one who screwed up. Your ex is."

"Clearly he's able to move on. I want that," Marissa said.

"You want to get married?"

"No way. I want to move on, but I have all these emotions I don't know what to do with. Panic and fear and anger and confusion."

"Want to know what I do to cope with those feelings?"

Marissa nodded.

"I get out my secret weapon," Deb said.

"Cherry Garcia ice cream?"

"No. My Nerf baseball bat. It's this big green foam bat. I get it out and I hit the couch with it. It's out in the car if you want to borrow it. I think you need it more than I do tonight."

"No, I couldn't take your secret weapon."

"I've got another one at home."

If Marissa couldn't dance even when she was alone, would she be able to bash her couch with a kid's toy? There was only one way to find out.

An hour later, Marissa stood in her apartment. She was still wearing the khaki pants and white shirt that she'd worn to Cups Café. She wasn't sure what the proper attire was for couch bashing. It wasn't like her couch had done anything wrong. Maybe she should bash her bed?

She moved from the living room to her bedroom. The covers were still rumpled from her massive make-out session with Connor earlier. She tentatively tapped the bat on the foot of the bed.

Perhaps this was poetic justice after all because her troubles had all started with a bed back when she'd found her husband in bed with another woman. This time, she whacked the bed harder. Once she started, she found she couldn't stop.

Whack, whack. Wham, wham, wham! Over and over again until her arms trembled from exhaustion.

Deb was right. The anger was dissipated. Now Marissa was too tired to feel anything.

Even so, she ripped the bedding off and put new sheets on the bed. She could still smell Connor's clean scent so she stuffed the old bedding into a big black garbage bag and put it in a corner of the dining room to wash it tomorrow.

Connor's scent might be gone and Marissa's anger at her situation might have diminished, but her memories of Connor's mouth on hers and his body blanketing hers stayed with her throughout the night, taking hold of her dreams and leaving her aching with unfulfilled need.

• • •

The trouble with a small town was that whenever you didn't want to see someone, they were there right in front of you. Hopeful was no exception to that rule. There was no escape. Connor knew because he tried. But he kept running into Marissa. Not that they'd spoken. Not yet. But they'd have to at the teen meeting at the library tonight.

Weeks ago, Marissa had given him an agenda with each meeting's scheduled topic. Tonight's was the July Corn Festival, which Ruby Mae claimed was even bigger than June's Rhubarb Festival.

She also claimed that Connor was being crabby. She didn't seem to understand that he was the sheriff and she was supposed to answer to him. That was the chain of command. On paper, maybe. But clearly not in Ruby Mae's mind.

"Something is going on with you," she told him Wednesday morning. "You've spent the past four days doing double overtime. You've practically moved in here at the office."

"We're short-staffed." One of his full-time deputies was on vacation in Mexico and two others had come down with food poisoning so bad it landed them in the hospital.

"Yes, we're short-staffed and you're short-tempered," his assistant said. "Your mom isn't coming back to town for the Corn Festival, is she?"

"No."

"Then you've got no reason to be such a pain in the butt."

Connor glared at her.

She glared back but looked away first. "Usually you've got this kind of easy-guy-next-door machismo thing going on that makes you so likeable."

"Likeable?"

"That makes you a sexy chick magnet," Ruby Mae said tartly. "Does that sound better?"

He shrugged. The one sexy librarian chick he wanted didn't seem to be feeling his machismo magic.

Not that he was telling that to anyone. Not even his best bud, Sully. But then, Connor was a pro at keeping things to himself. After all, he'd had years of practice.

"This perpetual bad mood of yours wouldn't be caused by a woman, would it?" Ruby Mae asked.

Connor resumed his glare, adding icy disapproval this time.

"Fine. Be that way. But be that way on your own time, not on ours." Having stated that, she marched away in a huff.

Connor's mood hadn't improved by the time he walked into the library several hours later. Marissa appeared surprised to see him. She also looked damn great in a simple black skirt and light blue top.

"I wasn't sure you'd come," she said.

"I honor my commitments." He gave her a look intended to communicate the fact that he didn't promise one thing and do another. Like her taking him into her bed and then kicking him out just when things were getting really hot.

He would never have taken her to be a tease. He didn't know what her problem was and he didn't care. So what if she was still hung up on her ex? Not his problem. Getting hooked up with her would clearly be a big mistake. So he really shouldn't be looking at her as if he wanted to devour her with whipped cream and a cherry on top. He immediately stopped.

Marissa blushed and looked away.

Jose observed the interaction with interest. Connor directed a glare in his direction. "What are you looking at?" he growled.

Marissa immediately came to Jose's defense. "Don't talk to him that way,"

"The sheriff is in a bad mood," Nadine muttered under her breath as she no doubt tweeted that info on her smartphone before setting it down on the table.

Connor was tempted to pick it up and throw it against the wall.

"Let's get things started," Marissa said briskly, avoiding eye contact with Connor. "The Corn Festival is coming up next month and once again the library will have a booth at the event. And once again, the teen group will have a presence there."

Marissa paused to pass around a bowl of wrapped granola bars and packets of trail mix. Connor had deduced that she'd managed to scrounge enough money to pay for snacks and drinks at their meetings. She tried to keep them on the healthy side and they all went fast. You'd think the kids hadn't eaten in a week.

Now that it was summer and classes were over, the school lunch program wasn't in effect. Connor knew Marissa worried about the teens' well-being. He'd heard how Marissa had assisted Tasmyn's mom with filling out the necessary paperwork to get food stamps until she got another job. But times were tough and jobs hard to come by.

Connor had pitched in and brought food, too—junk food, which the kids all grabbed and consumed in seconds.

"Potato chips have a high sodium content," Marissa told them all.

"So you've said," Connor replied, popping a chip into his mouth. He noticed the way she was staring at his lips. Good. He hoped she was wishing his mouth was on hers right now.

"We're hoping that things go even better at the Corn Festival than they did at the Rhubarb Festival as far as our fund-raising efforts go," she said briskly.

"People are broke," Red Fred said. "They already donated last month. Why should they do it again?"

"Because we're going to have the sheriff in the dunking booth," Marissa said.

Connor's head whipped around to glare at her.

"Just kidding," she said weakly.

"It was an idea of ours," Red Fred said. "But Marissa said you wouldn't go for it."

"She's right," Connor said. "I'll be working during the festival."

"So will we," Red Fred said. "It's hard work trying to get people to hand over their money. I don't think it's going to go well."

"I did a new T-shirt design," Jose said. "Corn never looked so good." He proudly pointed to the T-shirt he wore. "This is a bad-ass cob of corn."

"This time they don't have to buy anything," Red Fred said. "Anyone can just make a donation to help out those in need."

"We're donating the money we raise to the local food pantry." Snake spoke up for the first time, shifting his focus from his laptop to his surroundings.

"I thought you weren't supposed to be on the computer during meetings," Connor said.

"I was just putting the finishing touches on our web page." He turned the laptop so Connor could see.

The kid had talent. Connor knew that Spider and Nadine had pointed out gaps in the sheriff department's computer system. He shouldn't take out his frustration on them. They were good kids.

"Nice job," he said.

Spider smiled at him. "Thanks. I thought so, too."

Connor spent the rest of the meeting focusing on interacting with the teens and ignoring Marissa. The Fourth of July festivities were next on the calendar—before the Corn Festival in mid-July—which meant there was another parade and another chance for Marissa . . . No, he wasn't going to think of her giving that royal wave at the Founders' Day Parade her first day back. Instead he talked about the danger of messing with store-bought fireworks.

"Sully already dropped by with a batch of brochures about this subject," Marissa told him.

Connor wasn't happy to hear this news. He sure as hell didn't appreciate the fact that Sully was interacting with Marissa. Was he jealous? No way. Sully was his buddy. That didn't mean, however, that Connor wanted him within a hundred yards of Marissa.

"I heard the library book cart drill team is going to perform in the Fourth of July parade," Molly said. "Are you going to participate, Marissa?"

Marissa shook her head.

"She already was in the Founders' Day Parade," Jose said. "With that loco lime car of hers."

Connor hadn't been the same since she'd crashed that parade back in May, and he was starting to wonder if he'd ever be the same again.

• • •

Three and a half weeks later, Marissa found herself once more manning the library booth for the Corn Festival. For the most part, she'd managed to limit her exposure to Connor to the teen meetings. But that didn't stop her from thinking or dreaming about him. And it didn't stop her from wanting him. She missed him.

His black Mustang was absent from his parking space at their apartment building more times than it was present. She'd worried about bumping into him coming or going but that rarely happened and when it did he barely acknowledged her with a nod. Not that she could blame him.

She'd spent the Fourth of July with her family, remembering that the last time they'd all gotten together Connor had been there at Jess's birthday party. Her mom and sister noticed his absence. "He's working," she'd said before quickly changing the subject.

Since then, Marissa had focused her energy on the Corn Festival event this weekend. Centennial Park was packed with wall-to-wall people. One of whom was Brenda from Marissa's divorce support group.

"We invite artists young and old to create art that best represents their interpretation of corn. We're open to all types of mediums including not only drawings and paintings but also jewelry, garden ceramics, clothing, music and poetry to name just a few," Brenda was saying.

"I had no idea," Marissa said, even though she sort of did know all that. But Brenda was on the organizing committee and seemed a little nervous or lonely or both.

Some might not understand how it was possible to be lonely in such a large crowd but Marissa did. The sight of a couple walking hand in hand reminded her that she wasn't part of a couple any longer. The sound of laughter from a young woman drove home the fact that Connor hadn't stopped by the library booth to tease her. He'd stayed out of touch and out of reach, although he'd managed somehow to help the teens set up last night during the brief period of time when Marissa had had to take a bathroom break.

"So far the attendance this year is above last year's," Brenda said before abruptly changing the subject. "My date fizzled out at the last minute. His wife called. The joke is on me because I thought he was divorced like me. But no, he just lied and told me he was. You'd think in a small town like this that I'd know who is divorced and who isn't. I mean, it's almost like we have giant *D*s plastered on our foreheads that scream 'Divorced!' judging by the way some people look at us." She paused to do a fake smile and wave at someone who walked by. "I

26 • Cathie Linz

refuse to fall into a pity pile just because I was deceived. Again. Thankfully we hadn't gotten intimate yet. In fact, we hadn't even kissed yet but still . . ." She sighed. "Well, look at it this way. At least I'll have plenty to talk about at our next support group meeting. How about you?"

"I'm good," Marissa said. "Busy working here at the booth. Our teen group is gathering donations for the local food pantry." Marissa pointed to the sign that Jose had painted and the container that Molly and Tasmyn decorated with photos of kids and food.

"At least I don't have to go to the food pantry myself," Brenda said. "Not yet, at any rate." She reached into her trendy leather shoulder bag and dropped a few dollars into the donation bin. "I'll see you at the meeting next week," she told Marissa before moving on.

"She doesn't look very happy," Molly noted.

"I know," Marissa said.

"But she's pretty."

"Being pretty doesn't automatically make you happy," Marissa said.

"It would make me happy," Molly said wistfully.

"Me, too," Tasmyn agreed. "So would having a purse like that. It looked like a Sharif design."

"Purses don't make you happy either." Okay, that may have been a bit of a lie. Marissa could still remember getting a Coach purse from Brad for Christmas and being delighted. But the feeling hadn't lasted and neither had the purse. She'd had to sell it on eBay to pay off her bills after the divorce. "Not a happy that lasts."

"What can make you a happy that lasts?" Molly asked.

Marissa was still trying to figure that one out herself.

Luckily, they were interrupted at that point by Roz's

arrival. Molly and Tasmyn retreated to their corner of the booth.

"I just wanted to give you a heads-up that our library board president isn't very happy with all the activities in our booth," Roz quietly said with a subtle nod toward the teens. "I told Chester you have my full support, but he may still stop by and say something."

"Thanks for the warning. I appreciate it."

"And I appreciate the way you've really pitched in at the library. I realize you've put in plenty of extra hours and gone above and beyond," Roz said. "Even though you haven't been with us that long, you've really made a difference."

"A good one, I hope," Marissa said.

"Definitely." Roz tilted her head toward Molly and Tasmyn, who were talking to a family about donating. "Especially with the teen group."

"I just wish I could do more."

"You do plenty. How is it working out with Connor?" Roz asked.

"What do you mean?"

"The two of you overseeing the teen program."

"Right. We're okay. Why? Did he say something to you?"

"No. Should he have?"

"No." Marissa nervously fiddled with her silver dangle earring. She hadn't worn moonstones since that fateful night when Connor had been in her bed. Now she stuck to turquoise, which was supposed to relieve mental stress. Her dad had already stopped by earlier to remind her that turquoise jewelry dated back to the ancient Egyptians. He was once again manning the mummy booth.

"Well, I'd better be off. I have to go judge something in the Food Hall—corn relish, I think it is." Roz waved and took off.

Marissa expected the other members of her family to stop by. Since her mom loved the Rhubarb Festival best, she didn't participate in the Corn Festival as anything other than an observer and consumer. Ditto for Marissa's sister, who came strolling by on the arm of one of the Roberts brothers.

Jess shook her head at the sight of Marissa working the booth. "You lead such an adventurous life," Jess said.

"I'm not looking for adventure," Marissa said.

"What are you looking for—the reason you can't dance?"

Marissa was looking for peace and quiet but she obviously wasn't going to find it today at the festival.

"That's right," Jess told the teens at the back of the booth. "My big sister can't dance."

"My big sister can't sing," Molly said, immediately leaping to Marissa's defense.

"I don't have a big sister," Tasmyn said. "But if I did, I wouldn't make fun of her."

Jess grinned. "Yes, you would. That's part of a sister's job."

"What's the other part?" Tasmyn said.

"To have your sister's back through thick and thin." Jess wiggled her fingers in a teasing wave and took off.

Marissa spent the next hour answering questions about library services and programs while silently mulling over Jess's words. They'd surprised her.

She hadn't thought of her sister as someone who had her back. Not that she thought of her as someone who'd necessarily stab her in the back, either. But Jess just wasn't the first person Marissa would call if she needed moral support.

Maybe that would change. There was always the chance that their relationship would continue to grow and flourish.

Marissa's thoughts turned to her relationship with Connor. She missed him. She missed watching the way that sexy mouth of his moved when he was smiling. She missed having his mouth on her body. No. No, she didn't. She pulled herself away from sex fantasyland and focused on her job.

Sure enough, Chester stopped by as Roz had warned. "A reminder that you weren't hired by the library board to baby-sit a bunch of teens. You're supposed to assist all the people of Hopeful."

"I realize that. My time with the teens doesn't reduce my attention to other library patrons in any way." Marissa had made sure of that. She suspected her job depended on it. So she researched new titles for Reluctant Readers on her own time, listening to *Booklist* podcasts on her laptop at her apartment on subjects like graphic novels and Young Adult award nominees.

"I'm watching you," Chester said before moving on.

"Are you in trouble because of us?" Molly came closer to tentatively ask.

"Not at all. Don't worry." Marissa shifted the conversation. "It looks like the crowd is growing even bigger, doesn't it?"

Molly nodded. "And it's getting hotter."

The temperature had to be in the upper nineties with matching humidity. Marissa had set up two electric fans in the booth but it was still extremely sticky. Molly and Tasmyn wore tank tops and shorts but Marissa didn't have that option. Her sleeveless dress was a chili-pepper red, which Flo had informed her at last week's divorce support group meeting was a power color. In an effort to stay cool, Marissa had gathered her hair up into a ponytail.

During a break from people stopping at their booth, Marissa paused to look around. She remembered coming to these festivals as a kid. She'd been so excited at the prospect of booth games and special food and rides. The young kids seemed to be enjoying themselves on the various rides being offered—from a merry-go-round with colorful carousel horses to the tilt-a-wheel. A new attraction, in which kids crawled around in large, clear spheres, reminded Marissa of something a gerbil would love.

The accident happened so fast that Marissa was completely unprepared. The rides were set up near a paved walkway through the park. A boy around eight was racing down the path when he tripped and fell, hitting his head on the cement and bleeding profusely.

Connor was there an instant later and the EMTs showed up shortly thereafter. By the time they took the child and his hysterical mother away, Connor's shirt was covered in blood.

He stood there frozen, for a second staring down at his chest. Marissa saw Sully say a few words before drawing him away. But it was the look in Connor's eyes that hit Marissa so hard. Sully was assuring everyone that the child would be okay, and that head wounds bled a lot. Marissa was relieved to hear the kid would be okay, but she was worried about Connor. She'd never seen him so devastated. The expression on his face had only lasted a moment but even so . . .

"Are you okay, Connor?" she asked as Sully rushed Connor past the library booth to the exit. "Are you hurt?"

Neither one of them answered her but she could tell that Connor wasn't okay and that he was hurting in a soul-deep sort of way that she'd only seen on the faces of soldiers returning from war.

She saw Connor at a distance a while later. He'd changed into a clean uniform shirt and had his sunglasses in place as well as his warrior cop face. You'd never know by looking at him now that he'd been through some sort of personal hell earlier.

But she knew. And she knew what she had to do about it.

After the festival closed for the night, she waited for his car to pull into the apartment lot. She refused to get cold feet again. She had no doubts this time. She'd changed her clothes but she was not changing her mind.

She knocked on his door.

"What do you want?' he growled.

"You." She reached out to trail her fingers down his cheek. "I want you."

Chapter Sixteen

. . . .

Connor didn't appear surprised or pleased. His expression remained remote. "Why?"

Marissa blinked. She hadn't expected this reaction, hadn't expected having to explain her actions. But she wasn't about to back down now. "I want to pick up where we left off."

"You mean when you kicked me out of your bed?"

She looked around nervously. "Can we discuss this inside your apartment?"

For a moment she feared he was going to refuse, but he backed up and let her in.

"Are you offering me pity sex?" he said bluntly.

"Were *you* offering me pity sex?" she countered.

"Hell no."

"Why should I pity you?"

"Lots of reasons," he growled.

"There's been something between us since I came back to town. You know it and I know it. The time has come for us to do something about it," she said.

"Like what?"

"Do I have to show you?"

He shrugged and crossed his arms over his chest. She did notice that he couldn't help glancing at *her* chest, however. She'd chosen her ruffled blouse carefully. She'd noticed his interest in it when she'd worn it before. Actually his interest was in her cleavage. She leaned closer, giving him a better view.

She took one of his hands and guided it to her breast. "Can you feel my heart beating?"

"Is this some kind of trick?"

She shook her head and sent her own hands under his dark blue T-shirt. "I'm not going to get cold feet this time."

"Are you sure?"

Leaning her lower body against him, she nodded emphatically and smiled. "I'm positive."

"You better be." His voice was becoming husky and that distant expression had definitely disappeared. Now those awesome eyes of his were more smoky blue than green.

"How can I convince you?"

"This way . . ." His mouth covered hers.

She responded to his hunger with an equal passion.

A second later, he had her backed up against the wall and was peeling off her ruffled top. She reciprocated by removing his T-shirt. They left a trail of clothing en route to his bedroom.

Marissa didn't know where their relationship was going but she knew that making love with him tonight was the right thing, and the only thing she was concerned with at the moment.

She was soon naked and so was he.

"Resistance is futile," she said with a husky laugh.

His grin was appreciative. "Who's resisting?"

He swept his hand from her breasts down to her hip and below. Foreplay was all well and good but she was about to go up in flames here.

She helped him put on a condom and guided him to the part of her body that was aching for his entrance. "Now," she moaned. "I want you now."

He obliged, sliding into her with one thrust. Her gasp of pleasure was incorporated into their kiss. Those gasps increased as he reached down to caress her where they were joined. The erotic friction he was creating with his body and his fingers was more than she could take.

Her orgasm grabbed hold of her, starting with sweet spasms deep within her womb and spreading to powerfully clenching waves. She felt more in that moment than she had in years. "Flashes of lightning," she gasped.

"Where?"

"Inside me."

"Is that a good thing?"

"Yes, yes!"

The crescendo sent her soaring over the edge of satisfaction into pure bliss.

Connor's shout followed soon after as his body stiffened and then relaxed in her arms.

She couldn't speak for some time. And when she finally did, she simply said one word. "Wow." Her voice reflected her amazement.

"Double wow." He tucked a loose strand of her hair away from her face.

"Triple wow. Was it like this between us before?" she asked.

He rolled away from her.

"Never mind," she said. "I shouldn't have asked you that."

"You can ask me anything you want."

"I can?"

He nodded, his back to her. "I'll grant you three questions."

"What are you doing?"

"Counting how many condoms are left in this package. I bought it the day you came back to town."

"You did?"

"Yes, and that's question number two," he said. "You only have one left."

"What happened today?"

He gave her a heated look over his shoulder. "We had sex."

She pulled him back down to her and ran her fingers over the faded scar on his shoulder. "I know we had sex. That's not that I meant. What happened?"

"I got in the middle of a knife fight my rookie year back in Chicago."

"Is that why you left?" she asked.

"Hell no, and that was question number four."

He lowered his head to string a line of kisses from her mouth down to her breast. She arched her back as shards of intense pleasure shot through her.

"I think we need to work on that triple wow again," he murmured against her skin.

"A repeat sounds like a good idea."

"I was thinking more along the lines of a three-peat," he said.

"Oh yeah?"

"Yeah." He trailed his fingers down to her intimate feminine folds, brushing her clitoris with his thumb in a way that set her entire body soaring. "What do you think?

"I think that's an . . . *oh yes* . . . right there . . . excellent idea."

"Excellent, huh?" He gazed down at her, his eyes dark with hungry passion. "My idea or this?"

He caressed her with his wicked tongue. She clutched his shoulders and held on for dear life as the earlier inner flashes of lightning returned with a vengeance.

By the time dawn came, Connor had more than delivered on his promise of a three-peat and Marissa had never experienced such utter and total satisfaction.

The four-peat took place in his shower, where he soaped her naked body with naughty enjoyment. Twining his fingers through hers, he held her hands over her head as he kissed her all over. The cool ceramic tiles were at her back while his hot, aroused body was pressed against her. Foreplay had never been so much fun or so powerful. He released her hands to widen his explorations to her hips and beyond.

By the time he turned off the shower, Marissa was saturated with satisfaction. Her sexual hunger had been totally appeased but her stomach growled. "I didn't eat any dinner last night," she said in embarrassment.

"I love it when you blush," he said, grabbing a huge bath towel and drying her off. Her entire body was tingling by the time he was done. He handed her one of his chambray shirts. "Let's get you something to eat."

She followed him into the kitchen, where he made her a batch of toast with strawberry jam.

"Do you have to work today?" she asked before remembering the Corn Festival was still on.

"Yeah, but not for an hour or two."

She watched him move around the kitchen. He had only a bath towel tied around his waist.

He caught her staring at his scar. "It's not pretty, I know."

"It looks serious."

"Nah. It was just a nick." A nick that had almost killed him. Connor knew Marissa was dying to ask him more questions. He was just as eager to avoid them.

He didn't want to talk about what had happened to him at the festival yesterday when that kid had bled all over him.

The bottom line was that the kid was going to be okay. That's all that mattered. Finally a kid would be okay, after so many hadn't made it. Like Hosea.

The blood had gotten to him yesterday. The sticky warmth of it and the metallic smell. Which was stupid. He'd never been one to cringe at blood. Cops couldn't afford to have weak stomachs. They saw too much.

As a third-generation cop, he had quickly developed the gallows cop humor and emotional calluses that numbed him to the painful realities of his job.

"What are you thinking about?" she asked him.

"You," he lied.

"I sure hope not," she said. "Because you had a really sad expression on your face for a moment there."

"Maybe it's gas."

She socked his uninjured shoulder. "Go ahead, try to humor your way out of telling me the truth."

"Humor my way?" he said. "How about seducing my way?"

"You think I'm that easy?"

"I think you're that incredible."

"Really?"

"Yes, really. Do I need to convince you again with a five-peat?"

She gave him a demurely sexy look. "Well, I wouldn't want any of those condoms to go to waste."

He swooped in for a kiss but, just as things were getting interesting, his cell phone interrupted him. Swearing under his breath, he checked it. The mayor was calling. Connor wasn't officially on duty for another hour but as sheriff he was always on call. "I have to take this," he told her regretfully before answering the phone.

"Sheriff, we have a problem. I need you to come down to Centennial Park and the Corn Festival right away."

"What's wrong?"

"I'd rather show you than tell you."

"And I'd rather you told me," Connor said. "Was there some kind of accident?"

"No, I believe this was deliberate."

"What was?" Connor's growing impatience was reflected in his voice. He couldn't help it. Why couldn't people just get right to the point instead of running this fifty-question routine? "What's the emergency?"

"The damage has already been done."

"What damage?"

"To the festival. If word of this gets out . . . I've got people cleaning things up now before the event opens."

"Cleaning what things?"

"The vandalism. Spray-painted graffiti on several booths."

"Are you messing with a crime scene?"

"We're not messing it, we're cleaning it."

"Well, stop right now," Connor growled. "You're tampering with evidence."

"We already know who did it."

"Who is we?" Connor was already in his bedroom, yanking on clothes while speaking into the phone.

"Chester. He's here with me. He saw who did it. He saw Jose Martinez running from the area but he didn't know that there was any vandalism or he would have called the police at the time. And there's more. There's money missing from the food pantry booth's cash box."

"Don't touch anything," Connor said. "I'll be there in five minutes."

"But—"

"Don't touch anything," Connor ordered.

"What's going on?" Marissa asked as she joined him in the bedroom, his chambray shirt barely covering her upper thighs.

"There was vandalism and robbery at the park last night."

She frowned. "I thought the vendors hired a private security firm to patrol the area after closing hours."

"They did."

"Then what happened?"

"That's what I'm going to find out."

• • •

Connor arrived at the park to find the mayor and Chester waiting for him. "Why aren't you at Jose's house arresting him right now?" Chester said.

"Because I have to investigate a crime before I arrest anyone."

"But I saw him," Chester said.

"Did you see him spray-paint anything last night?"

"Well, no, but . . ."

"No buts. There are no buts in police work," Connor said. "So why don't you just step aside and let me do my job."

"If you were doing your job properly, you would have made sure Jose wasn't included in the Corn Festival at all," Chester said. "I told you that those kids would be trouble, and now you see that I'm right."

What Connor saw were footprints. A *lot* of footprints.

"How many of you stepped here?" Connor said.

"I don't know." The mayor appeared a bit chagrined. "Chester and I did for sure."

Connor took photos with his smartphone of the footprints and the graffiti. Then he took notes on what Chester and the mayor told him. "Why were you here so early?"

"I always check on our festivals before they open," the mayor said. "I walk the grounds and make sure everything is shipshape."

"What about you?" Connor asked Chester. "If I recall correctly, you are on the planning committee for the Rhubarb Festival but not the Corn Festival."

"I just had the feeling that those rowdy teens were up to something."

"So you have ESP now, do you?" Connor said.

"It doesn't take ESP to know that there would be trouble."

"Where is the person in charge of the booth with the missing money?"

"It's the local food pantry. Flo is volunteering there for today."

Flo stood nearby. Upon hearing her name, she moved closer. "I'm madder than a hornet! Can you imagine, stealing money from the mouths of babes? Not that they were going to actually eat money, that isn't healthy."

"Show me the money box," Connor said.

"It's gone."

"Vendors are supposed to take their money boxes with them when the event closes for the night," Connor said. "Why didn't you do that?"

"I wasn't working the booth last night."

"Who was?"

"Brenda. Your landlady, Sally, was going to do it but she got food poisoning. We think it was from the sushi booth in the Food Hall. Anyway, Brenda stepped in."

"Where is she?"

"Right here." Connor had seen Brenda around town but didn't know her well. She was one of those women who valued her looks. "I forgot to take the money box with me. I'm so sorry," Brenda said.

"You're sure you left it at the booth?"

Brenda nodded.

Connor continued his line of questioning with Brenda and Flo before moving on to the security detail charged with securing the area after hours. And all the while, he was praying that none of his teens was involved with this incident, no matter what Chester claimed to have seen. But that spray-painted tag had looked like Jose's work and that didn't bode well.

• • •

Marissa snuck out of Connor's apartment in the clothes she'd worn last night and quickly scuttled into her own place right next door. In a way, she was glad that he'd gotten called in to work because it gave her a moment to catch her breath. She certainly hadn't been doing much of that last night. Instead, she'd been involved in all sorts of wildly satisfying acts of pleasure.

She felt delightfully wicked.

She didn't want to think about where this was going. She just wanted to bask in the afterglow for once and not worry. She almost felt like dancing. She took a few tentative steps then stopped. No, she wasn't quite there yet. But for the first time, she felt confident that she'd work that out. That she'd work everything out. That she had a bright future.

She popped two blueberry frozen waffles into her toaster. She was still hungry despite the several pieces of toast and jam that Connor had given her. A few minutes later, she was sprawled in the armchair in the living room, eating waffles with strawberry cream cheese spread on them. She felt decadent eating in the chair instead of sitting up straight at the dining room table. At this rate, she'd be dancing in no time at all.

Hopefully she'd be back in Connor's bed in no time as well. She was really looking forward to that. Maybe next time he should come to her bed?

While trying to decide, her cell rang. Maybe it was Connor. She checked the screen. No, it was Flo. Marissa couldn't imagine why she'd be calling this early on a Sunday morning.

"Hi, Flo. What's up?"

"Did you hear what happened at the Corn Festival? The vandalism? And the missing money. They've had to delay the opening by half an hour. That's never happened before."

"Wait. What vandalism? What money?"

"The money box from the food pantry booth is missing. And there was graffiti spray-painted on that booth and several others. Chester is saying he saw Jose running away last night after closing time. Connor has gone to talk to him now."

Not without me, he's not. "I've got to go, Flo. Please keep me posted."

"Sure thing, hon. You know what they say. Flo always knows."

Marissa disconnected the call and quickly changed into a pair of jeans along with a red T-shirt. Red, the power color.

Ten minutes later, she and her loco lime VW were outside Jose's grandmother's house. Connor was just getting out of his police vehicle. He didn't appear thrilled to see her. "What are you doing here?"

"That same thing you are."

"I doubt that."

"Flo called me. She told me what happened. You can't trust anything Chester says about Jose. He's disliked him from day one."

"Do not block my investigation," he said.

"I wouldn't dream of it." Emboldened by the way he was staring at her mouth, she moved closer to murmur, "I loved the way you investigated me last night."

"I'm serious."

"So am I." She stepped back and put her hands on her hips. "Our kids didn't do it."

"How do you know?"

"I trust them," she said.

"Why?"

"I just do."

"Then trust me, too," he said.

"I'm coming with you to talk to Jose. I won't say a word."

"Yeah, right."

"Are you charging him with something? Should he have an attorney present?" she asked.

"I'm just going to ask him a few questions."

"Okay then."

"I'd rather you wait out here," Connor said.

"And I'd rather Chester hadn't tried to make trouble with Jose but there you have it. The reality is we're here and we need to work together."

He raised an eyebrow. "We do?"

She nodded. "Jose needs us. He's depending on us."

"How do you know?"

"Because he's standing on the front porch waving at us." Marissa waved back.

Connor moved forward. Marissa tried to keep up. She could tell he was already in his cop persona. "Where were you last night, Jose?" Connor said.

"At the Corn Festival. Why?"

"Until when?"

"Closing time."

"What about after that?"

Jose's defenses rose. Marissa could see his body language changing. The door behind him opened and his grandmother poked her head out. "What's going on? Why is there a police car in front of our house?"

"Hello." Marissa held out her hand. "I'm Marissa

Barrett, the librarian in charge of the teen group at the library."

"I'm Lola Martinez." She shook Marissa's hand. "Why is the sheriff here?"

"He co-sponsors the teen group with me," Marissa said.

"Oh, right." Lola nodded. "Jose told me but I forgot."

"What time did Jose get home last night, Mrs. Martinez?" Connor asked.

"I was out playing cards with my friends so I'm not sure. I got home around eleven and he was already in bed."

Connor continued his questioning. "Did you see him in bed?"

"Well, no," Mrs. Martinez admitted. "His door was closed and I didn't want to wake him."

Connor turned his attention to the teen. "What time did you get in, Jose?"

"Before eleven."

"Someone tagged several booths at the Corn Festival last night," Connor said. "Any idea who that might have been?"

"I don't hang out with other taggers," Jose said. "I do my own thing."

"And does that 'thing' include taking the money box from the food pantry booth?" Connor said.

"Not that he's accusing you of anything like that," Marissa quickly inserted.

"It sure sounded like it to me," Jose said. "I don't know nothing about no missing money."

"A witness saw you running from the park after-hours," Connor said. "Were you there?"

Jose refused to answer.

They were interrupted by Red Fred running up onto the porch, panting frantically from his sprint down the block. Marissa remembered that Red Fred lived on the same street as Jose. "It's me," Red Fred gasped. "I'm the guilty one. I did it!"

Chapter Seventeen

. . . .

Marissa stared at Red Fred in disbelief. She'd been so sure that her teens had been innocent.

"Shut up," Jose growled at Red Fred.

But his friend didn't back down. "I'm not gonna let you take the fall for it. That would be wrong," Red Fred said. "It wasn't Jose's idea. It was mine."

"Why?" she asked him. "Why would you vandalize and steal?"

"What?" Red Fred frowned in confusion. "We didn't do that. Tell them, Jose."

"They don't believe anything I say, man," Jose said.

"You haven't actually said much," Marissa reminded him.

"What's the point? Cop Dude doesn't believe me," Jose said. "Look at him. You can read his face like a book."

Marissa looked at Connor. Yes, he was wearing his impassive don't-mess-with-me expression. "That's his cop face," Marissa said. "He looked at me that way when I was in the Founders' Day Parade. It doesn't mean he thinks you're lying." Marissa nudged Connor. "Tell them."

"It means you're in trouble." He expanded his glare to include Marissa. "All of you."

Jose immediately leaped to her defense. "Library Lady didn't know what we were planning. Don't involve her or she'll lose her job."

"What are you talking about?" Marissa said.

"Molly told us that she heard that crabby old library board dude threatening you yesterday at the library booth."

"He didn't actually threaten me," Marissa said.

"Then what did he actually do?" Connor asked.

"You already know that he's not a happy camper about our teen program," Marissa said. "He was just spewing off steam about that."

Connor returned his attention to Red Fred. "So if you're not confessing to the theft and vandalism, then what are you confessing to doing?"

"*Dios mio.*" Mrs. Martinez sank into a faded plastic chair on the front porch.

Jose turned to her in concern. "You need to go inside and take your medicine. It's too hot out here for you. Let me help you."

Mrs. Martinez shook her head. "I won't desert you if you're in trouble."

"It's okay," he said. "Marissa will look out for me, right?"

"Yes," she said. "Absolutely."

"Don't say a word until I come back," Jose ordered Red Fred.

The instant Jose was inside, Red Fred said, "He's my bud so he's looking out for me as best he can."

"Were you at the festival after closing time?" Connor asked.

Red Fred nodded.

"Why?"

"We heard that a number of the booths in the Food Hall were tossing their leftover food to start fresh the next day. So we hid until after closing time and went Dumpster diving. My mom is having a really hard time lately. She's too proud to go to the food pantry or get food stamps or ask for help."

Marissa's heart broke at the thought of her teens having to grub in the garbage for food. "Why didn't you say anything? You know you're not the only one who's having money trouble right now."

"My mom made me promise not to say anything to anyone."

Jose rejoined them. "I should have made you promise me the same thing."

"Are we going to jail?" Red Fred asked, fear making his voice tremble.

It was all Marissa could do not to pull him into her arms and give him a reassuring hug.

Connor's response was slightly different. "That food can make you sick," he said.

"We only took stuff that was still wrapped and non-perishable. They were wasting it. We didn't steal it because they'd already tossed it. We heard them say something about the town regulations not allowing anything that was already opened. Even hot dog buns and stuff."

"What about the graffiti and the food pantry money box?"

Red Fred stared at him blankly. "We only took food from the Dumpster. Nothing else. No money box. And we sure didn't stop to leave any graffiti. We're not stupid. Why leave a message that we'd been there? Tell them, Jose."

"We're not stupid," he said. "You want us to swear we didn't tag nothing or steal no money, we'll do it. We'll swear on my grandmother's Bible." Jose went inside the house and returned a moment later with a well-worn Bible in his hand. He thrust it at Connor. "You hold it." He placed his hand on it, as did Red Fred. "We swear we didn't steal any money or vandalize nothing."

"Anything," Connor corrected.

"Huh?"

"Didn't vandalize anything," Connor said.

"We didn't vandalize anything," the two teens said in unison.

Jose glared at Connor as he retrieved his grandmother's Bible. "That good enough for you?"

Connor nodded. "For now."

"Don't tell my grandmother," he said. "Or Red Fred's mom."

"Where do they think the food came from?" Connor said.

"That we were paid with groceries for helping at the library booth," Red Fred said. "My mom doesn't ask a lot of questions."

"Unlike you," Jose said, with another glare at Connor.

Connor's expression remained impassive. "I'm just

doing my job. Someone went to a lot of trouble to make the tag look like your work. Who has a grudge against you?"

"Old Library Dude was not pleased that I won that poetry jam at the Rhubarb Festival," Jose said.

"I remember," Connor said. "He complained to me about it. Anyone else seem angry with you lately?"

"Besides you?" Jose said before stepping back at Connor's glare. "No, not really. No more than usual."

Fifteen minutes later, Connor and Marissa were sitting together in his police SUV.

"They didn't do it," she said. "You believe that, right?"

His cell phone rang, preventing him from answering. It was the mayor calling. Connor put him on speakerphone. "I heard you're in front of Jose Martinez's house," the mayor said. "Did you arrest him?"

"No."

"Why not?"

"Because I'm still conducting the investigation," Connor said.

"I don't want anything ruining the reputation of the Corn Festival," the mayor said. "We've got folks coming from all over the state. Rumors are already circulating about the robbery and vandalism. I need to assure everyone that the culprit has been caught."

"And that will happen when I find the culprit."

"It's Jose."

"I lack sufficient evidence to prove that," Connor said.

"Chester told you he saw him running away."

"Chester had an ax to grind with Jose, so he's not what I'd call an impartial witness," Connor said. "Look, I'll let you know when I have more information."

"It better be soon," the mayor warned. "*Real* soon."

After disconnecting the call, Connor told Marissa, "Someone went to a lot of trouble to make that tag look like Jose's work. I can't see Chester risking his position in the community by pulling something like this."

"I can't believe the mayor is eager to throw a fifteen-year-old kid in jail."

"He's eager to pin the blame on someone."

"Then we have to find the right someone, the real guilty party."

"What's with this 'we'?"

"Don't sound so panicked. I'm not talking about picking out wedding china for us. I mean, you're my rebound guy."

"Is that all last night meant to you?"

"Why are you sounding crabby? I thought you'd be reassured that I wasn't trying to build a white picket fence around you."

"I already knew your views on marriage," he said.

"I'm not real eager to jump back into that. And I know you're not interested in marriage. You've made that clear. So trust me, you don't have to worry that I'll be needy. I can stand on my own two feet."

"So you wouldn't mind if I dated other women?"

"Would you mind if I dated other men?" she countered.

"Hell, yes!"

"Then you're saying you want this thing between us to be exclusive and monogamous?"

"Damn right," he said emphatically.

She smiled. "That works for me."

"Good. Now, getting back to this case . . ."

"Right," she said. "All we have to do is figure out who is trying to frame Jose."

"I'd prefer you didn't get involved in the investigation."

"I'm already involved. I care about Jose and Red Fred and the rest of the gang."

"I know you do."

"And I know that you care about them, too, even if you do have your own unique way of showing it."

"I'm not going to respond to that comment."

"I don't expect you to. If Chester wasn't involved, then who else had an ax to grind from the poetry jam?"

Connor shrugged. "Anyone could have been upset at Jose's taking the Lord's name in vain or using the word *penis* in his poem."

"Did anyone other than Chester complain to you?"

Connor shook his head. "I can check to see if anyone lodged a formal complaint with the department but nothing Jose said or did was illegal."

"I heard something about someone else thinking they should have won."

"The mayor's granddaughter," he said.

"Really? That's interesting."

"You think the mayor planned the vandalism?"

"No, but his granddaughter might have had a hand in it."

"She's never been in trouble before."

"There's always a first time." Her words reminded her that Connor had been her first and here she was, sleeping with him again. And it was as good as ever. Better. They were both older and more experienced. Well, he was probably more experienced than she was.

She was still rather amazed at the way she'd gone to his place last night and told him she wanted him. That was so Rissa the Rebel. Not that she'd ever done that back in the day.

True, she'd kissed Connor before he'd kissed her when they were teens but that was as far as her bad girl act went. After that Connor had made the moves and she'd appreciated them. Okay, she'd done more than just appreciated them. She'd encouraged them.

But the bottom line was that she hadn't been the one to make such a bold move. To come out and state what she wanted.

As far as her ex was concerned, Brad had been the one to chase her. And it seemed that once he had the wedding ring on her finger, she was no longer a challenge for him. She hoped the day would soon come when her ex would no longer play any part in even a passing thought of hers.

As she'd told Connor, she wasn't foolish enough to think he was the One. Or that even if he was, he'd feel the same way about her. She just wanted to live in the moment and enjoy every single orgasm as it came.

Was that so wrong? Did that make her a wicked woman? Did she care if it did? She was single and so was he.

Okay, what were they talking about before thinking about having sex with Connor distracted her? Who had framed Jose. Right. She could probably think more clearly if she wasn't sitting next to Connor.

"I need to go question more people at the Corn Festival," he said. "And no, you may not come with me."

"I wasn't going to ask to."

"Liar." He made the accusation sound like a sexy

compliment, which went a long way to appeasing her irritation at his dismissal. Not that she needed him. She had contacts of her own.

"I've got plenty of things to do," she said as she exited his vehicle.

He got out and accompanied her to her demon VW, opening the door for her and closing it once she was inside. The second she started the car, the music started blaring.

" 'Boulevard of Broken Dreams' by Green Day," Connor said. "This is where I came in."

"I still can't get the damn thing to stop. It's possessed. It plays whatever song on the CD playlist I did up. I can't get the CD to eject or the music to stop."

When Connor leaned toward her she thought he meant to kiss her. Instead he reached for the CD player on the dash and forcefully punched the eject button. To her amazement, the CD obediently popped out and silence ensued.

"I can't believe you did that," she said.

"I have the magic touch," he said with fake modesty.

"Yes, you do." She gave him her best version of a sultry look. "I'd kiss you but I suspect that half the neighborhood is watching us. So I'll owe you one tonight."

"I'm holding you to that," he said huskily.

"I'm counting on it," she replied. "I'll see you later."

He nodded and stepped away from her car.

Had he stayed a moment longer, she doubted she'd have been able to resist giving him that kiss she'd promised. This was starting to feel a lot like love and not just lust. She felt a moment of panic before shoving it aside. Living in the moment meant not worrying about the future.

Jose was the one she needed to be worried about clearing. The sooner she did that, the better.

• • •

Connor spent the rest of the morning re-questioning people of interest working at the festival. The security people hadn't seen anything. Since the event was a temporary one, there was no monitoring from video cameras. He spoke with Brenda and Flo again as well as people working the neighboring booths.

"The mayor said that Jose did it," Flo said. "Why are you still asking questions? I thought the investigation was over."

"It's not."

"You don't think I stole the money, do you?" Brenda demanded.

"We're not ruling out anything at this point," Connor said.

"But you are ruling out that I stole it, right?" Flo said.

"Like I said, we're not ruling out anything."

Flo glared at him.

Connor put on his sunglasses to ward off her evil eye. He'd told his deputies to be extra vigilant today. "I expect you to wrap this thing up ASAP," the mayor told him before hurrying off to moderate one of the many presentations going on at the main stage.

Connor was able to grab some award-winning grilled corn on the cob for lunch. As he passed the Kernel Fabulous popcorn stand, he remembered Marissa's sister, Jess, getting some for her birthday. He wondered if Marissa liked it, too. There was still a lot he didn't know about her.

He was looking forward to making more discoveries

tonight. In the meantime, he headed to headquarters to file required paperwork about his investigation. En route, his cell rang. It was his paternal grandfather, Buddy Doyle.

"I heard via the grapevine that the two Polish broads from Chicago visited you a few weeks back," Buddy said.

"Logan told you, didn't he." Connor made it a statement not a question.

"He said something about you calling him crying from your balcony."

"Logan is delusional. I was not crying."

"I'm glad to hear that, boyo. Not that your mother hasn't made grown men cry before. She sure made your dad weep in his beer on more than one occasion."

"I don't think she ever forgave him for not giving up alcohol for her," Logan said.

"It wasn't that easy," Buddy said. "Your dad had a disease and it took him years to acknowledge that and get help. But he's sober now."

"Yeah, I know."

"What about you?" Buddy asked. "Have you forgiven him?"

"I don't think about stuff like that."

"Right. That sissy emotional stuff, huh?"

"Look who's talking. The man who'd rather walk on hot coals than admit to emotional stuff," Logan said.

"Ingrid has taught me a lot."

His grandfather had married Ingrid West more than a year ago. Ingrid was Logan's wife's grandmother so once again the family tree got tangled. God knew his dad's various marriages and Connor's much younger half brothers already created a complicated web.

"Is Ingrid still talking about the Swedish mob?" Connor asked.

"Ingrid talks about all things Swedish. She's very proud of her heritage."

"As are you. Irish through and through, eh?" Logan said.

"Ingrid and I make a good combo. Logan seems to have found a good combo in Megan as well. I don't know why he fought meeting her for so long. Stubborn. That's what you boys are."

"My mom blames that on my dad."

"Ha!" Buddy paused a moment before sheepishly admitting, "She may have a point there."

"I hope you're taking your meds and going to your doctor appointments."

"Ingrid is worse than a Marine drill sergeant regarding those things."

"Sounds like she's taking good care of you."

"Yeah. It's mutual," Buddy said. "How are things going with you?"

"Good."

"Logan said there's a new woman in your life."

"We already confirmed that Logan is delusional."

"Don't make me come down there," his granddad growled. "You know my interrogation skills can't be beat."

"You don't have to come to Hopeful."

"Then tell me what's going on."

"Why this sudden interest? First Mom grills me and now you."

"I'll bet she was trying to matchmake, wasn't she? That's nothing new. Why did that spook you?"

"I am not spooked," Connor said.

"Because Doyle men don't get spooked?"

"I don't know about the rest of you, but I sure as hell don't."

"Right. And that's why you left your job in Chicago and hightailed it out of town."

"Being burned-out isn't the same thing as being spooked. Undercover work is . . ."

"I know what it is," his grandfather, a longtime veteran of the Chicago Police Department, said. "You don't have to tell me."

"I know you don't approve. Logan stayed and I left. So that makes me what . . . a coward in your eyes?"

"No way. Sometimes the most courageous thing you can do is move on. I know too many cops get professionally numb over the years. They have to, in order to survive. But it can make them less of a cop. You always wanted to do good and to make a difference. You were always like that. Even as a little kid. I'm guessing that's easier to do where you are now?"

"Yes."

"So how does the woman fit into this?"

"We're working together on a program to help teens at risk."

"A lot of the local departments have a special school liaison. So she's a police officer?"

"No."

"A teacher then?"

"No. She's a librarian."

"Uh-oh," Buddy said. "Your brother married a librarian."

"I'm aware of that," Connor said. "I was there. What does that have to do with anything?"

"Don't you think it's strange that you're having trouble with a librarian?"

"Who said I was having trouble?"

"Logan."

"Don't the two of you have anything better to do than gossip about me?"

"Maybe I could give you some help, you know . . . in the romance department."

"I don't need any help in the romance department."

"Well, you never have in the past," Buddy said. "But you seem to have run into some difficulty with this new girl."

"I've got to go."

"If you need help, you know you can call me."

"Right. Bye, Granddad."

"Hold on. That offer goes for cop stuff, too," his grandfather said.

"Thanks."

"Don't let something eat you up inside like Logan did."

"His partner died. I didn't have that experience."

"Maybe not, but you had something happen that hit you hard deep inside, where healing doesn't come easy. Like I said, you can talk to me anytime."

"Thanks. Bye."

Connor knew all about the intervention his granddad had staged with Logan, who was having terrible nightmares and suffering from guilt about his partner's shooting. The guy had died in Logan's arms.

There was something about having someone die in your arms that changed you forever. Connor was trained to deal with emergency situations but there was nothing like the trauma of a kid's bloody death to destroy any idea that life was either fair or predictable.

Connor's undercover work had ended that day. He'd stayed on the force for a while longer, working with kids. He'd tried to steer them away from gangs and drugs and toward programs and places that could help. But he'd failed so many times that something inside of him had atrophied.

He'd ended up walking away. Just like he'd walked away from Marissa all those years ago. He'd made a mess of things. He hadn't expected or wanted to fall for Marissa back then. He'd just had his heart broken by his first love, who'd dumped him, and he wasn't looking for complications.

He still wasn't looking for complications but he sure as hell had them. Only this time Marissa was the one who'd had her heart broken by her cheating ex and he was the one with questions.

Earlier today, Marissa had cheerfully explained to him that he was her rebound guy and that she wasn't looking for anything serious. Her statement should have reassured him instead of irritated him.

What the hell was wrong with him?

Connor didn't have time to ponder that question because Spider and Nadine were waiting for him at the station.

"We need to talk to you," Spider said. "In private," he added. "It's urgent."

Chapter Eighteen

· · · · · · · · · · · ·

"Where are Nadine and Spider?" Marissa asked
Molly. Marissa had raced home from Jose's to exchange
her jeans and T-shirt for black cotton pants and a turquoise sleeveless shirt for her shift at the library's booth.
The day was another one of those steamy kind guaranteed to make you wilt and sweat. "They're supposed to
be volunteering now, not you and Tasmyn. Did you get
the schedule mixed up?"

"No. Nadine said she needed us to fill in their slot
because she and Spider were doing something else."

"Something else?" Marissa felt her anger rising. They
were already shorthanded because Connor had told Jose
and Red Fred it would be best if they stayed away from
the Corn Festival today. "I can't believe she'd be so irre-
sponsible. Is she tweeting from somewhere?"

"They're helping Jose and Red Fred."

"By doing what?" Marissa could imagine all kinds of outrageous scenarios, most involving wild tweets, posts and photos.

"She didn't say. Tasmyn and I don't mind spending more time here at the booth. Don't be worried. We've got this."

But Marissa was worried. The minute Flo stopped by the booth, Marissa went from worried to agitated with a dose of panic thrown in for good measure. It wasn't the wild corn–covered T-shirt and earrings that Flo was wearing. It was what she said.

Pulling Marissa aside, she quietly said, "So you and Connor finally hooked up last night. Don't look so shocked. I told you, Flo always knows. Someone saw you leaving his apartment early this morning. They also saw you going in last night."

Marissa was too stunned to speak.

"I didn't say anything to anyone else. But the word does seem to be out. I thought I'd give you a heads-up." Flo patted Marissa's arm reassuringly. "This silent routine is probably the best. Or maybe you should think of an alibi. Of course, your other option is to just fess up. Not that I'm saying you should brag about it or anything. Of course, the sheriff is one of Hopeful's most eligible bachelors. He was even listed as winning that title in the local paper last year but that was before you came home. Would you like me to issue a statement on your behalf?"

Marissa shook her head. The day had started out so well and with such promise. She'd had soapy shower sex with Connor, flirted with him, even thought she might be confident enough to try dancing.

Then things had gone bad when Flo had called to tell Marissa about the vandalism at the festival.

Now things had gone from bad to worse.

"You might not want to look so guilty," Flo advised. "If you change your mind about issuing a statement just call me. You've got my cell number." She paused as a group of kids approached the library booth to ask about the summer reading program. Standing back, Flo held her two fingers to her ear in the universal "call me" signal before leaving.

Marissa went on automatic pilot as she answered the kids' questions. No, it wasn't too late to sign up for the reading program. Yes, graphic novels counted toward the number of books read. Yes, some books earned them double points. No, Jose's T-shirts weren't one of the giveaways for the summer reading program but they had other promo items from Scaredy Squirrel for younger readers and *Glee* bookmarks or Twilight saga posters for older ones. She handed them the sign-up info and the brochure. The booth got busy for the next hour, leaving Marissa little time to worry about the rumors about her and Connor swirling around Centennial Park.

Her mom was the first family member to stop by. Luckily she did so during a lull in patrons asking for info at the booth. Like Flo, she tugged Marissa to the far corner of the booth.

"Is it true?" her mom asked in an undertone.

"Is what true?"

"You and Connor." She studied Marissa's face before exclaiming, "It is. Flo said you looked guilty and you do."

Marissa put her hands to her cheeks. "I do not."

"You're blushing."

"I'm hot. It's ninety degrees out here."

Her mom aimed her handheld battery-operated fan at

Marissa before directing it back at her own red cheeks. "I should have brought you one of those ice packs to stick between your breasts."

Marissa felt like sinking through the ground. "Mom, I'm trying to work here."

"Right. I heard that one of your teens is about to be arrested for the vandalism. Is it one of the girls over there?"

"No, of course it's not," Marissa said.

"Right. Girls aren't vandals. Boys are."

"That's not true. And none of the teens committed that vandalism."

"What about the missing money?"

"They didn't steal any money either."

"You sound pretty sure about that," her mom said.

"I am sure."

"What about Connor? Are you sure about him? Is he the One?"

Marissa looked over her mom's shoulder to see her dad approaching. She welcomed his arrival. He'd never interrogate her about her private life the way her mom was. "Hi, Dad. How's the traffic at your booth? It seems pretty busy today. A big crowd at the festival."

"Have they found the culprit who defaced the booths and stole the money?" her dad said.

"Not yet," Marissa said.

"You know what the ancient Egyptians did with thieves, don't you?"

"No and I don't want to know," Marissa's mom said. "I'm sure it involved bloodshed of some sort. Forget about the pharaohs and concentrate on your daughter."

Her dad frowned at Marissa. "They don't think you did it, do they?"

"No," Marissa said.

"They think one of her teens in trouble did it," her mom said. "But that's not important."

"Yes, it is," Marissa interrupted her. "My teens aren't in trouble. They're good kids."

"I just meant that I wasn't talking about the vandalism. I was referring to Marissa and Connor," her mom said before rolling her eyes and sighing. "Forget it," she told her husband.

"I just stopped by to see if I could borrow a pen," Marissa's dad said. "I seem to have lost mine."

"Of course you did." Marissa's mom's voice reflected her growing agitation. She moved her fan closer to her increasingly red face. "You are so wrapped up in that silly booth of yours that you can't even see what's right in front of your nose."

Marissa's dad automatically reached up to the brim of his hat. "My pen's not in front of my nose."

"I give up!" Marissa's mom said dramatically. "We'll talk later, Marissa."

"She doesn't seem like a happy camper," Marissa's dad noted as his wife marched off. Turning his attention to Marissa, he abruptly said, "Do you have any idea what it was like being the only male in our otherwise all-female household? The estrogen levels were through the roof. They still are, as far as your mom is concerned."

She gave him a pen along with some advice. "Whatever you do, do not bring up what ancient Egyptian women did to handle menopause."

"Most didn't live that long," her dad said.

"I wouldn't say that either."

"I can't say anything right so I don't even bother

anymore," he said. "Thanks for the pen." He wandered away.

Marissa returned to the main section of the booth. "How are you girls doing? Do you need some water?" The library provided bottled water in a cooler for staff and volunteers.

"No one is donating any money," Molly said. "It's like they don't trust us."

"Someone actually told us that," Tasmyn said. "They said we'd just take the money and buy something at the mall instead."

"I'm so sorry," Marissa said. "People can be idiots sometimes."

Marissa tensed up as she saw her mom returning. "I forgot something," her mom said before dropping a twenty into the donation box. "I'm going home. It's too hot out here."

Marissa suspected it was going to get a lot hotter.

• • •

"It's urgent, huh?" Connor invited Spider and Nadine into his office and closed the door. "What's going on?"

Ruby Mae knocked on his office door and popped her head in. "The mayor is on line one. He say's it's urgent."

Connor gritted his teeth. As much as he wanted to blow off the mayor, he couldn't do so. "I'll be with you in a minute," he told Nadine and Spider before picking up the phone.

"Doyle, here."

"Sheriff, I'm hearing disturbing rumors here at the festival." Mayor Bedford's voice was thick with disapproval.

"There's no law against gossiping," Connor said.

"The gossip is about you and a certain librarian who works alongside you regarding the teens. There's talk that the two of you are . . . an item, shall we say. And some are complaining that that's why you won't arrest Jose. Because of that certain librarian and your relationship with her. That she convinced you to go easy on him. What you do in your own time is your own business, Sheriff. But as mayor, I cannot allow you to have your personal prejudices color the investigation."

"I'm not the one allowing personal prejudices to color anything."

"Are you denying you and Marissa Barrett are a couple?"

"As you said, what I do in my own time is my own business." Connor's voice was curt.

"If the two of you are having an affair . . ."

"My personal life has no bearing on my job or my investigation. I've got to go." Connor slammed the phone down.

"Did you just hang up on the mayor?" Spider asked.

"Yes, I did. And that info does not leave this office. No tweets," he warned Nadine.

"Tweets helped us break this case," she said. "You see, your brain isn't wired the way ours is."

Connor was about to say "Thank God for that" but held his tongue.

"Spider and I are digital natives. That means that, unlike you, we've always had digital technology. We are pros at multitasking. This is our world and we hold the keys to it," Nadine said proudly.

"And if we don't have the keys, we know how to unlock certain areas," Spider said. "Jose isn't guilty. Someone framed him."

"I am actually smart enough to have figured that out on my own," Connor said. "Even though I'm not a digital native."

"You may have figured out he was framed, but have you figured out who did it?"

"Not yet," Connor said.

"We have." Spider's face beamed with pride.

"Do I want to know how you did that?" Connor said.

"Probably not," Spider admitted.

"See, the thing in law enforcement is that I need evidence I can use in a court," Connor said. "Not something illegally obtained."

"The mayor's granddaughter was our first suspect," Nadine said. "She was very angry that she came in second and that Jose got first place in that poetry jam at the Rhubarb Festival. She's been holding a grudge ever since then. It's all here on her Facebook page." Nadine turned the open laptop to show Connor.

"How did you get access to her Facebook page?" Connor asked.

"She friended me. I was using an alias and said I was a huge fan of the TV show *Vampire Diaries*, as is she. Ian Somerhalder is her fave, so we posted about that."

"There's nothing illegal about holding a grudge," Connor said.

"Or liking *Vampire Diaries*," Spider added. "Although there should be."

"I don't see a confession that she framed Jose. And she has an alibi. She was home with her family," Connor said.

"It wasn't her. She's a senior in high school but has a nineteen-year-old boyfriend." Nadine switched screens to another Facebook page. "He's not very smart. He posted some photos of himself at the festival."

"With a can of spray paint?"

Nadine nodded. "Like I said, he's not real smart. Did you question him?"

"I'm about to," Connor said and headed for the door.

Nadine and Spider got up to go with him.

"No, you don't. You two stay here. Or better yet, go home. And don't breathe or tweet or post a word of this until I tell you to. Got that?"

"Yeah," they said in unison.

"I just have one more thing to say to you both. Good job." He gave them both a high five and a low down. "You should consider jobs in law enforcement."

"In that case, we should come with you to observe your interrogation techniques," Spider said.

"No, you shouldn't. Remember, not a word. We don't want to spook the suspect."

"So you plan on ambushing him. Smart move," Spider said.

"I'm so glad you approve," Connor said. "Remember, not a word. I'm trusting you."

"We got that," Nadine said. "Go book 'em, Danno."

• • •

Marissa had barely made it home and changed out of her work clothes when her mom called. She sounded on the verge of a panic attack. Marissa could relate. She felt that way herself since hearing that the news of her and Connor was now public gossip.

"I need your help!" her mom repeated.

"What's wrong? Are you okay?"

"No, I'm not okay! I need you to come over here and talk to your father immediately."

"Why? What happened?'

"I'll tell you when you get here."

"But . . ."

"I'm your mother and I'm saying that I need you." Her mom's agitation was growing by the second. "And you're saying you can't be bothered?"

"I didn't say that," Marissa protested.

"Then stop talking and get over here. It's an emergency."

Her mom was starting to freak Marissa out. "Should you call 911?"

"Not that kind of emergency," her mom said. "Just get over here." She hung up.

Marissa hoped her parents were okay and that this wasn't some lame attempt to set her and Connor up. He had his hands full investigating the vandalism and theft. He needed to clear Jose's name, not deal with Marissa's crazy family. She tried calling him on his cell but it went to voice mail.

She decided against leaving a message and grabbed her car keys. It looked like she and her rust bucket VW were heading over to her childhood home on Tranquility Lane.

• • •

Connor sized up Todd Newman. The nineteen-year-old was nervously shifting from one foot to the other. He looked like the defensive lineman that he'd been in high school, from his buzz cut to his thick neck to his GO EAGLES tattoo.

"We have reason to believe that you were the one behind the vandalism and theft at the Corn Festival last night. I get it. You were pissed that your girlfriend didn't get the poetry prize she deserved. Again, I get that. But I've got to tell you that posting that picture of you with the spray paint wasn't a good move."

"How do you know about that?" Todd's nervousness increased.

"Here's the deal, Todd. If you confess now and give me the money box we can keep this as a misdemeanor offense instead of something a lot more serious like a felony robbery. It's your choice."

"No one saw me."

"Are you sure about that? We have surveillance camera footage." There was a security camera on the bank across from the park. Connor never said that Todd was on the footage or where the cameras were.

He didn't have to.

Todd swore and then crumbled. "Don't tell my parents."

"If you give me the money box, it will go better for you."

"I didn't spend any of the cash," Todd said. "Not a penny."

"Good. Where did you stash it?"

"In the trunk of my car. I was gonna move it."

"Show me."

Todd did.

"You're going to have to come down to the station," Connor said before reading him his rights.

"Don't ever drink vodka and energy drinks together," Todd said. "It makes you do crazy shit."

"Yes, it does."

An hour later, Connor had processed Todd. He'd called Jose and Red Fred to let them know they were cleared of this offense and warned them about the dangers of trespassing on city property after hours. "We'll talk more tomorrow," he told each of them.

"Tell Marissa I'm sorry I took her lunch from the library that one time," Red Fred said. "Did you know she eats avocado and banana sandwiches? That's just weird. But I was so hungry . . . I only did it the one time."

"Make sure you don't do it again," Connor said in his best cop voice while writing a note to himself to find help for the food situation with Red Fred and his mom.

"Don't forget to tell Marissa," Red Fred said.

"I won't."

Connor barely hung up the phone when his office door flew open and Marissa stood there in shorts and a sexy tank top. She was breathing hard, making her breasts rise and fall in a way he found irresistible.

"I need to report a crime!" she gasped.

Chapter Nineteen

. . . .

"What happened?" Connor almost leapt over his desk in his hurry to get to her side. "Did someone hurt you?"

"It's my parents."

Connor frowned. "Someone threatened your parents?"

"*I* did. And then I locked them in a room in their house and told them to talk to each other."

"That doesn't sound like a crime to me." Connor closed the door on his nosy staff and guided Marissa to the chair in front of his desk.

"My dad was threatening to call 911 because I took away his tech toys. His iPad and iPhone. I made sure there was no landline in the room and neither had their cell phones. It's not like I plan to lock them up there for days."

"How long do you plan on locking them up?"

"A couple of hours."

"What if they need to use the bathroom?"

"There's one attached. The bedroom used to be my sister's. My parents put a lock on the outside of the door when she was thirteen and started sneaking out when she was grounded. The lock was still there and I used it."

"Okay, just calm down and catch your breath."

"I shouldn't be bothering you with this," she said. "I know you're busy working on the vandalism case."

"We solved it."

"You did?"

"Yeah. It's a long story. I'll tell you later. Let's get back to your parents. What made you . . ." He paused, searching for the right word.

"Go off the deep end?"

He nodded.

"It was them," Marissa said. "They were driving me crazy. My mom called and demanded I drop everything and go over there. She said it was an emergency. So I get there and find the two of them bickering. I tried to reason with them but they didn't want any part of it. They refused to listen to me. So I sort of conned them into going upstairs with me to my sister's room. That's where I confronted them." She drew in a deep breath. "I'm telling you, you're lucky your parents live in Chicago."

He squatted in front of her and reached around her to rub her back reassuringly. "I know."

"At first I thought maybe they were trying to con me into meeting you the way your mom and grandmother did. I called you to warn you but it went to voice mail."

"I haven't had time to check my messages," Connor said.

"That's okay. I shouldn't be bothering you with this. It's just going to increase the talk about us."

"Who cares?" He looked over to glare at Ruby Mae, who was peeking through the open blinds on the glass partition window into his office.

"I don't want you to get in trouble because of me," Marissa said.

"Don't worry about me," he said. "What about your parents?"

"I'm tired of worrying about them," she said. "I mean, I love them but they were driving me crazy."

"How long ago did all this happen?"

She checked her watch. "About two hours ago. I went right home from their house but then I started thinking about it and panicked and came here. I wouldn't put it past them to write out a sign reading CALL POLICE and hold it up to the window or something. The windows in the room have been painted shut for a few years now so I knew they couldn't scream or anything. What if there's a fire?" She grabbed hold of Connor's arm. "It's dangerous to leave them in there. I shouldn't have done that. I'm a terrible daughter."

"No, you're not."

"Yes, I am. I've made a mess of things. Again."

"What do you mean, again? You've locked up your parents before?"

"No. I meant with relationships."

"I don't know." He smoothed her hair away from her face. "I think our relationship is pretty damn awesome."

"Do we have a relationship?"

"Yeah, I think we do. And I want to be more than just your rebound guy."

"You do?"

He nodded.

Marissa realized Connor was already more than her rebound guy. When in trouble, seek shelter. When she'd panicked about her parents, she'd sought him out. Connor, not Jess or Deb. He was the one she'd come to.

She didn't even realize that she had her cell phone clutched in her hand until she felt it vibrate. The text message read:

urgent, call me now

"It's my sister," Marissa said.

"Go ahead." Connor stood and took a few steps back to prop his hip on his desk.

Marissa called her.

"I just walked in on Mom and Dad locked in my old bedroom." Jess sounded freaked out.

"Were they fighting?"

"No, they were half naked on my old bed and doing the nasty."

"What?"

"I'm telling you, they were about to have S-E-X."

"Why are you spelling it?" Marissa said. "You're usually liberal about that subject."

"Not when our parents are doing it. What did you say to them?"

"I locked them in the room and told them to be nice and talk to each other. I told Dad to pretend Mom was the Egyptian queen Nefertiti. I told Mom to pretend he was Jon Bon Jovi."

"What did they say?"

"They both claimed they didn't have that much imagination."

"Clearly they *do* have that much imagination," Jess said. "I may be traumatized for life by what I saw."

"So they weren't fighting? They were getting along okay?"

"Hello," Jess said. "What part of they're having sex did you not understand? Of course they were getting along. Enough about that. I need to talk to you."

"You are talking to me."

"No, I mean face to face. Are you home?"

"No, I'm at the police station."

"What did you do?" Jess said. "Crash another town event?"

"No."

"So the rumors about you and Hottie Sheriff are true. Are you with him right now?"

"Yes, but I'm leaving. He has work to do."

Marissa saw Connor raise an eyebrow at her comment.

"Meet me at your place in fifteen minutes," Jess said before disconnecting.

"Everything okay?" Connor said.

Marissa nodded. "My sister . . . uh . . . went to the house and unlocked the door so my parents are free now."

"And they're okay?"

Marissa nodded again.

"Good," Connor said. "How about I stop at your place after work and fill you in about the vandalism case? I've still got a few things to tie up here yet."

"Sure. That sounds fine." She quickly stood. "I'll see you later then."

The second Marissa opened the door and stepped out of the office, the conversations stopped and all eyes turned to her. She wished she could think of some brilliant and sassy comment like the kind Jess would come up with, but her mind went blank. Instead she kept her head held high and walked out of the police station. Okay, so she may have walked at a fast-almost-jogging pace but she had to get to her apartment to meet her sister.

Jess arrived at the same time Marissa did. "What did you want to talk about?" Marissa asked as she let her in.

"You." Jess opened the fridge and grabbed two Vitamin Waters. She opened one her for herself and handed the other to Marissa. "Ever since you told me about how you can't dance, it's been bugging me."

"Bugging you?"

"Yeah. So I've been trying to figure it out. First off, let me say that it wasn't my fault," Jess said.

"What wasn't?"

"You not being able to dance."

"I never said it was your fault." Marissa sat on the couch and Jess joined her there. Jess kicked off her sequined flip-flops and curled one leg beneath her in her customary pose. Marissa kicked off her own sandals and made herself comfortable. "I actually talked to my friend Deb about it a few weeks ago. She said my dancing phobia sounds like people who have the naked dream."

"Like you dreaming about Connor being naked?" Jess said.

"No, like nightmares where you're out in public and you suddenly realize you're naked. But it's not really about being naked. It's about a fear of exposing your worst weakness—something you're ashamed of. She thought my fear of dancing could be the same thing."

"Hey, analyzing you is *my* job, not hers," Jess said. "Is she a therapist or psychologist?"

"She's a self-proclaimed self-help book junkie."

"Yeah, well sometimes a penis is just a penis, you know?" Jess took a deep breath. "Okay, here's what I think happened. I don't remember any of this but apparently when I was three, Mom entered me in one of those beauty pageants for little kids. Like the kind you see in the cable TV show *Toddlers and Tiaras*. Anyway, she wanted to enter you, too, in the section for your age group of eight-year-olds. I was going to do a dance routine but you were so paranoid at the thought of dancing onstage in front of an audience that you freaked and threw a temper tantrum and refused to go."

"That's it? Why didn't Mom remember this?"

"Are you kidding me?" Jess said. "Mom can't even remember where she parked the car in the Kroger parking lot."

"What about pictures?"

"Of you throwing your tantrum?"

"No, of you doing your toddler tiara thing," Marissa said.

"Apparently they were ruined a few years later when the hot water heater broke and flooded the basement, where Mom stored extra photos."

"If Mom didn't remember and there are no photos then how do you know all this?"

"Daddy told me."

"When you caught him and Mom today?" Marissa said.

"No. Yuck." Jess made a face and hit Marissa with a

small throw pillow that read "Chocolate Is a Vegetable."

"I talked to him last night about it."

"Is he a reliable source?" Marissa had to ask.

"You mean, he may have made it all up to make you feel better?" Jess paused a moment to consider it. "I suppose he might have but that's not really like him. He'd just say he doesn't know and talk about how ancient Egyptians danced."

"You're right." Marissa took a sip of her drink as she contemplated this info. "So I've been traumatized all this time because I didn't want to dance in front of a crowd as a kid. I was eight. I should remember that."

"You must have blocked it from your memory. I mean, it was over twenty years ago."

"What a wimp," Marissa said.

"Hey, I was only three," Jess said.

"Not you, me. I was sure there was some kind of big trauma."

"I'm sure you thought it was big at the time."

"I'm surprised Mom didn't refer to it over the years," Marissa said.

"The way Daddy told it, it was right after Mom's mother died suddenly and she had a hard time coping with that."

"I wonder if I thought somehow that my refusing to dance had something to do with Nana's death. I barely remember her."

"It's not always the trauma dramas that cause trouble," Jess said. "Sometimes it's just the everyday fears that do it."

"You're sure you're not making this up?"

Jess frowned at her. "Paranoid much?"

"I'm sorry."

"You should be. I'm your sister. I've got your back. I want you to dance. Not this second maybe, and not in front of me at first. But soon. Now that you know the reason, you should be able to figure out the rest. Think about it. I know I did. And it made me realize that I want to do my graduate work in psychology. I want to figure out why people do the things they do. I think I'd be good at it, don't you?"

Seeing the way that Jess was looking at her for approval, Marissa felt a sudden lump in her throat. "Yes, I do. You've always been a people person."

"Thanks, sis." Jess gave her a full-blown gigantic hug, which Marissa returned. Stepping away, Jess reached into her bag and handed her a CD. "I burned this for you to practice your dancing. It's just an idea. If other songs hit you more, then try those. I just don't want your fear to hold you back from anything," she said fiercely. "You're so brave about so much stuff."

"I am?" Marissa had no idea her sister felt that way about her.

"Sure. You didn't go to college here despite the pressure from Mom and Dad. You followed your dream. Okay, so the marriage part didn't work out as you'd planned. But you weren't afraid to try. I stayed. I wasn't as brave."

"You're brave in so many other ways," Marissa said. "You're willing to take risks and put yourself out there. You don't apologize for being you."

"Why should I?"

"That's what I'm talking about," Marissa said. "And there's no reason you should apologize . . . except maybe for pulling my hair all those times when we were kids."

Jess grinned and reached out to give Marissa's shoulder-length hair a gentle tug. "Old habits are hard to break."

After her sister left, Marissa inserted the CD in her player. So she'd been afraid to dance because of a beauty pageant? No wonder she didn't want to participate in the Rhubarb Queen rigmarole.

The first song on the CD was Florence and the Machine's "Dog Days Are Over." The sound of harps at the opening had Marissa tentatively putting her hands up over her head in a mimic of a ballerina. Tears came to her eyes. But she didn't give up. Next came applause on the song so Marissa started hesitantly clapping.

When the music picked up, Marissa cupped her face with her hands, and she started turning her head. The next thing she knew, she was stomping her feet. But she was pretty much stomping in place and not bouncing around the room.

The music slowed, allowing her to breathe and think. That's when she heard a voice in her head. "You dance like a dork. You look stupid." And the sound of kids laughing at her. Was it Jess? She squeezed her eyes shut and focused on the flashback. No . . . it had come from the kids next door. A bunch of kids.

Marissa remembered now. She'd been dancing on the front porch. She didn't know anyone was watching her. Jess was still just a baby and Marissa felt left out and wanted to be a ballerina. A family with loads of kids had lived next door and they'd seen her and all laughed at her.

Maybe both Deb and Jess were right. Maybe Marissa felt ashamed at being laughed at, at being so bad at something that she never wanted to do it again. She didn't even remember having a momentary ballerina dream but tons of little girls did.

She certainly wouldn't want to repeat that in front of an audience, which would explain her temper tantrum. It had probably been more like a full-blown panic attack since Marissa wasn't really prone to temper tantrums.

So she was a failure at dancing and at marriage. But she was tired of always allowing her fear of failure to hold her back. She didn't want what had happened in her past to have so much power over her present and her future. So she started the CD over again.

This time, she deliberately focused on "Dog Days Are Over" as a healing song. Fear wasn't going to be the boss of her. She clapped and stomped her feet so hard the power vibrated clear up her leg. She circled, she was a whirlwind, and she made herself dizzy. There was no one here to laugh at her. The only laughter came from her before she sang, "The dog days are over . . ."

She belatedly realized that some of the bass beat was actually someone knocking on her door. She flung it open and found Connor on the other side.

"Are you okay?"

"I will be." For the first time since returning to Hopeful she truly believed it. "I definitely will be."

"I'm glad to hear that."

"I'm glad you're here," she said. She turned the music off.

"I don't recognize that song."

"It's by Florence and the Machine. Jess burned a CD of songs for me." She curled up on the couch and patted the space beside her. "Tell me about the case. Can I get you something to drink?"

He shook his head and sat beside her. She was close enough to see the lines at the edges of those special eyes of his.

"Despite what you see on TV, most cases aren't solved this quickly," Connor said.

"I'm glad this one was, for Jose's sake. Who did it?"

"The mayor's granddaughter's boyfriend. She's a senior in high school and he's a nineteen-year-old. He got drunk and wanted to impress her by trying to get Jose in trouble for getting the poetry award she thought should have been hers."

"He's nineteen, huh? That's the age you were when I was a senior in high school," she said.

"That's right."

She wanted to say more but didn't know how to express what she was feeling. Just that morning she'd been thinking that she wasn't foolish enough to believe that Connor was the One yet here she was at the end of the same day thinking otherwise. Was she brave enough to admit Connor was the One and had been all along?

Not yet. She had to work her way up to that. "I'm glad that it all worked out. About Jose, I mean."

"I told you to trust me."

She found the courage to ask a question she'd been wondering about for some time now. "You talk to me about trusting you but when are you going to trust me enough to tell me what really happened back in Chicago?"

"You don't want to know."

"Why not?"

"Because it's brutal."

"It involves a child, doesn't it?" she said. "A child and a lot of blood. I saw your face at the festival yesterday when that kid was injured."

"As a cop, you do your work and feel later."

"What happens when you eventually do feel?"

"I may have some trouble in that department," he reluctantly admitted.

"So you don't allow yourself to ever feel?"

"It's a slippery slope."

"Not feeling? Being immune? I would think so."

"No. *Feeling.* You can't allow yourself to go down that slippery slope or you'd fall apart every time a gang-banger on a power trip decides to kill a kid on a drive-by as a thrill kill or an initiation. I'd seen it happen so many times I should have been immune. Hosea was a good kid. He didn't deserve that. None of them did." His words were clipped, his expression closed. "Maybe it was the cumulative effect or something. But Hosea's murder hit me hard. The blood. So much damn blood." Connor paused and shook his head. She saw the flash of despair in his expressive eyes. "A week later, another eight-year-old was killed as retaliation."

Eight years old. The age Marissa had been when she'd refused to dance at the pageant. So young. She couldn't imagine having to deal with what Connor had.

"I should have stayed," he said. "I should have done more. Instead I walked away and came here."

"Maybe fate brought you back here to Hopeful because you'd done all you could in Chicago. If it hadn't been for you, then Jose would be in juvie right now."

"Spider and Nadine are the ones who helped break the case."

"But you listened to them. Another cop wouldn't

have. You've taken the time to build the relationships with these teens. And I know you probably did the same thing in Chicago. I bet there are plenty of kids that you saved."

"Not enough."

"It would never be enough for you. Not in Chicago. There are other great cops carrying on your work there. But you . . . you were meant to come back to Hopeful. Just as I was meant to come back to Hopeful. This is where we're supposed to be. Right here."

"Right here on your couch?"

She shifted and in doing so inadvertently hit the remote control on the CD player. The classic song "Have a Little Faith in Me" started playing. "Sorry. My sister did a playlist of dance songs," she said. "I'll turn it off."

"Don't." Connor stood and held his hand out to her. "Dance with me."

She slowly put her hand in his. "I'm not good at this. I'll probably step on your toes," she warned him.

"That's okay."

"I'll probably mess up."

"That's okay, too."

"I'll never be a ballerina," she said.

"Me neither."

"I'm afraid of storms. And relationships."

"Me, too. About the relationship stuff."

"I've got baggage."

"So do I."

His arms encircled her, giving her strength and courage. She moved with him, her arms looped around his neck, her fingers brushing the silky dark hair on his nape. They were never going to be contestants on

Dancing with the Stars but that was fine with Marissa. She felt as if she'd won that disco-glitzy glitter-ball award by doing exactly what she was doing—having faith in Connor.

"One day at a time?" she asked.

"Then a week at a time and then a month at a time." He twirled her in his arms. "Then a year and a decade at a time. Have a little faith in me."

"You're asking me to have a *lot* of faith in you."

"Because I'm putting a lot of faith in you."

Her first love could end up being her forever love. This was her chance to find out providing she was brave enough to take it, to take Connor into her heart.

Who was she kidding? He was there all along. He always had been. She'd had to come home to Hopeful to discover that. When in trouble, seek shelter . . . the shelter of her true love's arms.

• • •

One year later . . .

"Another Corn Festival bites the dust," Connor said as he slid into the booth across from Marissa at Angelo's Pizzeria. "Without incident this year."

"I can't believe it's been a year already." She fingered her favorite moonstone earrings. "The time has gone by so fast."

He grinned at her. "And they said we wouldn't last."

She frowned at him. "Who said that?"

"Nobody. I was teasing you."

"You've been hanging out with Red Fred too much."

"Who knew the kid had such a great sense of humor?"

"You did." Marissa reached across the table to link her fingers with his. "You knew."

"I am pretty brilliant," he noted.

"One of the many reasons I love you. What?" she asked as his eyes widened.

"That's the first time you said that."

"It is not."

"I'm a police officer. It's my job to take note of details like that. This is the first time you've said it in public. It's a huge red-letter day."

"Yes, it is. Because of what's going on with the teens. Can you believe that Nadine and Spider have created over thirty apps now? And how about Molly and Tasmyn creating the steampunk jewelry using old watches? They can't keep up with the demand. And what about Jose's artwork? The professor at Midwest College is so impressed with him and Jose loves being involved in the art program there. I love the cool book logo he put on my formerly-lame-lime-now-shiny-red VW."

"No more rust buckets for you. Amazing what a body shop can do. It's a win-win situation all around. But that's not why this is a red-letter day."

"It's not?"

He shook his head and nodded to the pizzeria owner. "Hit it, Angelo."

Suddenly "Have a Little Faith in Me" played over the sound system.

"They're playing our song," she said.

"I know. I planned it that way." Connor slid out of the booth and took her hand in his before dropping to one knee. "I already asked your dad for your hand in marriage. He told me that in ancient Egypt, a woman could actually make up her own mind about marriage. So now I'm asking you at the place where we first met all those year ago, where we first fell in love. I love you so much more now. So Marissa, aka Rissa the Rebel, will you marry me?" Reaching into his shirt pocket, he removed a ring. The diamond sparkled in the classy gold setting. "What do you say?"

This was her moment. She hadn't known it would be coming tonight. But she knew that this was the man for her. She'd known as a teenager and she knew it even more deeply now. Past mistakes were washed away by the love she saw in those blue-gray-green eyes of his. Her reply was confident and without hesitation. "I say yes."

He slid the ring on her finger and stood to pull her into his arms. Lights flashed around them as the crowd eating dinner burst into applause.

"Your mom made me promise to e-mail her photos," Angelo told Marissa as he took another picture with his iPhone. "She'll send them to your mom too, Connor."

"One big happy family," Connor said as he slowly danced with her. "We've come a long way for two people who weren't fans of marriage, but the best is yet to come."

"I know. And I can't wait," she murmured against his lips.

"Hey Angelo, make that pizza to go," Connor said.

"You got it."

Marissa and Connor ran out of Angelo's Pizzeria

with the cardboard box of pizza in hand and the sound of the cheers from the people who called Hopeful home.

Twenty minutes later, Marissa was in bed with the man she planned on loving for the rest of her life. There was no place else she'd rather be.

From *USA Today* bestselling author

CHRISTIE RIDGWAY

Can't Hurry Love

**The three Baci sisters are on a mission to save
Tanti Baci—the winery that's been in their
family for generations—by transforming it into
the perfect wedding destination.**

But love doesn't come easy for everyone...

The pivotal event of the wedding season is the fiftieth anniversary celebration of the winery's bridal bubbly—a shared glass of this sparkling wine supposedly keeps couples in love forever. But worries about the festivities fly straight out of Giuliana Baci's head when she finds her apartment ablaze. Homeless and practically possessionless, Giuliana is forced to live in the house next to the winery. Unfortunately, there's already someone in residence there...

Liam Bennett staked his claim in Tanti Baci after stepping in to help the Baci sisters save their family legacy. But Giuliana questions his motives. They've been at odds ever since a hot summer long ago ended in heartache. With the fate of the winery on the line, the former lovers must control their barely leashed hostilities. And with a tangled past and powerful emotions simmering just below the surface, the road back to love will be the biggest challenge of all.

M873T0411

Discover Romance